Praise for
Accidental Adulthood

Jeff Gephart's novel is a "coming of age" story. The age Michael (Mick) Collins is coming to is generally a bit old for that genre, but he's got a lot of growing up to do, so his story fits. Mick has a way of looking at things that can be hilarious and profound simultaneously.

The best stories have great characters, and *Accidental Adulthood* has Mick Collins. He's a little like Ted Mosby from the TV show, *How I Met Your Mother.* Like Ted, Mick thinks he's in search for the perfect woman, but he's really in search for his adult self. Combine that story-line with Gephart's edgy sense of humor and the result is a fabulous read.

~Steve Lindahl, author of *Motherless Soul, White Horse Regressions* and *Hopatcong Vision Quest*

An entertaining read. Gephart has a way with words that make you feel you are there as the narrator tries to decipher the opposite sex and his actual goals in relation to them. Hs characters are believable and fun. Enjoy!

~ Glenn Oliver Parkhurst, author of *Love and Laughter*

There's a witty edginess to this story that carries the reader along, with hints of Augusten Burroughs and Philip Roth. Mick's journey is more than one of becoming; it's toward an identity that opens up possibilities, rather than crushing them, and ultimately, a sense of belonging.

~Mary Clark, author of *Miami Morning* and *Tally: An Intuitive Life*

Accidental Adulthood

One Man's Adventures with Dating and Other Friggin' Nonsense

Jeff Gephart

ISBN: 978-0-9980717-4-9

Library of Congress Control Number: 2017934366

Cover design by Jeff Gephart
Author photo by Roland H. Brady III, PhD, ImageQuestPhoto@msn.com

For sharing ideas and encouragement,
I'd like to offer special thanks to:

Julie Gephart
Kyle Housel
Jennifer Mattson
Chris Buscher
Brent Homman
Joseph Rodriguez

"Not everything you read on the internet is true."
~Thomas Jefferson

1__estrogenical treachery

Most guys I know eventually arrive at the same conclusion: that women, as a gender—a species?—are insane. Most of us get there gradually, as seemingly unrelated actions by the females in our lives over a long period of time begin to reveal themselves as a pattern that suggests dubious mental stability. For me, it wasn't gradual. I vividly recall the exact moment I felt certain about their craziness. It was when I was being patted down like a suspected drug dealer outside of a seafood restaurant on a busy street in Sacramento by one of their demented minions at the conclusion of our first date.

I had just paid triple digits for dinner, and she had admirably kept up the ruse of being a rational person while we'd eaten. But for some reason, once we stepped outside the restaurant and she'd offered me a lift in her car, she decided to morph into Kiefer Sutherland from *24*, seemingly convinced I was a cleverly-disguised terrorist sleeper agent about to activate. As more pedestrian traffic noticed the spectacle and registered double-takes, my total shock at the stunning turn of events had begun giving way to the shame of public humiliation, and my epiphany about the hallucinogenic effects of estrogen had established itself in my mind as fact.

Then again, maybe it was gradual. I suppose that—like most revelations—this moment of clarity was more like the appearance of leaves and fruit upon a prominent orchard tree, when all along its roots had been stealthily taking shape somewhere out of sight. There I go again with the trees. I have a tendency to think in metaphors, to get trapped in their world like Jeff Bridges in *Tron*. And lately, they seem to involve trees.

For example, I could admit that, a lot of the time, all I see are trees. You know the old expression. Too often, in conversation, I get caught up in the details and tend to miss the proverbial forest. Words, phrases — they kidnap my attention and transform me into some sort of grammar psychopath, obsessive and compulsive over semantics at the expense of extracting the intended general meaning. For instance, I clearly recall the closing seconds of my first high school basketball game with the varsity squad. I brought the ball up the court, drove the lane, and when the behemoths approached to squash me like the indolent little garden pest that I was, I dished the ball to the first open man I saw, which happened to be my best friend Derek, who was also playing his first varsity game. He tossed up a jump shot that bounced and danced around the rim like a skittish cat at the precipice of a gopher hole before it finally decided to drop through. It was a tense couple of seconds, but the shot put us up by one, leaving our opponents something like two seconds to try to win or get fouled.

Timeout was called, and on our way to the bench Derek caught up to me and apologized for "almost missing" that open shot. During the time out, I heard not a word of Coach Woodring's brilliant plan to prevent the Burbank Titans from scoring; my mind was up to its elbows in paperwork trying to reconcile Derek's apology. "Almost missing" a shot is, in the end, exactly the same thing as "making" a shot, and who the hell apologizes for scoring the points that put us ahead? I have no memory of the ensuing defensive stand we took, because my brain was busy racing through all the psychological implications that would induce Derek to utter such a statement.

Anyway, I said all that to make a point about my sister.

My older sister Maggie's latent insanity was one of the first that manifested itself to me, and must have been instrumental in forming my belief about the overall mental state of females. About a month ago, she and I were engaged in one of those cringe-worthy sibling dialogues that I try so desperately to avoid—you know, the ones that deal with something real, rather than safe topics like which brand of peanut butter is best, or which actor will be next to overdose and be fawned over posthumously—when in the course of the conversation she told me that my "door of opportunity" was closing. I was so distracted by her mangling of a common metaphor that I missed the bulk of what came next, but she was talking, once again, about my diminishing chances of finding a wife and thus ending up with what she would call "a normal life."

If you are single and over the age of thirty, I don't need to tell you how often this subject comes up. It's like your educational years—when you were told you needed to take personal responsibility for your future and put yourself in the best position to succeed—all of that turns out to have been a hoax because "you" and "yourself" don't actually matter at all. What you really should have been preparing for is a series of diminishments. In your twenties, the world makes it clear to you that all you're destined for is to go from being a complete entity to being merely one-half of a couple, and, later, an even smaller fraction of a family. This entire concept seems contradictory to what I'd been taught for the first twenty years of my life, and I'm still having trouble buying into it, but my sister subscribes to the theory with unquestioning, patriotic devotion.

Which is strange, because Maggie in her youth gave no indication that she would turn out to be the person she is now. As a high school student, she seemed fated to end up as a brooding performance artist hanging out in smoky French cafes complaining about people who enjoy life, or, in the worst case scenario, as a well-respected prison inmate, but definitely not the Fox News-watching, S.U.V.-driving, PTA vice president that I get irritating phone calls from on a regular basis today. I remember doing my homework at the dining room table when I was twelve years old, and she walked in, decked out in the safety-pin adorned black leather jacket that was a staple of her retro-Ramones phase, and fixed me with the kind of pitying gaze a dog trainer reserves for the dimwitted beagle who just can't manage to wrap its head around the "sit" concept. I was immediately consumed by the icy feeling of inferiority that is common to younger siblings everywhere who had older ones that grew up never allowing them to feel as if they were in on the joke, and my head dipped unconsciously. Maggie let out a disaffected sigh and said, "Don't believe their lies, Mick."

Pretty much everyone calls me Mick these days, but Maggie was the first. My parents christened me Michael Collins—yes, named after "the big fella" himself—and my mother still calls me that. My dad, to the best of my recollection, hasn't called me by an actual name in decades. I try to ignore the possibility that he doesn't remember my name anymore, but it lurks in the back of my mind, believe me. My sister just decided, with the unambiguous conviction of a self-confident nine-year-old, that her brother should be referred to as Mick, and then proceeded to do so from that point on, as if she'd never heard me called anything else. My mother continued to call me Michael, but neither she nor any of the rest of us dared challenge my sister's application of the nickname.

That precocious little girl ended up getting married and undergoing a startlingly Transformers-like evolution into a stern, over-organized, aggressive mother of two. She married a man with money, and evolved first into a fiscal conservative, then into a social one, in the grand tradition of reformed liberals who turn out to only be interested in helping others until they actually have the financial means to do so. These days she dresses like a rich person who's trying to give the impression of being merely upper-middle-class but can't quite pull it off. You know those "casual" clothes the top designers put out—the blouses and shorts purported to be perfect for a day at the park, yet you can't imagine them with grass stains or wrinkles. Maggie looks a lot like the models in Lands End catalogues, and wears the same severe expression on her face. The accessories she so painstakingly chooses to complement her outfits make her style seem somehow flamboyantly understated. The makeup she wears is thicker these days, but always immaculately applied, and she keeps her strawberry blonde hair pulled back tightly into a ponytail or braid no matter what the occasion, giving the impression that she has successfully wrestled her prettiness into submission and intends to keep it in check.

When Maggie made the "door of opportunity" comment all those weeks ago, it had been during another of her attempts to impress upon me the necessity of conforming to her version of becoming a proper grownup. Settling down with a woman is an integral part of achieving this utopian status, and her campaign to get me on board with her vision is a task she approaches with the zeal of a Catholic missionary. She had clumsily worked the name of Alice, a new member of her book club, into the conversation enough times that I knew she was up to her old tricks. She tries relentlessly to set me up with any single woman she meets, from casual acquaintances from her yoga class to total strangers she encounters in the line at Starbucks. In her mind, a single person is a problem that needs to be fixed. Putting me together with another lost soul would be killing two birds with one stone. Compatibility does not seem to be part of the equation. On the rare instances when I've actually met one of the poor candidates she's tried to cattle prod in my direction, I have immediately and wholeheartedly disliked them. It's as if she's an animal trainer attempting to breed a Golden Retriever with a canary because they're both yellow. I suspect my sister has begun to view others as if they were photos of people in one of her catalogues, and a suitable match in her mind depends solely on the hypothetical attractiveness of the offspring the two single people would one day produce. Either that, or she's just stupefyingly clueless about what kind of person I really am.

"I know what you're trying to do," I'd said at the time. "I'm not remotely interested in meeting your friend Amber."

"Alice," she corrected.

"Whatever. I'm ninety-nine percent sure I'd hate her. In fact, I'm eighty percent sure I already do."

"The fact that you approach these situations with such pessimism is probably one of the main reasons you haven't yet been successful."

Did you catch what she did there? Successful. As if my love life was a competition and she was the judge. "When was the last time you and Marc had sex?" I asked, hoping to land a stinger.

"Stop being crude, Mick. I'm only trying to help."

"I know. And I appreciate it. It's just that your taste in women is so consistently awful. You'd make a terrible lesbian."

Maggie was silent, and for a moment I feared that I'd offended her. "Actually, I doubt that," she finally said. "I could see me ending up with an Angie Harmon type."

2__ex-men

I'm pretty shoddy at being a grownup. The pervasiveness of the whole "fraction of a person" mindset convinces me of this. I'm still stuck on the impression that grownups are supposed to have some sort of life plan, something that gives their life a trajectory to follow. Shouldn't the sum total of someone's life stand on its own as a worthwhile contribution to the world while they were in it? Somewhere on a high, dusty shelf toward the back of my mind rests a notion that I'm supposed to be a writer. Not the middling blogger that I currently am, but a novelist. I'm not one of those starry-eyed delusionals that thinks I'm going to write *the* Great American Novel. Obviously John Steinbeck beat me to that. But I do think I have a Really Good American Novel inside me somewhere. Something that a lot of people will read and then say how much the movie sucked compared to it. I must admit, however, that so far it's pretty slow going.

The first book idea I had was about a priest's secret marriage to a nun. It was called "The Lies We'll Tell on Sunday," but eventually that title sounded too much like a cheesy country song from the '80s, and later I ended up abandoning the whole idea. My current venture is about a guy who falls for a beautiful, mysterious art thief and reluctantly becomes her cohort. At least that's the main plot line, but underneath the surface it will be a biting satire about consumerism and greed in our culture that will send critics scrambling to come up with a unique way to laud my genius. I was an English major in college, so I know enough about writing to know that the linchpin of the whole project has to be the beautiful art thief, so the book needs to start out with a proper description of her, through the eyes of the narrator. Something that will immediately hook the reader into the story. The problem is the first sentence. So far I've got:

Angelina was mysterious.

I know, I know. It's too pedestrian; it doesn't even begin to capture the essence of this incredible woman. Let me tell you, it's extraordinarily difficult to think of yourself as a writer when so far the entirety of your epic novel consists of one woefully mediocre sentence. Maybe my problem is that I've never known a woman in real life who riveted me as much as the idea of Angelina does, so I have no real point of reference at which to begin. But this thought is distressing, because it triggers the cycle again, the one where I question the validity of my existence because I'm single. Lately I'm having a tough time resisting my sister's theory of only being a fraction of a person, and thus doomed to be incomplete until I partner up with another fraction.

At the moment, I'm meeting my friend Ethan for coffee at Weatherstone's, a little pseudo-hippie café in my neighborhood. He excels at making me feel better when I'm bummed out, because he's an excellent listener and endures my various rants with grace and seemingly genuine interest. I'm regaling him with the disastrous results of a Singles Mixer I attended three nights ago. In the alternate reality universe of the internet, the day before Valentine's Day has become known as Singles Awareness Day. It's an attempt to make single people feel less left out of the Valentine's festivities, but I find the title they've chosen to be depressingly ironic. In my little corner of society, I find it impossible not to be pretty damn aware that I'm single, and I don't need a special day to remind me. Also, the day's initials are S.A.D., which I'm not sure I believe could have been unintentional.

The SAD Mixer was a terrible idea from the start, and I'm not sure how I let myself be coerced into attending. It was my friend Witt's idea, and he hasn't had a good idea since at least the Clinton administration. What I found out was that the ubiquity of the "fraction of a person" concept has begun to breed desperation in single people. And desperation, as you're probably aware, is the gateway state of mind that leads to the more hardcore ones, like insanity.

"One woman I met," I tell Ethan, "suggested we get our portrait taken together. She had some sort of coupon for the photo lab at Sears that was about to expire."

Ethan is about four inches taller than me and disgustingly handsome. His polished-gun-barrel-colored hair is usually oiled and piled thickly on his head, like those old drawings of Superman, but even when it's disheveled and splayed across his forehead like it is right now, it has the look of something it took a Hollywood stylist hours to perfect. His posture seems unnaturally erect, and he's one of those born athletes that's capable of making me look foolish in anything from tennis to Jenga with minimal effort. He would have been a star actor back in the days of silent movies; his ability to translate his emotions into facial expressions is the most transparent of anyone's I've ever met. He doesn't even need to respond to my comment in words; the disbelief he registers at it shows plainly in his steely grey eyes.

"Yep," I continue. "This was less than ten minutes into the conversation."

"So what are you going to wear?"

"Very funny." I stop. We had made our way to a table out on the patio since it's the first day it hasn't rained in a week, and Ethan has now proceeded to tilt his mug halfway over the side of the table, dumping the coffee he'd just paid for. "Everything copacetic, Ethan?"

"The sugar tends to stay at the bottom," he explains calmly, "so only the bottom half of the coffee is sweetened the way I like it. So I order a size bigger than I want and dump out the top half."

"Isn't that kind of a waste of money?"

"It's a waste of coffee, but in the end, I'm getting exactly what I want, so I consider it to be worth what I paid for it."

I blink. "Why don't you just add more sugar?"

He blows softly on his half-cup of coffee, and then answers in a tired voice, as if it's absolutely draining for him to have to navigate through the dense swamps of my elementary intellect. "Because then the bottom half is too sweet, Mick."

"Why don't you just..." I trail off, stumped.

"Exactly."

Anytime desperation about my love life tries to pry its way into my consciousness, I can put it in its place by thinking about Ethan. He's five years older than me, although he looks younger by a few years, yet he doesn't appear to have a life plan that's any more lucid than mine. He's an assistant manager in a bank, and he's dating a woman named Georgelle who's currently married to her second husband. Dicey situation to begin with, but throw in the fact that she's a homemaker raising her husband's kids from his first marriage, and you've got a situation that would give most people pause. But if you try to detect whether the absurdity of his circumstances bothers Ethan, he will look at you blankly, as if you've just asked him if the water at his house is wet. It does not even occur to him that there's anything abnormal about his relationship. It's this sort of serene acceptance of the bizarre that makes the rest of the country pigeonhole us West Coast people as nuts. In fact, I'd wager that half the guys I know are crazy, but I just shrug it off, because my mind seems far more able to tolerate insanity than my body does illness.

Unfortunately, the single friends in my life are joining the polar bears in the endangered species department. As their numbers dwindle, I cling to people like Ethan to reassure myself that it's still okay that I don't have a steady relationship or a master plan.

Actually, I've been questioning lately whether *anyone* really has their shit together or not. My theory is that most people don't, so they get married to disguise this fact, then have kids so that the focus shifts further away from themselves and onto their children. It's all a clever sleight of hand trick. Ever since jobs were invented, there have been men who have defined their entire existence by claiming everything they do all day is intended to provide their children with opportunities they never had. Nobody ever seems to call them on the fact that they aren't capitalizing on the opportunities *they* have been provided by carving out a life—or at least an identity—for themselves. Nobody ever says that stuff out loud, because it sounds pompous to admit that you want something for yourself out of this world. Society tends to find it more palatable when a person can define their life as being a husband and father, rather than having to explain that you run a second-rate motel but you're an aspiring novelist with one sentence to your credit.

What bothers me is that these guy friends of mine, who used to seem like complete people to me, have so willingly embraced the evisceration of their personalities. I mean, my roommate from college has a picture of his kids instead of one of himself as his Facebook profile picture. That says it all, and it seems tragic to me.

He was the guy back in college who allowed our dirty dishes to pile up to the point where he loaded them in the back of his pickup and drove through the car wash. Now he posts photos of his new S.U.V. and other ex-men comment on its roominess and how it's perfect for transporting his kids, their friends, and their soccer gear to and from their stupid games. And he also posts these painfully bland anecdotes about the adorable things his kids do, and their pseudo-accomplishments, like how his son won a "Best Spirit" award at his art camp. To me, this is a fake award that basically says, "Kid, you have no artistic ability whatsoever, but we're really glad that your parents continue to pay us so you can persevere in a field in which you have no discernible potential." My old roommate would have seen it that way too at one time, and I'm not sure what happened to him, or when.

Anyway, I don't really hang out with my old friends anymore once they have kids. I tend to bristle at that look they give you—you know, that look parents like to throw at us non-parents, as if we just don't get it. I prefer the company of a guy like Ethan. He and I have sat in silence for a few minutes, watching girls pass on the sidewalk, dressed in shorts as an obvious act of defiance against the rain and chilly temperatures that have held us hostage for the past week. "Let me ask you something, man," I say.

"Hit me with your best shot." Ethan is mildly obsessed with Pat Benatar. I daresay he knows more about that woman than her own parents do. I guess everyone needs to be an expert on at least one subject.

"You ever think about having kids of your own?"

He pauses long enough to make me anticipate that one of his startlingly insightful answers is on its way, but then he just says, "Sure."

"Sure? And?"

"And ... maybe a dog?"

"Don't be obtuse, Ethan! You know what I mean. Do you think you will have kids at some point? Do you want to?"

"Look, I was just trying to keep up my end of the conversation. Having kids crosses my mind from time to time, but I haven't taken time to analyze how I feel about it."

I constantly doubt the authenticity of this laid back, unintellectual persona Ethan takes pains to project. He's too smart to have lived the unexamined life he'd have you believe. It's like he sees himself as a guy who was lucky enough to have been placed into this dizzyingly mad world for no other purpose than to take a good look around, fold his arms across his chest, and let out the occasional non-committal "Hmmm." Sometimes I think he maintains this image just to make me feel like an over-obsessive worrier.

He adds, "How do you feel about it?"

"The thing is, I don't have any desire to have kids."

"Is that bad?"

"I don't know. It seems more normal to want to have kids. Everybody does. At least, any woman I meet is going to want to. But once you have kids, that's it for your plans. I mean, it becomes all about the kid. I'm too selfish to give up on all my plans."

"How *is* the book coming along?" he says wryly.

I can never tell whether Ethan is subtly needling me about my writing, or whether he possesses a genuine interest in the subject. I avoid looking him in the eye. "Good. Slow, but good."

"So have you got a woman I don't know about who's pushing you to have kids?"

"What? No."

"So you're not in a situation where you're likely to have to make a decision about this anytime soon."

"No! I mean, hopefully not. Not on purpose."

"Was that a dig?"

Ethan was an accident. He's very sensitive about this fact.

"God, no. I'm just saying, sometimes I feel immature for wanting to do something on my own. I want to finish forging my own life, feel like I've accomplished something, you know? I want to feel like I've contributed something to the world, some sort of legacy, on my own, before I settle down and start living for someone else."

"And all I'm saying is this." Ethan pulls his chair closer and adopts his theatrical, I'm-giving-you-the-straight-dope posture. "When I said I haven't analyzed it, it's because the idea of having kids is not relevant to my present situation. And I don't think it's relevant to yours, either. So what good is all this *overthinking* doing you? You'll know what to do when the time comes."

I wish I had half the optimistic confidence Ethan has. Despite a spotty history littered with the carnage of at least as many poor decisions as I've made, he still seems to approach making new ones with the same wanton fearlessness he's always had. I wonder if he realizes what a gift he's got: to be able to coast through life with that level of cavalier poise.

I press on. "Don't you think sometimes that most people secretly feel like me, that they want a legacy or to feel like they've contributed something to history? But they can't think of what to do or make or accomplish, so they pop out a miniature version of themselves and say, 'Okay, Junior, you take it from here.'"

"Hmm." He blows softly on his coffee. "There could be some truth to that."

"I just always pictured myself living in New York City or someplace like that, writing."

"Pat Benatar was supposed to go to Julliard, you know. But she quit school and became a bank teller."

It's mystifying how often he's able to work her into one of our conversations. "I'm going to go ahead and wait for you to make your point," I say.

"My point is, you want to be a writer in New York? Then keep heading in that direction. If somewhere along the line the plan needs to change, you'll know. Stop thinking so much."

Stop thinking. I should get that tattooed across my chest. But then again, I'd probably spend the rest of my life second-guessing the color I chose for the ink.

3__this is not my beautiful life

When I get back to my apartment, the phone is ringing. My father's name appears on the caller I.D. but I know it's my mother's voice I'll hear when I pick up. She's the talker. Until she retired last year, my mom had worked as a receptionist in a law office for nineteen years. She spent all day either on the phone or talking to visitors who showed up at the office. Her retirement effectively cut off that source of constant conversation, so since then the frequency of her phone calls to me has increased. I adore Mom, but she can drag out conversations to the point where time seems to slow, like the day itself is running low on batteries.

My father, on the other hand, would rather burn to death than speak up to ask for water. Sometimes I suspect that his decision to marry my mom was partially motivated by his desire to have someone do the talking for him for the rest of his life. Which is just as well, because he rarely has something coherent to contribute anyway. My dad's name is Tom Collins, and, believe me, the irony has not been lost on any of us. For most of his adult life he's been engaged in a systematic fermentation process that will one day qualify the blood running through his veins as a confirmed alcoholic liquid, and now the project is nearing completion. Not that any of us complain. Dad is a highly genial, functioning drunk with no trace of ill temper or negative impulses. My mother will usually force him to pick up the extension when she calls me, but he only makes his presence known with the occasional random interjection that may or may not be relevant to what's being discussed.

When I answer, Mom asks me if I saw the episode of some family drama she watches that aired last night. She already knows I have no interest in the shows she watches, but this fact doesn't dissuade her from keeping me up to date on the storylines. I know this isn't the real reason she's called today, but sometimes you just have to wait it out until she maneuvers closer to her actual point.

During the description of her television show, I haven't heard a peep from my father, so I ask, "Is Da on the line?"

A long moment of silence ensues, until my mother says, "Yes. I thought he was going to answer."

"How's it going, Pop?"

"Oh, yeah, you know, it's like everything else," he replies affably.

Mom says, "So what's new, Michael? Anything exciting happening lately?"

"Are you trying to root out whether or not I had a date for Valentine's Day?" I ask, convinced that I've deduced her real reason for the call.

"I'm not rooting for anything. I just want to know what's happening in your life."

"I went to a singles party; it was pretty lame, actually."

My dad pipes up, "Maureen O'Hara was a handsome woman, that's for sure."

"Well, that sounds wonderful," my mom says. "You're so good at conversations with new people."

"A woman showed me a photo of her son, and I told her he looked like a probable future serial killer."

Mom laughs. "I'm sure she knew you were kidding."

"Cheerios!" my dad blurts.

"She asked security to have me removed, Mom."

She laughs again. "I don't know where you get your sense of humor from, Michael. Certainly not from us. It's a gift."

"Are you kidding me? Listen to Da, he's like a running monologue."

He says, "Ha! You haven't listened to my advice in forty years, champ!"

I'm thirty-three. "That's because your advice always involves drinking more and waiting to see 'how things shake down'!"

"Ha ha," Mom laughs. "He's teasing you, Tom. Michael, do you want some tomatoes? We have too many."

"How do you have tomatoes this time of year?"

"In the greenhouse. Your father put the windshield from the jeep over the plants and they started growing like wildfire."

"Like a magnifying glass," the old man adds.

I'm sad to hear this. That jeep was the first vehicle I learned to drive. "What happened to the jeep?"

"Nothing," Mom replies. "It's sitting in the garage."

"It's not running?"

"Well, it doesn't have a windshield."

Talking with my parents is always a rigorous test of how well I can maintain my sanity. "I'm so glad you guys adopted me," I say. "Yeah, I'll take some tomatoes. I'll stop by this weekend. I gotta go for now."

"Okay, Michael, behave yourself. We love you."

"You guys too. Buh-bye." Before I click the phone off, I hear my dad yell, "The Quiet Man!" He sure does love that Maureen O'Hara.

◎◎◎

That evening, it's not busy at the motel, so I open my laptop and pull up my novel. I own and manage The Shady Spot Motel on the north end of 16th Street in Midtown Sacramento. I am fully aware that it's possibly the worst name for a budget motel that's already located in a rather dodgy part of town, but the enormous sign hanging above the building features the name in a casual, handwritten-style font beneath two lazy palm trees, so the double-meaning doesn't immediately register with most people. At least I hope that's the case, because it would be inconceivably expensive to replace the sign, as well as the plastic room key tags and all the other little things on which the logo is already printed. That's too big of an investment for a station which I consider to be a temporary phase of my life.

How the motel came to be mine in the first place is a story that makes as little sense as anything that's ever happened to me. During the summer between my first and second senior years of college, my burgeoning drinking habit began to require funding that exceeded what my meager student loan surplus could support, so I sought a part time job. The total absence of writing or editing job listings in the classifieds should have been my first clue that the English degree I was pursuing at UC Davis was in fact preparing me only for a conspicuous spot in the overeducated unemployment line. The only job I could see that didn't look like it would interfere too badly with my insatiable pursuit of college girls was as a part-time desk clerk at a local motel of dubious reputation. The owner, a perpetually sweaty Iranian named Remi Rangini, took an immediate liking to me. Remi was a compact, swarthy specimen who tended to talk loudly and constantly dab his balding forehead with a handkerchief. The ever-present Hawaiian shirts he wore did little to hide the belly that protruded from his midsection like a massive pumpkin, and whatever perspiration he failed to eradicate with his damp handkerchief soon disappeared into implausibly bushy eyebrows that perched above his deep brown eyes like giant tufts of grey cotton candy. His conversation and sense of humor were so wildly inappropriate and disgusting that I couldn't help liking him. He kept me in stitches, which I suppose is what kept me returning to the job on semester breaks and the occasional weekend.

By the time I graduated and was no closer to starting a career than I had been before I started school, The Shady Spot had become a second home to me. Moving back to my parents' place in nearby Carmichael seemed counterproductive to my efforts to prove myself as an adult, so Remi allowed me to stay in the room closest to the motel's office free of charge. He taught me every last detail about running a motel, which I felt was superfluous since I still didn't think of the job as anything but a temporary stepping stone toward something greater, but I endured it out of affection for Remi. He occasionally spoke of his failure to start a family as his one true regret, so I supposed it was important for him to feel like a mentor to someone.

And that's all the more I thought about it, even after I became a full time employee and found an apartment of my own, until about three years later when I showed up to work and found the office closed in the middle of the afternoon. I quickly located the maintenance man, who informed me in an emotionless voice that Remi had suffered a massive heart-attack while cleaning the pool and was dead before he hit the water.

The melancholy I felt at hearing this news was mostly for Remi, but also because I assumed the motel would close or be sold, and that would be the end of my cushy job, and then I would have to stop ignoring the fact that finding a job in my field had become a laughably impossible task. It wasn't until the day after the funeral that a lawyer contacted me and said that Remi had bequeathed the motel to me in his will. It is impossible to overstate how surreal this revelation felt for me. I remember actually pulling the phone away from my ear and looking at it, half expecting it to be some fantastic gizmo from a Bugs Bunny cartoon instead of a regular phone. Motels were owned and operated by grizzled, business-savvy grownups like Remi, not know-nothing twenty-four-year-olds with useless college degrees. The only other experience in my life I can compare it to is when I was eleven years old and had spent the six months leading up to the holidays begging my parents for a Super Nintendo, only to be surprised on Christmas morning when the Nintendo-sized present I opened instead contained a pudgy little Boston Terrier with outrageously oversized ears and Type 1 canine diabetes. I knew it was one of those *Important Gifts*, one that signaled my parents' faith in my growing maturity. I didn't want to seem ungrateful or skew their image of me, but I was just a kid who wanted to stay inside all day and play Super Mario World, and all I could think of were daily walkings, feedings, and insulin shots. A present like that was something you got for a grave, responsible kid, not somebody like me.

And so here I am, nearly a decade later, still running this shabby motel and stuck on the first sentence of my masterpiece. It's odd to be in this position, feeling like an actor who's miscast in a role—think Glen Campbell in *True Grit*, or Ethan Hawke in anything—and then stuck in that role for an endless series of steadily worsening sequels. Thinking about this gives me an idea:

Angelina was misunderstood.

That could be promising. The narrator could feel like he's the only one who truly "gets" her, and it drives his passion for her wild. I type it in and hit save, but I haven't yet started typing the next sentence when

I'm interrupted by the raucous entrance of Reena, one of my maids, into the lobby. She's bobbing toward me with exasperation almost visibly tumbling from the chubby joints of her body, the way that character from *Peanuts* used to radiate a cloud of dust wherever he went.

"I got to go, Meester," she puffs, plopping a handbag the size of a cheetah down on the counter beside me. I'm not immediately clear on what she's talking about. She usually checks in and out with DaLisa, my head maid, and I don't often deal directly with her. I'm surprised she's here this late in the evening anyway. DaLisa usually makes up the schedule for herself and Reena, and I'm not sure how it works, but I can't remember usually seeing the maids around by the time it starts to get dark. At least I don't think so. I hate to admit it, but the maids sometimes fade into the background for me.

"Okay. Did you run it by DaLisa?"

"I ron over nobody!" she says incredulously. "I got to go. Please for my moany."

Then it hits me. "Wait, you're quitting?" This is just what I need. Paperwork and the hiring/firing process are my two least favorite parts of the hotel management business. Well, those and maintenance problems. Don't get me started.

"Jess! Please for my moany, Meester."

"Hold on a second, Reena. What's the matter? Why do you want to quit? What happened?"

Her eyeballs make an exaggerated orbit around the unbefitting blue sparkly area that surrounds them on her face. "I no work wit de ghost. Too moch. Please for my moany."

"Did you say ghost?"

"Jess!" she erupts, as if this is something she's grown aggravated with having to repeatedly explain to me. It's the first I've heard of it. "De ghost! I make de beds and de ghost, dey unmake!"

"You've seen ghosts?"

I must seem like an extraordinarily dim gringo to this poor woman. She spreads her elaborately-manicured fingers on the counter, as if trying to stave off a mental breakdown. "All de time, de ghost. I got to go." I can tell immediately that there will be no talking her out of this. At least not by me, and as quickly as I think of calling DaLisa, I dismiss the idea. She has a tendency to ignore her ringing phone, and besides, I'd just as soon cut Reena loose for now and ask DaLisa to talk her into coming back tomorrow.

"Okay, Reena, I understand. I'm sad to see you go, though."

"Please for my moany."

"Yes, you'll still get your next paycheck. Not a problem."

"No paycheck. I gon to Joota. Please for my moany. Cash."

I can't tell whether she's saying she's moving to Utah, or whether it's some Dominican threat I just haven't heard yet. Either way, I'm not in the mood to argue, so I hesitate before I say, "Reena, I doubt that I have enough cash on hand to pay you. And the bank is closed by now."

She makes no response. She just stands with her fat arms resolutely folded on the countertop and stares at me quizzically, as if she's trying to spot scars from a lobotomy on my forehead. For a moment I consider trying to explain that most people pay with credit cards, and the actual on-site cash supply is usually meager at best, but I suspect that would be like trying to explain the benefits of veganism to a lion. I bring up her timesheet on the computer. It's been less than a week since she was last paid, so I only owe her three hundred and eighteen dollars. I check the register drawer, and a couple of my hiding spots in the office, and combined with the money in my own wallet I'm able to come up with three hundred and seven. I hand it to her and explain it's the best I can do, unless she's willing to take a check instead.

She takes it and flashes me one of those forced frowns that some people seem to use in place of a smile. "Okay, Meester. I come back for de ress."

Okay, so it didn't mean she was going to Utah. I'm so relieved that I placated her instead of trying to argue. Dominican curses are not a brand of tea I'd care to sip. As I watch her waddle out the front door, I'm plagued by a brief moment of pessimism that DaLisa won't be able to convince her to return, and that I won't be able to find another maid with such a tolerable level of insanity.

As I'm pondering this, my cell phone rings. It's my friend Witt. My mind races through the Valentines Singles Mixer and every other possible topic—from the ridiculous to the downright lewd—that he may be calling about, and none of them appeal to me, so I send him to my voicemail. Spending time with him or even conversing on the phone is like an Olympic sport; you have to be mentally prepared, and don't forget to stretch. Instead, I try to regain my grasp on what I was going to say about Angelina, but my peripheral vision spots a car pulling up outside the window.

It's my friend Stacy's Camaro. This is highly unusual. Stacy used to be one of those guys I'd only meet up with at bars, in various stages of evaporating sobriety. Then about six months ago, he started dating a girl named Terry, and now they have a kind of symbiotic relationship; if you ever spot one without the other, it's a newsworthy photo-op. I hate to admit it, but I've come to expect seeing the two of them together, so when I only see Stacy at first, he does momentarily look incomplete. Like a fraction, dammit.

I blame him for causing me to think that way, but I take comfort in the fact that fate has gotten back at him by putting him together with a girl who has a man's name. When they're being talked about, it's unclear who's the guy, or if there is a guy, or if they're both guys. Anyway, Stacy doesn't normally track me down in person, so his showing up here unnerves me. We'd attempted to make plans to hang out a couple of weeks back, but it didn't work out, which is not uncommon among friends when one of the friends is busy running a motel and the other friend is attached at the hip to a chatty, hyperactive gadabout. But his relentless attempts to reschedule have been uncharacteristic of a guy who used to register mild surprise when he'd run across my name in his phone, tending to forget about my existence when I wasn't sitting next to him on a barstool. It makes me suspect an ulterior motive is at play. Since meeting Terry, Stacy has quickly become a devout convert of the Fractions mindset, and thus an enthusiastic participant in the coupled person's favorite pastime, match-making. He's not as dogged in his determination as my sister, but his dedication is enough to have prompted me to dodge a few of his recent texts like they were paintball pellets.

The reason I bring up the match-making thing is because the last time I saw the two of them, we were watching the Super Bowl at The Zebra Club, and during the third quarter one of Terry's friends showed up, and it didn't strike me as coincidental. Since then I've had a hard time shaking the notion that if I were to agree to meet up with Stacy and Terry, they'd show up strapped with an I.R.D.—an improvised romantic device. Besides Sumo Wrestling and prostate exams, a blind date is the most awkward and unpleasant activity that you can engage in with a fellow human being. I'm on terror alert status yellow when Stacy and Terry enter the lobby.

"What up, yo?" Stacy, who is white, tends to speak as though he were raised in a daycare run by N.W.A.

"Hi, Mick!" chirps Terry.

"What's up, guys? What are you doing here?"

"On our way to DeVeres," Stacy says. "Gonna serve some fools in pub trivia. What time you outta here?"

This definitely sounds like an I.R.D. situation. "Oh, I gotta be here all night," I say with theatrical dissatisfaction.

"Oh," whines Terry. "We wanted to take advantage of your vast knowledge of the insignificant."

"Um, thanks?"

"You been hard to get a hold of lately, yo."

"Yeah, there's been this ghost situation here that I've had to deal with. Very time consuming."

"No shit. Well, listen, next weekend is the Amador County Winter

Wine Extravaganza at the Community Center. You'd love it, yo. You gotta come."

I release my I.R.D.-sniffing dogs. "Who's going?"

"So far it's us, my friend Ruth, and you," Terry says with forced innocence.

"Yeah," Stacy pipes up, as if the previous sentence had been his cue. "She's totally cool."

"Isn't that the girl I met at the Super Bowl? I don't know."

"She was all pissy about some shit that day, man. Usually she's *right*!"

"She's great. You'll love her," Terry adds. "Trust me."

This girl has known me for only a few months; we have never had a one-on-one conversation. As I'm stammering for a reply, Stacy runs his hand through his blond curls and lets it drop to his side, where it finds Terry's. He casually hooks a pinky finger around hers. It's an unconscious, unrehearsed gesture, yet it looks so natural and charming that it makes me resent my singledom. My staunch anti-Fractions position begins dissolving faster than a Tums tablet dropped into lava. "I don't know, maybe," I say sheepishly.

"Fat booty," Stacy says with utter conviction.

Terry rolls her eyes. "She does have an outstanding butt. But if you don't like her in *that* way, whatever, it will still be fun. We haven't got to hang out with you in so long."

"What the hell," I say. "I like wine."

"Tight," Stacy nods. His face flushes slightly, as if he was unprepared for the possibility that their plan would work, and now he doesn't want to risk saying something that could make me change my mind. "Uh, so, you sure you can't make it over for trivia?"

"If I weren't behind this counter, you'd be able to see the ball and chain."

"A'ight. I'm a call you soon and remind you." Which is not exactly the truth. As is the case with many of my friends, Stacy and I have fallen into the habit of conducting our brief conversations almost strictly through texting, because the strain of actually having to use our voices might be unbearable. We say our goodbyes and they swiftly retreat to the Camaro. As I watch them drive off, imagining them congratulating one another on their cleverness, I decide to email my doctor to schedule a CAT scan, so I can find out just which kind of brain tumor induced me to agree to their idea.

4__princess leia

If I were a politician, they'd murder me in the press for all this flip-flopping. Most of the time, I'm content to be single, even proud of it, feeling superior to the ignorant masses who drank the Fractions Kool-Aid. Other times, I find myself detesting the loneliness that keeps springing into view from the shadowy corners of the single life. Maybe on an unconscious level I'm finally starting to agree that people by themselves are incomplete entities, and I'm just too stubborn to admit I've been wrong all this time. There has to be some reason I only put up a feeble protest before I agreed to hang out with Terry's friend Ruth, so, in my typical fashion, I spend the next hour after they leave probing my subconscious for possible motives.

Is my being single really a conscious choice? I consider the possibility that I view dependence on another person as a perverse sort of weakness. My parents are the perfect examples of people who would be utterly lost without one another; they wear their codependence on their sleeves like my gay friends rock the rainbows. My mom has no idea how to pump her own gas, for Pete's sake. And my father, forget about it. Not only is Mom his mouthpiece, but she also serves as his secretary and substitute memory. As far as I know, he hasn't remembered an appointment without her help for at least as long as I've been alive. Without her, it's altogether possible he would starve to death because he'd simply forget to eat. My righteous indignation labels these behaviors as weaknesses, convincing me that they are things my parents could have—and should have—learned to do for themselves.

On the other hand, I suppose it could bring my parents some level of satisfaction to be needed by someone else to such a degree. Maybe there's a kind of indefinable joy in allowing oneself to rely so heavily on another person that I simply haven't experienced yet, so how could I understand it? I'm not ruling these possibilities out, but none of it jives with the image of a romantic relationship that exists in my mind's eye.

My first love was Princess Leia, from *Star Wars*. Even as a child, I realized I would never actually end up with her, but I assumed that one day I'd meet someone just like her. You know, an independent girl, playing hard to get at first, but ultimately won over after hearing a clever line or two. It would all fall into place so neatly and effortlessly, we'd turn out to be perfect for each other, and I'd get to enjoy the sense of accomplishment at having won her heart. A girl who's refined and feminine, yet with a healthy mix of tomboy thrown in. Somebody who looks amazing in a bikini even when chained to a slobbering, oversized slug. Oh, and she wouldn't turn out to be my twin sister.

That was my romanticized vision of love, and needing the princess to change a tire for me or remind me about my cardiologist appointment had no place in it. The problem, as I see it, is that I've never outgrown that childish vision of romance. It still makes sense to me, so I find myself bumbling through my adult life, still looking for Princess Leia.

It's interesting how movies you remember from your childhood seem better than they actually were. Try watching *E.T.* as an adult, and you'll see what I mean. The fact is most things from back then seemed greater, more consequential, because when we were younger the future was still unwritten. We didn't know yet what we'd turn out to be, so we were convinced that every little thing we saw or experienced might turn out to be a vital piece of the mysterious masterpiece we were constructing. The endless possibilities injected even the most minor incidents with the gravity of *potential*. The most deflating part of growing older is that now you've found out what you're going to be, because you're already it, and now you realize that ninety percent of what happens to you isn't leading up to anything, and is therefore utterly meaningless.

I miss the optimism that teachers and parents and movies and commencement speeches crammed down our throats, brainwashing us to believe that, although our destinies were still up in the air, they would inevitably turn out to be blockbusters. We were adorned like gaudy Christmas trees in our younger days with the hope and anticipation of the untold adventures that surely lay in store for our futures. And then we got out into the real world, and all the people and the responsibilities and the bullshit started taking down and boxing up our ornaments, one by one.

Even when I'd complained about the stressors of high school and college, deep down I'd still actually been certain that everything would ultimately work out, even though all of us knew it was totally uncool to acknowledge that aloud. To a degree, we all had to pretend that our problems were serious, because in the back of our minds we knew they'd one day turn into nothing more than funny stories we'd look back and laugh about, after we'd all "made it." The only time I see that kind of thinking today is on reality TV, where adults manufacture drama out of events they secretly know don't matter, simply for entertainment value. And it all seems ridiculous and tragic, because we know they should've grown out of that by now.

The lack of responsibility is another thing I miss. Random hook-ups were acceptable, and even funny. College students are allowed to be careless with another's emotions, because they know that no one involved is taking the situation seriously. I remember waking up on a weekday to find a girl I didn't recognize picking her clothes up off the floor and getting dressed. At one point, she stared confusedly at me and asked, "Where's your garage?" There was no garage, but for reasons I can't recall, I told her it was about a half a block away, on the left. I never saw her again, but I repeated the story often for my friends' amusement. Nowadays I'd be wracked with guilt if I treated someone so callously, but the terrible part is that I can't honestly say there's no ambivalence mixed in with the pride I feel about how much I've matured. The rudeness is gone now, but did it take the joy with it?

I can't help wondering what it was we gained or lost that makes us better as men than we were as boys.

◎◎◎

The Amador County Winter Wine Extravaganza is one of those events that make me feel like a grownup in a good way. A classy way. The Convention Center is packed, mostly with people from the generation that still considers T-shirts to be undergarments. There are lots of people around my age—mostly broken off into couples, of course—but I can't spot anyone younger than us. No frat boys, no chugging, no loud or animated behavior. It's weird to have switched sides like this. I'm now one of the people who casts disapproving sidelong glances at exuberant young morons who act exactly like I used to. And I remember how foolish and insignificant we *old folks* seem to them, too.

The vendors aren't strictly from Amador County; tables and displays are set up featuring wineries all the way from Lodi to some places in Oregon I've never heard of. Some vendors have gone all out. They've decorated their space with affectations like oak barrels, pine cones, wine bottles displayed in rough wooden mini-crates filled with straw. They're bringing the vineyards to us, to make us forget that right outside the Convention Center's doors the rain is washing the urine smell off J Street while scattered homeless people huddle under the overhang hoping not to be noticed and chased off. Although thinking about stuff like that would probably also inspire people to buy copious amounts of wine. Stacy and Terry will probably end up purchasing a bottle or two, but I'm content to just walk around and sample the wares, tending to gravitate towards the vendors that offer free cubes of cheese. A gray-haired couple passing a few feet away from us is clearly stocking up for the rest of the winter; they're both toting boxes nearly filled with an assortment of different bottles.

It's been a harmless experience so far. Although Ruth and I have exchanged a few pleasantries, I've stuck close to Stacy and she's hung mostly with Terry. Long before the wine entered my blood stream, I'd noticed a big difference in Ruth's appearance from what I remember from meeting her a few weeks back. She's obviously put in more prep time before leaving the house today than she had before showing up for the Super Bowl. The pony tail is gone, and her long auburn hair falls in wavy curls just past her shoulders. There must be some sort of glitter in the plum eye shadow she's wearing; it seems to make her wide eyes sparkle. I couldn't tell you what color her eyes were. For some reason I'm terrible at noticing things like that, but, believe me, the lovely shape that's revealed by her clingy beige sweater does not evade me. She's sporting stylish short boots and wearing tight pants that not only match her eye shadow but prove that Stacy was spot on in his praise for her prominent rear end. The fact that she dressed in such an alluring way today gives me confidence that she found me worthy of trying to impress, and now I'm actually somewhat pleased that I decided to come along.

I was not blessed with a distinguishing palate, which means I'm not your typical attendee at a function like this. Just as with food, I enjoy most any wine, but in a blind taste test I'd probably guess the same wine on all five samples, just so I'd be right once. Serious wine drinkers pride themselves on being able to notice and identify a multitude of different flavors present in a good glass of wine. I'd think that was an impressive skill if I could convince myself that it enhanced their enjoyment of the product even one iota. I'm amused by people who appear to take their status as a connoisseur so seriously, and as the afternoon wears on I develop a head buzz that persuades me not to hide this fact. Terry has already bought a bottle of Cabernet from a vendor when I wasn't paying attention, and seems to be close to securing a purchase from the Stonehouse Vineyards table, but she can't decide which one. She's putting on quite a performance for the rest of us as she samples a Petite Sirah. Watching Terry, I'm once again baffled by her and Stacy ending up as a couple. She couldn't be more different from him, at least from the Stacy I *thought* I knew. It's like Kate Middleton dating Slim Shady. But maybe that's what makes her so appealing to him. If I'm honest, I'll admit I've gotten together with a lady or two simply because they were so different than me. Of course, I ended up breaking up with them for that same reason. I've passed the age where I'm constantly being invited to the weddings of my friends and have entered the age where I'm the shoulder they cry on about their divorces. So I haven't really brought up my misgivings about Terry with Stacy, because nowadays when any of my friends lands a new girlfriend I tend to take a wait-and-see attitude towards the relationship.

"I definitely taste the nutmeg," Terry informs the bespectacled bald gentleman on the other side of the table, nodding thoughtfully. "Is that a hint of blackberry as well?"

"Absolutely," he replies good naturedly. I can tell he's not impressed, but he's polite enough to let Terry show off for her friends. Something strikes me about his expression, like he's barely containing an unspecific exasperation that's liable to unravel him at any second.

Stacy takes a sip. "That's dope," he offers. After he's reached a certain level, Stacy tends to drop the pretense and morph back into the Bud Light drunk I used to know and love.

A momentary look of chagrin flutters across Terry's face, but she maintains her poise. "Something bittersweet, too, I'm thinking," she says. "Vanilla spice?"

"Chocolate, actually," the bald guy says with unmistakable self-satisfaction. "Believe it or not." He's clearly impressed with himself, yet there's still a trace of that bizarre vexation that makes me think he'd be the guy riding up on the escalator flipping out because the people in front of him are just standing instead of doubling their progress by climbing.

I draw a sip from my own glass. "Ah, yes, chocolate," I say, squinting at the wine as I hold it up to the light. "I'm quite certain I also detect a hint of ..." I pause to suggest I'm working it out in my head. "Pork gravy," I conclude. "Probably aged in a barrel of Georgia Pine, along with shavings of some Crayola crayons." I set the glass down gently and look the bald man in the eye. "Cerulean blue, if I'm not mistaken."

Stacy nearly spits his wine, and Ruth makes sure to lay a hand on my arm as she's laughing. A line of perspiration appears on the Stonehouse guy's upper lip, but he feigns polite amusement. Terry's face clouds over, but Stacy puts his arm around her and she seems to loosen up. We try a Zinfandel, and I insist that I taste lemon peels and Tang. This even gets a smile from Terry. The bald guy produces a cloth and begins fastidiously wiping away spills that aren't there. Stacy joins in, declaring that he tastes at least fourteen of the same twenty-three flavors found in Dr. Pepper, and suddenly we are having more fun than we've had all day. I challenge Stacy to identify all fourteen flavors, and, as he gives it a whirl, Baldy scrubs a dry spot with such fury that his elbow knocks an open bottle of Sirah off the edge of the table. A younger female employee stoops to prevent the bottle from gushing its entire contents onto the carpet, but the left half of the poor bald man's reddened face begins twitching spastically and he sputters something incoherent about his grandfather having been a winemaker.

Our gazes all abandon the stain on the carpet and settle on the twitching face of Baldy, who seems about to pop like one of those canisters of biscuit dough you can buy from the refrigerated aisle at the grocery store.

"He was Polish!" he blurts, and I can tell from their silence that my friends are stuck where I am: in the no man's land between perplexity and the desperate attempt to stifle a laugh that needs to erupt.

"From Poland!"

Part of Stacy's laugh escapes in the form of a muffled snort, but we remain frozen.

"So I'll take one of these," Terry says, grabbing a bottle of Zin and extending a twenty towards the quivering man, who seems unable to respond. As if we'd rehearsed it ahead of time, the other three of us gingerly place our tasting cups back on the table, but we can't take our eyes off Baldy, who vibrates in front of us like the loose-fitting lid balancing atop a pot that's about to boil over. The beleaguered female employee steps in front of the proud Pole and completes Terry's transaction, allowing us to back away and turn our backs before exploding into laughter. Stacy and Ruth practically shove me in the direction of another vendor, almost giddy to hear what I'll say next.

Our observations about the spazzy bald guy get funnier each time we tell them, and even Terry lightens up. The glasses of wine flow faster as all hints of sophistication and earnestness abandon us in our wine tasting adventure. When I'm goofing off and someone gives me the slightest bit of encouragement, I can't be stopped. Making people laugh is as addictive as crack. We're all tipsy before long, and Ruth's hands are all over me as she complains that her cheeks hurt from laughing. When I ask the lady from Sobon Estates Winery if their Cougar Hill Zinfandel contains any sweat from the brow of Courtney Cox, Stacy guffaws so hard he actually drops his glass. As soon as it hits the floor I screech, "I'm from Poland!" and we all nearly piss ourselves. At this point we decide it's probably time to depart.

Outside, the rain has stopped, but the late afternoon still has a damp chill to it. Stacy and Terry decide getting something to eat is a priority before we offend anyone else, so we head towards the nearest sushi joint, about a block and a half away on 15th Street. Ruth sidles up to me on my left and laces her arms through mine, saying she needs me for warmth, and I stride down the sidewalk wearing the exhilarated grin that only the possibility of impending sex with a beautiful girl can bring to a man's face.

5__an inconvenient ruth

The chilled sake at Zen Sushi goes down like water. The sushi is delicious, but it crashes and burns in its mission to sober us up. I wish I could describe the details of the rest of the afternoon and evening more accurately, but my memory is spotty from this point on, so I can only give you the highlights.

At some point between platters of sushi, Terry becomes convinced that Stacy would rather hang out with me than with her and adopts the whiny voice of an overtired seven-year-old in order to get this point across to him. I make Ruth laugh so hard she cries by telling the story of Reena and her purported ghost sightings in a perfect non-regional broken Latino accent. The four of us get into a heated debate over the staying power of One Direction; my comparing them with David Cassidy and the Jonas Brothers does not go over well with the ladies. Stacy is dared into eating a spoonful of Wasabi and turns a shade of crimson that we all find alternately alarming and hilarious.

When Terry's drunken poutiness becomes intolerable, Stacy grudgingly consents to take her home. Ruth, who has impressed me with a respectable knowledge of non-Top 40 music, suggests we go next door to a blues joint called the Torch Club, and I readily agree. On the sidewalk outside between the two venues, Terry grabs me by both shoulders and makes me swear that I'll see Ruth safely to her car, with a gravitas that suggests I'll need to navigate through a minefield in order to do so. With ersatz solemnity, I vow that it shall be so, and we watch the two of them wobble down the block, arguing in animated fashion. Ruth hustles me out of the cold and into the warmth of the dim, rollicking club. Ray-Ray, the door man, gives Ruth a thorough appraisal and nods approvingly at me as we walk by. My apartment being a scant six blocks away, I am somewhat of a regular at the Torch Club, and being greeted by name several times on the way to the bar gives me an air of celebrity, which I hope does not fail to impress Ruth. On stage, a four- piece band wails Texas-style blues. We secure a couple of draught beers and grab one of the last remaining tables at the rear of the club; it's surprisingly crowded for this early on a Saturday evening. The volume of the music prohibits much in the way of conversation, so we let our hands do the communicating for us under the table. My left hand eagerly examines the contours of Ruth's taut, shapely leg, thrilling with the increase in temperature it discovers as it moves further up her inner thigh. Her right hand is on a similar exploration of my leg, which causes the whole situation down there to stiffen. Her eyes—blue or green as they were, or possibly brown—have glazed over and taken on the look of one whose physical desires are in need of prompt satisfaction. It's an unmistakable, magnificent expression in the eyes of a woman, possibly because of the relative rarity of its appearance. I'm not sure what look appears in this situation in the eyes of men, but I'd suspect it's remarkably similar to the one we see each time we look in the mirror.

In between the band's sets, she tells me more about herself. She's a huge Kings fan, so we make eager, vague plans to hit up a game before the NBA season ends. She's not devoutly religious, but she enjoys going to church from time to time to experience "the high" of spirituality. She recently filed a restraining order against her ex-boyfriend, who has a tendency to construct creepy shrines made from found objects on the front lawn of her condo building. She's not on speaking terms with three of her coworkers, which makes for awkward silences at the copier and in the bathroom. Most people do not like to visit her at home because her cat, a jealous type, engages in terrorist tactics designed to make visitors feel uncomfortable. I know what you're wondering, but the answer is no. None of this registers as a red flag to me, because the girl has what appear to be fantastic breasts. Alcohol once again mounts a late game comeback to take the lead over Common Sense.

On the way out, I shake hands with Downtown Willie Brown, and when we emerge from the club, the sky is dark and the overwhelming silence is spanking my eardrums as if they've done something wrong. In a voice too loud I mention that I've got a nice bottle of wine at my place and suggest we have a nightcap. Ruth agrees, and in this fashion we are able to elegantly pretend that screwing each other's brains out is not foremost in our minds. She clings tightly to me on the walk, clearly finding taking turns putting one foot in front of the other to be a taxing endeavor.

Most of my time and energy is taken up by the motel, and the disheveled state of my apartment reflects this. The multitudes of spots in varying shades that have never been steam-cleaned make the carpet appear calico. The posters and framed art that adorn the walls do not represent a cohesive theme; they're more like a timeline of my evolving tastes: a framed poster of famous Irish writers, prints of cubist paintings, a 49ers poster, a ratty *Ferris Bueller* movie poster, a string of Christmas lights I haven't bothered to take down, and an autographed eight by ten of Chris Rock. A dilapidated sofa from the Salvation Army store squats against the main wall of the living room, not the least bit self-conscious about the fact that it doesn't come close to matching the carpet. A *Jenga*-like tower of DVDs rises precariously between the oversized TV and the pieces of the DVD shelf that fell apart three months ago.

Ruth plops down on the sofa and starts fumbling to remove her coat, while I disappear to the kitchen to pour two glasses of wine. I take one small sip from mine, which turns out to be one more than she does before we make our way to the bedroom. Undressing a woman for the first time is one of life's spectacular thrills, and Ruth is a sight for horny eyes. Her breasts are ample, perfectly spherical, without sag, and—as I excitedly find out when I first touch them—untainted by synthetic materials. Her muscles are toned, and she appears to be without body fat. As for me, I'm a booty enthusiast, and what I find when I turn her around makes me feel like I'm in a rap video. Her exquisitely round, firm buttocks protrude further in the third dimension than any Caucasian girl has the right to expect. They are a work of art, and I can't keep my hands off them.

My edge of the bed is only a nightstand's width away from the wall, and I notice Ruth bumps into said wall twice during the four steps it takes to guide her into the bed. We smother each other with sloppy, drunk kisses, and mumble the depraved nonsense you're supposed to say at this point. My coordination is almost as impaired as my mental capacities after a day of drinking, so when I lean over to grab a condom from the drawer of the nightstand I lose my balance and topple off the side of the bed, slamming face first into the wall on my abrupt journey to the floor. The dizzying fall, combined with the force of the impact, immediately clarifies to me the meaning of the expression "seeing stars," but I won't be deterred. Feeling my way back into bed since my sight has not fully returned, I ignore Ruth's concerned questions about my health and concentrate on getting the condom on so that we can commence with our main order of business.

At one point during the festivities, when I am writhing on top of her like a fish dying on the deck of a boat, I become aware of the words that are steadily streaming out of Ruth's mouth.

"Oh, god, I wanna be your girlfriend," she huffs, her eyes clenched shut and her head thrown back, "so you can tell me what to do."

"Um, what?" I ask indistinctly, not wanting to interrupt her in case she's trying to talk herself off in some bizarre fashion, rather than actually talking to me.

"I wanna be your girlfriend," she repeats with conviction. "I want to have your babies."

At least four glasses of wine evaporate from my system upon hearing these words.

"Oh, god, I love you," she declares. "I just love you, love you, love you!"

"Wow," I respond idiotically, "really?" If my thrusting motions had been a jazz song, the bass player has just begun a solo and changed the entire rhythm into something no one's able to dance to.

She has her hands braced against the wall behind her head, but now she wraps them tightly around my torso. "I love you so much," she whispers in a breathy voice that doesn't even sound like hers.

I don't respond. I'm nearing the end, so I speed up, determined not to let her unsettling monologue keep me from reaching the Promised Land. As I climax, over my groan I can hear her say, "I want to redecorate this place for you."

It shouldn't be possible for someone to get drunker the longer they go without drinking, so as I slide out of her and lie down beside her I wonder if she has been sounding this unhinged the whole time, and I'm only beginning to notice because I'm sobering up. Unlike a lot of men that get complained about, I usually have no problem with post-coital snuggling, but at the moment I'm feeling a lot less relaxed than I should be.

"God, I love you so much."

It feels like I'm supposed to respond to this. "Are you ... are you actually talking to God?" Hey, she did say she goes to church, right?

She turns in to me and wraps her leg around mine. "You're so funny," she purrs. "That's one reason I love you so much."

Silence. "Wow," I stammer, "that's ... it seems like it's a little early to decide something like that." I offer a half-hearted laugh.

Her head is tucked under my chin, so I can't read the expression on her face. I notice my sweat has turned cold; that's two clichés that I've now lived out. After about twenty years of silent unresponsiveness, she emits a small sniffing sound, and her back quivers. I realize she's crying.

"I just mean that ... you know, we barely—" I'm not able to finish the sentence because the fist she's using to push herself away from me has caught me right under the rib cage and knocks the wind out of me.

She retreats to the far edge of the bed and turns her back to me. "You're the meanest person I've ever met," she mutters through choked sobs.

Good. I was afraid she was going to say something irrational again.

"I hate you!"

Drawing shallow breaths, I manage to respond, "Look, I'm just saying let's not rush into anything. We've got time to—"

"You're the meanest person I ever met. Why do you think you're so much better than everyone else?"

"Why are you so mad?"

"You always think you're better than everyone else. You're so mean to me. You always do that!"

"Always? We've only hung out the one time, just today."

"See? You're always correcting people. I hate you so much."

It occurs to me that no one I tell this to later will believe this conversation actually happened. I mentally run through my options. I don't know where she's parked, but it's somewhere near the Convention Center. Not far. I could make her get dressed and take her to her car.

"That's why nobody likes you," she declares.

"Do you want some water or something?" I ask, starting to shift from being flabbergasted to being pissed off.

"Yeah."

I hop out of bed and locate my boxer briefs. Walking out to the kitchen, I argue with my conscience, which maintains that she's still too drunk to drive, and, as crazy and annoying as she's acting, I can't put her in harm's way like that. I grab a chilled bottle of water and head back to the bedroom, having decided to let her sleep it off and take her back to her car as early as possible in the morning.

"I don't feel good," she mumbles.

I hand her the water. "Drink some of this."

She obliges, then looks around confusedly. "Are these walls purple, or covered with fur?"

What the hell? "It's just dark in here. Try to get some sleep." I crawl onto my side of the bed and try to fall asleep with my back to her.

Less than a minute later she's clutching at my shoulder, leaning over me. "I want a goodnight kiss," she pleads.

"Are you crazy?" I blurt, shoving her away from me. "Have you ... do you even know what you've been saying?"

She blinks at me, uncomprehending. "Do you want a goodnight fuck?"

"No! Jesus, just go to sleep. You're really drunk. You need some sleep."

"You're the meanest person I've ever met."

"So I've heard." I roll back over and stare down the clock on my nightstand. With a clenched jaw, I vow to count down the minutes until six hours have passed. By that time, whether she's sober or not, I'm putting this girl into her car and shipping her back to Crazytown.

I hate blind dates.

6__saint paddy's lament

A little part of me dies as I walk into Romano's. I haven't seen Maggie for a couple of weeks, so out of a sense of sibling duty I agreed to meet her here. At Romano's Macaroni Grill. On Saint Patrick's Day.

It was her choice, as she is apparently unafraid of having her Irish card revoked. Not surprisingly, Maggie and her husband Marc are already seated at a high table in the bar area as I walk in three minutes late. When my sister was a senior in high school, she was sent home from school on Saint Patrick's Day for showing up wearing a nun's veil, rosary beads, a bright purple bra, but no blouse. She rocked. These days a Saint Paddy's celebration means one glass of house wine at a soulless, pseudo-Italian chain restaurant at 5:30 in the afternoon.

Marc is checking something on his smart phone when I join them at the table. Marc is always checking something on his smartphone. He's six or eight years older than my sister, and he appears to be going for the game show host look: fake tan, unnaturally white teeth, and an expensive-looking, Reaganesque haircut with stylish gray-frosted patches around the sideburns. He's the CFO of some big communications company whose clients include AT&T and Sprint. Or maybe Verizon. That's literally the most detailed explanation of his job that I can tell you, because each time he talks, or Maggie talks about him, I tend to zone out before the end of the conversation because I find him to be the most stunningly boring person I've ever met. In almost ten years of being his brother-in-law I have yet to find any common ground with the man. He doesn't like sports or movies. He says he has to read too much at work to have any desire to read a book when he gets home. To this day I haven't a clue what kind of music he listens to, if any. As far as I can tell, all he does for fun is play golf with his business associates. Or play poker with them. Or hang out in cigar bars with them. In fact, boring is probably not a strong enough word to describe how relentlessly Marc's flatlining personality will undermine your will to live whenever you're around him. One of my favorite hobbies is to try to get my sister to admit aloud that she finds him as boring as I do.

"Look who finally decided to show up," Maggie says in the unique tone she reserves for me, that's somewhere between lighthearted and reproachful. To Maggie and Marc, ten minutes early is pushing the limits of fashionably late.

"Mags, Marc," I say, hopping up into one of those aggravatingly tall bar chairs with no footrests that force you to swing your legs like a damn four-year-old.

"How's it going, Mick?" says Marc, flashing me that creepy grin of his that always makes me suspect he's about to try to sell me a vacuum cleaner.

"Oh, not so bad. I just spent almost an hour convincing DeLisa, my head maid, to take charge of hiring a new maid. The last girl quit because she claims the motel is infested with ghosts."

"What sort of ghosts?" Maggie asks.

I didn't know there were different categories.

"You know, you should always hire your own people," offers Marc. "Look them in the eye. That way you can tell whether you can trust them."

Thanks for the tip, Mr. Human Ambien. "Yeah, I'm not sure. DeLisa's been there longer than me, and she actually likes to choose her own staff. She just enjoys messing with me by pretending to be too busy to do it." They both stare at me expectantly, as if I'm forgetting a line. "So, yeah." I shrug. "I wouldn't know what to look for in a maid anyhow. I don't really know anything about that stuff."

"Don't they like to be called domestic workers these days?" asks Maggie with concern in her voice. This is just the type of nonsense that makes me wish the body snatchers would bring back my old sister.

"I'm not sure; I'd have to check one of your magazines."

"Oh, how cute," Maggie says, oozing smarm. "Those comedy classes are really starting to pay off."

A bright-eyed waitress glides over to the table and asks if she can get me anything. I know she's got bright eyes, because my gaze *eventually* lands there. I bet if more guys were honest, they'd admit that they always check out the whole package when they encounter a woman they don't know. Or maybe I'm just a pig. I ask for a Guinness, watch her ass walk away, and then remind myself that at least I'm an honest pig.

Maggie leans in conspiratorially. "Speaking of cute," she murmurs.

I know full well that this line of conversation will inevitably lead to Maggie pressuring me to ask out the waitress. Hitting on waitresses is one of the most futile ventures you could ever attempt. They get hit on all day, by guys a lot better looking than you, which means what you consider your most charming lines smack of tedium to them. Plus, they work for tips, which means they're only pretending to find your banter entertaining so that you'll falsely believe you have a chance and lay a hefty tip down to try to impress them. Inside, they're probably barely tolerating you. The only reason they appear to be paying such close attention to your awkward jocularity is so that they'll be able to accurately recount your pathetic attempts to charm them for the amusement of the other servers back in the kitchen.

At least, that is the theory I've worked out to explain my otherwise breathtaking lack of success in getting waitresses to go out with me. But complexities like this would be too difficult to explain to my sister, so I just pull out my standard counter. "You think so?" I ask, scrunching my face as if I've just detected a foul scent in the air and am making a show to convince people it didn't come from me.

"What, you don't? Come on, Mick, she's hot." Before I can respond with one of my patented "you'd make a terrible lesbian" digs, she turns to Marc. "Don't you think that waitress is cute?" she prods.

Marc looks up from his phone and casts a gaze in the general direction of where the waitress is standing at a nearby terminal, punching in my order. He shrugs. "I don't know; she has high lips."

Maggie stares at him. I must admit I'm impressed at how deftly Marc has eluded the trap of admitting he finds another woman attractive in the presence of his wife. And he came up with a flaw so bizarre that even Maggie couldn't argue with it. Maybe there's more to him than I thought.

"So what's been going on, guys?" I ask. "How are the kids doing?" This is another foolproof ploy on my part. Maggie is incapable of passing up an opportunity to brag about my niece and nephew, even if it means relenting on an attempt to manipulate me into dating someone.

"Well, someone is going for his green belt this Saturday," she says, beaming.

"Is it Ralph Macchio?"

"Mick, it's a big deal," she explains sternly. "In Tae Kwon Do there are a ton of belts. Keegan is moving up faster than most of his classmates, and he's very proud."

"Awesome," I say, with what I hope sounds like genuine enthusiasm. Keegan is actually a pretty cool little guy, even if I can't get over the fact that he's named Keegan. It seems like a haughty yet emasculating name, deserved only by guys who wear cardigans tied across their shoulders like the rich brats who were the villains in old John Cusack movies. The way I see it, any straight man that has a son named Keegan must have lost an argument with his wife in the delivery room. Considering that the wife in this case is my sister Maggie, well, I'd wager that Marc wins about as many arguments in that household as their tropical fish do.

"Wait, Tae Kwon Do?" Marc says. "I thought he was taking karate."

I should mention here that Marc is also a bit of a hands-off dad. In my observations, he seems to spend a great deal of time squinting confusedly at his children as they wildly run circles around him like looters terrorizing a beleaguered shopkeeper. Since there's no downloadable App for Parenting, the poor guy seems completely lost.

Maggie always tells me that I'd be a great dad, but I'm not so sure.

I adore the kids, Keegan and especially little Madeline. She's five and so implausibly cute and beautiful that she could never get cast in a movie because the producers would think she's not believable enough to portray a real child. I have this weird longing for closeness with the kids that probably has something to do with the magnificent vision I've conjured in my imagination of being the cool uncle—the one whose appearance lights up the eyes of the children and prompts them to throw themselves into my arms. I suppose yearning for a bond with innocent, precious young earthlings isn't such an unusual thing; after all, it's probably one of the main reasons so many people want to have kids.

Where I get hung up is that after spending even a short time with Maggie's kids, they start to annoy the snot out of me. Keegan's sense of entitlement becomes too much to bear, and Maddy gets whiny. Somehow actual children never seem to live up to my idealized expectations of them. But the tenderness of feeling them cuddle up on either side of me while we're watching a Disney DVD on the couch is enough to keep me coming back for more, like some tweaked-out snuggle junkie.

As I'm thinking all of this through, I've begun sipping on the Guinness that somehow appeared without my noticing it, and I gradually zone back in to hear that Maggie is rambling on about some horrific novel she's reading for her book club.

"And after the baby dies," she says, "her husband just grows distant and more detached, because that's what they do. No offense, Marc," she says, patting Marc's hand.

"What's that now?" he says, not taking his eyes off his phone.

"Anyway, she's left to deal with this unthinkable tragedy on her own, with no emotional support. It's heartbreaking. But then she meets this house painter, Jean-Pierre, who's in charge of the crew that's remodeling their downstairs."

"Don't tell me," I say. "He's the gorgeous, sensitive, European-type?"

"Ha, ha, Mick. Laugh all you want, but this author's already had two novels on the *New York Times* bestseller list. How many have you got?"

Ouch. My sister has been an artist in the medium of cruelty for so long it sometimes slips out without her realizing it. I don't have the strength at the moment to take issue with the comment, so I drain my Guinness instead.

"Just kidding. Anyway, it's a great book, and my friend Alice recommended it. You remember me telling you about Alice, right?"

"No," I say. By the way, "just kidding" almost never actually is.

"Sure you do. Alice. I told you about her, remember?"

Nope. "Oh yeah," I say, painting my face with what I consider a look of recognition.

"You know, she's started coming with me to the gym in the

mornings, after I drop the kids off." She eyes me for a quick moment, to try to surmise if I know where this conversation is headed. I do. My sister is about as predictable as cold winters and worthless politicians. "Speaking of which," she continues, "that's something you should think about, joining my gym. It'd be good for you! I could get you the first two months for free on the referral program. You could work out with Alice and I in the mornings."

Alice and *me*. I hate poor grammar. I motion to Bright Eyes for another Guinness. "That's not going to happen," I say. "Exercising in the morning has always made me queasy. As do your attempts to set me up with your friends."

"Who's setting you up?" My sister is a master at feigning incredulousness. "I just think it would be good for you."

"Marc, do you have one of those sturdy gold pens on you that wouldn't break if I shoved it into my temple?"

"Leave me out of it."

"Oh, whatever, Mick," Maggie huffs. "Just think about it, okay?" She catches the waitress's eye and gives her the "Check, please" gesture.

"What, are you going?" I ask.

Marc drains the last of his Chardonnay without looking up from his phone. "It's getting late," Maggie says.

It's 6:04.

"I just ordered another beer," I protest weakly.

"Oh," she says, scrutinizing her watch as if she were a general deciding that a change in plans might jeopardize the whole mission. "Well, we can stay until you finish."

She's starting to make me miserable. Plus the bar area is starting to fill up, and there's a good chance any of these strangers will turn out to be more fun than these two. "Nah, it's okay. Go ahead, you gotta get home to the kids."

"Are you sure?" asks Marc. "We'll stick around for a while."

"Nah, it's all good. I'm fine. I'll even hit on the waitress," I say to Maggie. "I promise." And I halfway mean it, too.

After they leave, I sit and nurse my beer, wallowing in a vague sensation of self-pity that's engulfed me. What a miserable start to Saint Patrick's Day. This used to be my favorite day of the year. Back in college, when so many demented and hilarious characters populated my landscape, on a normal day you could pretty much just sit around and wait for something fun to develop. On a day like Saint Paddy's, forget about it. You just knew that something would happen that would become a crazy story retold for years, and you considered yourself lucky if the cops weren't eventually involved.

Sometimes the best part of the story turned out to be the next morning. Also, that's the part that you can actually remember. Today included, I have never worked on a Saint Patrick's Day in my life. But during my final year of college, I'd been unable to avoid having an interview for a freelance writing job set up for the morning of March 18th. I lived in a big house at the time, with a revolving cast of roommates so transient that the front door was never locked because none of us had keys. The house was passed along from semester to semester; people moved out, other friends took their place. No one even knew who was on the actual lease anymore. The phenomenal thing was not that I'd actually found my way back to that crazy house on Saint Patrick's night, but that I'd somehow remembered to set my alarm for the next morning's interview. When it startled me awake, it took probably a full two minutes of extreme concentration for me to make the room stop spinning long enough to make out what time the clock said. 9:52. It turns out that I'd set the alarm to go off precisely ten minutes before the interview was scheduled. I believe that an epic state of drunkenness is as close as we humans are able to get to being immortal. To drunk Saint Patrick's night me, ten minutes to get ready and be at the paper's offices was not only feasible, it wasn't even going to be challenging. The spinning-headed me of the following morning—the one with the Tasmanian devil tap-dancing in my stomach—scoffed demonstrably at this proposition.

The newspaper at which I was scheduled to interview was a low budget, progressive outfit that projected a laid-back attitude, so I decided to gamble on their coolness. I called and told them I'd had to lend my car to one of my roommates under emergency conditions, and that there was no way I'd be able to come in for another couple of hours, until I could get a ride to my car. Unbelievably, they were okay with this, so I went back to bed for another hour and a half. When the alarm rang, it was every bit as disconcerting as the first time it'd happened, but I managed to bathe, shave, grab my portfolio, and stumble out the front door with just enough time to hightail it to my interview by noon. I had apparently done something the previous day to offend the sun, because it took a vindictive swipe at me as soon as I emerged from the house, half-blinding me and triggering an instant and hellacious headache. I fought back though, and valiantly staggered toward the curb, where my car was ... not parked.

I should own up at this point to the fact that when I was younger I was unflappable in my belief that my driving skills—even while intoxicated—were so vastly superior to those of most mere mortals that I assumed those pesky don't drink and drive rules naturally did not apply to me. As I stood swaying in that malicious midday sunlight, hopelessly confused, I tried unsuccessfully to reconstruct the previous night's events. I had assumed that I'd driven myself home and that's how I'd woken up in my bedroom. But focusing my eyes on both sides of the street, it was apparent that my car was nowhere to be found. I quickly attempted to narrow down the possibilities of which bar I'd been at last so I could calculate how long it would take to walk there to retrieve my car, but my muddled mind drew a blank. I summoned an image of me standing around a pool table, singing a Pogues song with all the other bar patrons, but I decided that could very well just be a memory of an episode of *The Wire* I'd seen on TV, so I shuffled dumbly back into the house. One of my roommates, Stokey, a guy who I wasn't sure was even enrolled in our college, was lying on the couch staring in the direction of the ever-glowing TV. I asked him if he'd seen my car, and he proceeded to laugh uncontrollably—a convulsion that finally stopped when he wiped his eyes, muttered "Classic Mitch," and stared back at the TV. I sighed. As if the guy who didn't even know my real name would have a line on my car. I wandered back outside. The panicky feeling of having no idea of the whereabouts of my car, combined with the realization that I was about to blow an interview for a pretty good job, made my churning stomach sink a few inches further down into my left leg, and I began to emit sweat that smelled faintly of Powers Whiskey. I scanned both sides of the street, the length of the entire block, hoping that maybe I'd just missed it the first time I'd looked due to having cut the amount of my remaining brain cells in half the previous night, but to no avail. The car had disappeared, like my pride. Unable to devise another reasonable excuse, I withdrew my phone from my pocket, having resolved to admit to the newspaper people that I had misplaced my automobile. I knew what a monumental idiot I would sound like, but I didn't have the energy to care. You'll remember my mentioning that in those days I was still fueled by the relentless optimism of youth, so missing out on one job opportunity didn't seem like that big a deal. As I held my phone out before me, I looked up, trying to remember the last four digits of the phone number that was written on an ATM receipt about a thousand miles away in my bedroom. It took a moment for me to register what my gaze had fallen upon. There, on the next block, parked halfway on the front lawn of some poor soul's property, was a vehicle that looked a lot like mine.

Then it all came back to me. Stumbling from my car up to the front porch, being absolutely astonished to find the front door locked. Angrily banging the front door knocker and vowing to kick the ass of whoever had locked me out for several minutes until it had occurred to me that our front door didn't have a knocker on it. My clamoring expedition continued laterally—through the front yards and shrubbery of our neighbors, not on the sidewalk—in search of my real house.

I was so overwhelmed with the relief of not having lost my most expensive possession that it didn't even faze me how spectacularly awful I did at the interview. How it turned out to be a walking tour of the facilities, and how I'd turned it into a never-ending quest to find low shelves to perch upon or sturdy walls against which to lean.

Sure, I hadn't gotten the job, but that's not the point of the story. The point is: that's what Saint Patrick's Days are supposed to be like! Even after I'd graduated college and moved to downtown Sac, I'd spend all day in Irish pubs waiting for friends to get off work, talking amiably and comparing March Madness brackets with total strangers. I'm not supposed to be feeling gloomy like this. I haven't even worked up the nerve to flirt with the hot waitress. As I leave cash for my tab, I console myself with the possibility that maybe tonight—when I meet up with Witt and Ethan somewhere less depressing than The Macaroni Grill—will prove to be more like what Saint Paddy's is supposed to be about.

7__super lothario brothers

If Olive Garden commercials have taught me anything, it's that corporate American chain restaurants are places where heights of fun so deliriously enthralling can be attained that it would be impossible to replicate the experience anywhere else, unless you're sniffing glue. Such was not my experience, however, at Romano's, so I'd gone home afterwards and taken my second shower of the day. I find long showers to be rejuvenating and sometimes cathartic exercises, and I'd needed a rebirth after the inexplicable blues that had enveloped me during Unhappy Hour with Maggie and Marc.

After using my Jedi mind powers, along with some Wolfe Tones and shots of Powers, to recover some semblance of optimism, I'd been picked up by Ethan, and we're now on our way to commence the *real* Saint Patrick's Day festivities. Our destination is Blue Cue, a club that in no way purports to be Irish the other three hundred and sixty-four days of the year, but tonight its exterior is decked out with green balloons, Bailey's logos, and Erin Go Braugh posters. This decision could turn out to be a catastrophe for two reasons. One is that I've noticed over the past couple of years that my desire to hang out at such establishments has waned to near non-existence. When I was younger, I was a mainstay at all the local clubs; my heart pulsed to a house beat. Now I tend to find them overly crowded, far too loud, and generally annoying. I don't like this about myself. I miss the old, fun me, the guy who thrived in these spots. When I was a kid, the saying went *If it's too loud, you're too old!* These days even passing motorcycles make me seethe inwardly. I find having to shout in a person's ear to be heard a rather taxing impediment to having decent conversations. Needless to say, this locale was not my choice, and I'm not sure how Ethan feels about it, because he projects an air of contentment no matter where he is, but if I had to guess I'd doubt that this club would be his first choice. And there's another thing. Although Ethan has steadfastly refused to confirm them, I have my suspicions that he's not that crazy about Witt, either.

My friend Witt is the one who made the plans to meet here tonight. If there were such things, Witt could pass for Ethan's total opposite. He's undependable and capricious, yet so damn charming that you can't help but like the guy. He's the friend who'd give you his last dollar as eagerly as he'd take yours. To Witt, everything is a game, and he revels in being a player. He's somewhat of a local celebrity; he's got a radio show on

KWOD where he spins cutting edge songs and chats up listeners for three hours, five nights a week. Like most radio personalities, his appearance is probably far different from what listeners would expect from his radio voice. He's of slightly shorter than average height, with a stocky build. He's part Latino, so he's got that whole exotic skin tone that American women seem to go for, with short, spiky black hair and an impeccably maintained goatee. I've known him for years, but I couldn't begin to guess his age; the mystery is part of his persona, and he's a mastermind at artfully dodging the subject whenever it comes up. Also, no one I know seems to be sure whether Witt is a real name or a nickname, or what. "Strong Nights with Witt Marten" is all I've ever heard. That's the name of his radio show—get it? Because it's on weeknights, but Witt makes them strong, or some crap like that. I've been very open with him about the incredible dreadfulness of his show's name, but he just laughs me off.

Ethan and I spot him across the room as soon as we reach the top of the stairs. The room is expansive, with high ceilings, a large dance floor next to a small temporary bar on the far side, and a lounge area beside the full bar in the half that we've entered. It's not quite standing room only, but it's getting there. The patrons are a sea of shades of green, decked out with shiny bead necklaces and shamrock pins that light up. The dance floor is relatively unoccupied at the moment; most people are lingering around the main bar, shooting pool, or relaxing around some of the many couches in the lounge area.

"It's pretty loud in here," I half-yell to Ethan.

"Not for a construction site," he responds.

Witt is standing beside one of the few cocktail tables that encircle the dance floor talking to two seated, scantily-attired twentysomethings sipping on what appear to be Cosmopolitans. When it comes to meeting women, this guy is always on the clock, and we know better than to interrupt him when he's at work, so Ethan and I amble over to the bar. Surprisingly, there is only one bartender working, a heavily made-up yet attractive girl wearing black slacks that hug her impressive figure and a tight green tank-top that manages to push her ample cleavage up to nearly chin rest level. She's engaged in pouring a tray full of at least a dozen shots, so Ethan and I wait our turn and survey the scene. Witt's posture and hand gestures evoke someone giving a sales pitch at a corporate business meeting. He is a total player. The guy's vanity plates read NE1469 for chrissake. He's got the two girls laughing, which is just one of his superpowers. You have to admire the guy's fearlessness when approaching strangers, and his acumen for smooth talking his way into a woman's good graces is unparalleled. Although I never approached his level, in the days when the two of us wing manned for each other I enjoyed a better than moderate success rate when attempting to woo strange women. As the years have passed, I find it enormously difficult to approach a woman with the same level of optimism I once did. Too many disastrous dating experiences will do that to a guy, I suppose. Lacking any expectation that beginning a conversation with a female will result in anything other than lunacy and calamity makes it extremely difficult to summon the motivation to even try. But Witt hasn't lost an ounce of his former aplomb, and I'm sure that confidence directly contributes to his remarkable winning percentage.

After a couple of friendly head nods have failed to garner the bartender's attention, I switch places with Ethan and make him try. She grabs something from our side of the bar and flashes Ethan a quick smile, but doesn't ask for our order before scurrying away. A sign posted behind the bar, scrawled in a mystifyingly haphazard combination of capital and lowercase letters, warns that Any crEdit cArd LEft ovErnight will hAve a 20% grAtuity addEd to it's totAl. The urge to take a white-out stick to that apostrophe nearly incapacitates me.

I'm mildly surprised that even Ethan has failed to put in an order by now, but before my surprise can morph into frustration, a hand claps loudly on my shoulder. Witt, beaming, has an arm around both of us. "What's the word, fellas?"

We both greet him, and he says to me, "Happy drunkard day, ya fuckin' Mick!"

"Oh, I see what you did there. Nice."

He turns to Ethan. "How's it going, big guy?"

Ethan doesn't return Witt's exuberance. "Pretty good, Witt. How are you?"

"Fantastic!" He looks over at the bartender and gives her a nod. She smiles and immediately fills three glasses with ice.

"I see you were up to your old tricks over there," I say, nodding in the direction of the two girls he was talking to moments before. "How's it look?"

Witt presses his lips tightly together and wags his head back and forth. "Not sure. We'll see." Witt nods hello to a couple of guys that just walked in. "Did either of you two go to work today?" he asks us.

"I did," Ethan says. "This one had religious differences with the idea."

Witt smiles at me. "So I figured."

The bartender sets three drinks the color of weak apple juice on the bar beside us. "Here you go guys," she says, smiling to reveal two adorable dimples on her cheeks.

Ethan looks at me, dumfounded.

"Unbelievable," I mutter.

"All right, all right," Witt says excitedly, handing one to Ethan, then me.

Ethan smells his. "Red Bull?"

"And Belvedere," Witt says, picking up his own drink. "Very Irish, huh?" He holds up his glass in a toast, and we clink ours to it. "Gentlemen, Happy Saint Patrick's Day!"

"Slainté," I say as we all take a sip. Starting the night with a Red Bull and Vodka is a tradition that goes back several years with Witt and me, back to the days when we used to patrol the Sacramento bar scene in tandem, like a NorCal version of Vince Vaughn and Jon Favreau. Those were good times, and they suddenly seem so long ago.

We move away from the busy bar and find a leaning spot in the lounge area beside a wall-mounted shelf. "So Mick," Witt says, "how did it go with that chick from Valentine's Day?"

Ethan softly snorts, having already heard my tales of woe from the Singles Mixer event. I'm not sure which "chick" Witt thought showed potential that night, but as I summarize the general misery of the overall experience to him, he listens so intently that I'm reminded why he's so damn hard not to like. His effortless ability to make anyone he talks to feel like they're the most important person in the room is a subtle gift that most people lack. He gives you the impression that whatever you're telling him is information he's been anxiously waiting to hear for weeks. I sometimes wonder how genuine the interest he projects actually is, but it's so convincing that I've decided it doesn't really matter. I occasionally wish I could develop this capability, but then I realize that I'm only wishing I could learn how to pretend to have it, which doesn't say a lot for my overall character.

Ethan, who has a knack for comical storytelling so refined that sometimes I think he should be the writer instead of me, begins describing a guy at his gym this morning that declined a row of unused stairmasters to take the one right next to him and immediately began climbing slightly faster than he was.

"He was trying to show you up?" asks Witt.

"That's what I wondered," Ethan says. "So I started going a little faster, and sure enough the guy speeds up."

"This is getting to be too hard to believe," I inject.

"What?"

"People going to a gym on Saint Paddy's Day."

They both laugh, and Ethan continues. "Now, I'm not the guy who's going to take the bait on something like this," he says, and I roll my eyes. Despite his claims to the contrary, we all know Ethan is a highly competitive person and will never back down from a challenge, no matter how trivial or absurd. "But I'm just so curious what this guy's deal is, that I speed up again, and sure enough, so does he. All this time, I'm trying to keep from laughing, because this guy is just so ridiculous."

Yeah, I think, *he's* the one who was ridiculous.

"After about fifteen minutes, I get off and move over to the bikes."

"Oh, no way," Witt says, his eyebrows lifting.

"Oh, yes way," Ethan continues. "After about five minutes the guy comes over and plops down on the bike right next to mine."

"Is it the last bike available?" I ask.

"No! There's like five empty ones. So almost immediately he starts pedaling just faster than me." Witt and I exchange grins, picturing this ludicrous scene. "So we take turns out-pedaling each other until we're going like fifty miles an hour!"

"But you're not competitive," I chuckle.

"I just think it's funny," Ethan exclaims. "That's why I kept egging him on."

"Did you say something to him?" Witt asks.

"Even better," Ethan says, then looks at me. "You'll love this!"

I find I'm on the figurative edge of my seat. Ethan always tells these idiotic stories, but he always manages to suck me in completely. That's the kind of novel mine is going to be.

"I hop off the bike, trying my best not to laugh," he says. "I head to locker room, but I stop for a second to say something to the girl at the counter."

"Was she hot?"

"Shut up, Witt," I say.

"So when I turn around to head into the locker room, this guy is just standing there staring at me."

"What?"

"Like he's waiting to race me into the locker room or something. I can't believe it."

"Don't tell me you still didn't say anything to him," Witt says.

"No, for some reason I think of something even better." He nods at me. "We're standing there facing off, and in honor of your people, I decide to dance a little Irish jig, like I'm gonna challenge him to a dance-off."

"No you didn't either!" I say.

"I did! Just like this." He sets his nearly-empty drink on the shelf and proceeds to do his best Michael Flatley impersonation.

Witt is laughing so hard he has to wipe a tear from his eye.

"What did he do?" I barely manage to get out between laughs.

"Nothing! He just stared at me, so I went back to the locker room." He's laughing, too, and he has to take a sip of his drink before he can continue. "He never came into the locker room, and when I finally came back out to leave, I didn't see him anywhere."

"Victory!" Witt says, offering a high five.

"That sucker got served," I say. This place is already about a thousand times more fun than Romano's.

An ultra-skinny brunette and her tall blonde friend who were standing nearby have turned toward us. "That's some pretty impressive line dancing," the skinny one says.

"Well, I was going more for Dublin than Nashville," Ethan says, "but thanks anyway."

"Do you girls line dance?" Witt asks.

"Oh, yeah," skinny says. "It's so much fun!"

"I want to learn how," says Witt, and I can't fathom that this could in any way be true, but he's back on the clock, so I say nothing. "I was working in Memphis a few months ago, and I was at this bar one night. Some popular song came on, and the whole crowd got into these lines and started doing the steps. It was the coolest thing I've ever seen!" He's gambling that he's struck upon a subject of interest for them, and making his play. Even though I'm not all that good at this game, I understand and recognize the moves.

"You totally should," she says. "It's a blast." She is returning Witt's smile twofold. The gamble appears to have been a wise one.

"You seem familiar," the blonde one says. "Do I know you from somewhere?"

"As much as I'd like to hope so," Witt says, "not that I recall. I have a radio show weeknights on Star 106.5; maybe you've heard my voice or something."

"Really?" both girls say. They are hooked. Witt has entered his zone, and I silently watch him work his magic.

"Yeah, but where can a guy like me learn to line dance around here?" he asks, cleverly shifting the topic of conversation away from himself. With some people, it's best to brag up your selling points; with others it's best to downplay them. Witt is the best I've ever seen at instantly assessing a stranger's personality well enough to know which technique to apply. "I also do a little music production on the side, and I got really into country music when I was in Memphis working with Taylor Swift."

The girls' jaws drop. Ethan rolls his eyes. I shrug.

"Wait, you know Taylor Swift?" the blonde asks excitedly.

"Well, I met her, that's all. I was only in the studio for three days, co-producing this one track with an old friend of mine." The apparent attempts to dismiss significant events and accomplishments only serve to make them seem more impressive to some people, while projecting an unassuming quality often turns out to be very attractive to the intended prey. So far, Witt's strategy is proving to be pitch perfect.

"That is so awesome!" the blonde says. "What's she like?"

"What song did you work on?" the skinny one asks.

"Oh, she was a real sweetheart. The song," Witt pauses midsentence, furrowing his brow in faux concentration. I think he's about to get caught here, midway through weaving his intricate tapestry of what I assume is total bullshit. If he had produced a song, I would have known about it. "Oh, my god, I'm completely blanking on the title." A look of mild disappointment registers on the girls' faces. "I'm such a newbie at country music. Those sessions were the first time I'd actually listened to the genre. It was a really good song though; it ended up making it onto her album. It was about how pissed off she was that her boyfriend had cheated on her."

Nice save. That could apply to probably seventy percent of all country songs in existence.

"Teardrops On My Guitar?" the skinny one asks.

Witt shakes his head.

"Picture To Burn?" asks the other girl.

Witt brightens. "That's the title! I can't believe I blanked on that." Making his participation in the creation of a song so obviously important to them seem like it's something so insignificant that he could forget the details is a stroke of genius. Watching Witt talk to women is like watching Michael Jordan slice through defenders in his prime.

"Holy shit," the blonde exclaims. "That is so cool!"

"Yeah, it was a blast. It got me really interested in country music; it's a really unbelievable market." He looks at me. "Best selling genre in the U.S."

"I had no idea," I say.

"Which is why I'd love for you ladies to teach me how to line dance sometime," Witt says with authentic-sounding warmth.

"Totally!" says the brunette.

"We'll work out the details later," Witt smiles, "but if you could possibly excuse us for a minute, there's someone I need to introduce my friends to."

The subtle look of guilt over having somehow screwed up an opportunity that marks their faces as we exchange goodbyes and walk away reminds me of the similar feeling I've experienced lately basically every time I talk to a new woman. I kind of feel sorry for these two, mostly because of how coldly they've been sold a pack of lies by someone who does not feel the slightest twinge of ambivalence about having done so. I'm no longer able to behave this way without being harassed by my conscience, and sometimes I miss the days when I could.

"Was any of that true?" Ethan asks.

"Hell, no. I can't stand country music."

"So who do you need to introduce us to?" I inquire.

"Oh, nobody," Witt says casually, "but let's go talk to the DJ to make it seem so."

As we amble toward the DJ booth, Ethan says, "Then why leave those girls? You were doing good, man."

"White girls? I don't date outside my race." We both look at him quizzically. He grins and slaps Ethan's shoulder. "Just kidding, bro." Ethan's girlfriend, Georgelle, by the way, is black. "No, the reason is you should always leave them wanting more. Right, Mick?"

"Ah, yes, I remember the routine."

We reach the DJ's table at the top of the stairs—a young guy sporting long black hair with blue tips—and Witt flashes an enormous smile and extends his hand as if he's known the guy for years. The DJ pulls one earphone off and leans down to shake his hand. "Hey, man, I'm Witt Marten from Star 106.5." I can't hear much of what he says because the speakers over here are deafening, but at one point he introduces both of us and we shake hands with the guy. I manage to catch Witt saying something about Taylor Swift, and although I wonder why he's using that line on this guy, it's too loud for me to bother inquiring.

Thankfully, we soon move away from the speakers and cross the outskirts of the dance floor. Ethan indicates a leather mini couch that's just been vacated in the lounge section and suggests we snag it. I'm all for it, but Witt protests.

"Come on, man, it's a good spot," I say.

After a slight hesitation, Witt shrugs. "Yeah, okay, for a minute. You gotta stay mobile to meet chicks, bro." I forgot to mention that hanging around a full time player can rapidly get tiresome.

◎◎◎

The next hour or so evaporates as we bounce around the club and brush up on our small talk skills. We don't move as quickly or as surgically as Witt would prefer, so from time to time he goes off on his own to circulate and work the room. It's like watching a politician at a fundraiser, as if he's the President of the country of VaginaPursuit. At one point, Ethan gets into a lengthy conversation with a couple of guys about the upcoming NCAA basketball tournament. Ever since I failed to make the team freshman year at UCD, I don't follow college hoops all that closely, so I'm only half paying attention. As I'm scanning the room for pretty faces, it dawns on me that I'm doing the same thing Witt's doing, only less successfully. I'm thinking of this conversation with these dudes as a lull between opportunities to hit on girls. When he's in a place like this, Witt considers a conversation simply a means to an end—and it's always the same end with him. If a conversation doesn't seem to be leading him into the good graces — read: pants — of an attractive woman, he quickly and deftly extracts himself from it and moves on. Ethan, on the other hand, seems genuinely interested in what people have to say — any people, it seems, and about any topic. There's no sense of urgency; he seems content to let a conversation develop organically, happy to follow it down whatever path it chooses. When I think about it, that's precisely how conversation is supposed to work. As this occurs to me, I vow to become more like Ethan in this regard. Then again, I think, maybe if Ethan was as unlucky in love as I am, he wouldn't be so easygoing. Either way, I decide to stop obsessing about meeting women and just enjoy my time here with my friends.

The guys talking to Ethan are suddenly spilling beer as they're being picked up off the ground in bear hugs by a couple more of their buddies who have just arrived at the bar. Ethan and I step back. These are Woo Guys, and it's best to keep your distance.

There is no shortage of Woo Guys in this bar tonight. You know the guys — the young ones that look like they spend way too much time in a gym and don't seem to own any clothing that wouldn't be appropriate for it, the ones whose voices grow louder with each shot of Jaeger, the ones that find an implausibly ample number of opportunities where they feel it's appropriate to shout "Woo!" in response to something that's been said or done whenever they're in a crowded bar. The kind who act as if they're attempting to set a record for most high-fives. It's hard to imagine that I used to behave that way in public when I was younger, but I probably did.

Ethan and I suavely slink away from the spectacle the Woo Guys are making of themselves and wander toward the bar for a refill. "Amateur night, man," I say. Ethan shrugs and rolls his eyes. It's gotten more crowded, but it doesn't take us nearly as long this time to get the bartender's attention. Being friends with Witt certainly has its advantages. We do shots of Jameson and order beers. I scan the bar but don't catch sight of Witt.

"What was that stuff about not dating outside his race?" Ethan says.

"That's just his way, man. He doesn't mean any harm. Chalk it up to the fact that he's an idiot."

Ethan looks like he's about to respond, but a girl bumps into his left arm so hard he spills almost a third of his beer. She's short, thick but not fat, and wearing about seventy green beaded necklaces.

"Oh, my gosh, my bad!" The music has been turned up, but she's still talking a little louder than necessary. The way she's looking up at Ethan makes me wonder just how accidental her bumping into him was.

"No worries," I say. "That's how he likes his coffee too."

She smiles, looking at me like she expects me to do a magic trick.

"It was probably your beads," Ethan says. "They probably threw off your balance. I hear Mr. T had the same problem."

"You guys want beads?" She clumsily lightens her load by one necklace and throws it around my neck.

"Wow. For free," I say.

"Oh, that's right," she says, pausing as she pulls the second necklace off. She looks up at Ethan. "Show me your tits!"

"Is that how you got all yours?"

She slaps him playfully. "Wouldn't *you* like to know!"

"I just wanna figure out the exchange rate. Do I gotta show both?"

"Of course!"

"If I show you my third nipple, do I win your car?"

"What?" She says this in more of an "I didn't hear you" way than a "What do you mean" way.

"What do I have to show you to get those earrings?"

"Oh, my earrings," she says with mock admonishment. "You have to buy me a beer for those." This poor child. She thinks she's engaged in some sort of flirting ritual. She has no idea that she's a ball of yarn and Ethan is the cat.

"Is that all?" he exclaims. For his part, Ethan probably has no idea he's being hit on; he usually doesn't. One thing is certain. There is no way Ethan will buy her a beer. He seems morally opposed to buying strange women a drink, but I've never understood his explanations of his objections. There's a lot about him that I don't understand, but I guess I could say that about everyone I know. Humans are a puzzling species. I have time to ponder all this because I'm pretty certain this girl has forgotten that I exist and was once part of the conversation.

"Do you want the beads or don't you?" She grins.

"No, I think they look better on you. But if you start giving away leg warmers or derby hats later, come find me."

"Are you sure?"

"Yeah, I'm pretty sure I would rather have had the rest of my beer back instead." Ethan says this with such innocence and charm that it doesn't sound as rude as she could have taken it. Or maybe she's just too drunk to decipher what he meant.

"You guys are weird," she says.

"It's nice that I got included in that." I smile.

"See you later, 'K?" she says to Ethan as she moves along. She still hasn't made eye contact with me.

As she passes, Ethan suggests we move to a different spot. "It's hack-a-Shaq in here, man." As we move away from the crowded bar, I inform Ethan that the bead girl was flirting with him. "I don't think so," he says matter-of-factly. "She was just drunk." Like I said, he has no clue. I can't help but wonder whether this ignorance works in his favor. He doesn't show the slightest interest in women who approach him, which they invariably interpret as his playing hard to get. What they don't realize is that it's genuine disinterest on his part. As far as I can tell, Ethan fails to notice or feel attraction to any female other than his girlfriend, an elusive ability that I'll admit I've so far not been able to master. Ethan doesn't consider talking to girls in bars to be a game that must be carefully played like Witt and I do. I can't speak for what goes on in the carnal mind of Witt, but with me there's always either the worry of how to say the right thing to a girl that interests me or how to avoid saying the wrong thing and seem cruel to a girl that's interested in me. I realize it's a shitty way to approach the art of communication, but I can't seem to get out of that mindset. This is another of the myriad ways that I wish I was more like Ethan.

After a few minutes of loitering near the pool tables, I move us over to the far table where two lady pool sharks, who look to be in their late twenties maybe—I'm wildly inaccurate when estimating people's ages—are holding court. They appear to be drinking whiskey-based drinks instead of green beer, which intrigues me. They are both very solid pool players, and they laugh a lot, seemingly oblivious of everyone around them. I make a few complimentary comments, and they respond graciously. After their game is finished they invite us to play them. "I don't know, you girls look like a couple of hustlers to me," I say.

The one who introduces herself as Brooklyn says, "Don't worry, we'll be gentle."

Ethan sets his beer down and adopts a theatrical pose. "It's a do or die situation, Mick. We will be invincible!"

I smile and pretend to get the reference—probably a movie line, or, knowing Ethan, a Pat Benatar lyric—then fish a dollar bill out of my pocket to feed into the pool table. Normally I'm pretty decent on the billiards table, not as good as Ethan because he's better than me at everything that requires the use of the hands or feet, but I can hold my own. But that's not how it goes down tonight. Maybe I can blame it on the distraction of playing with two attractive women wearing low cut blouses. Or maybe the Jameson has rendered me cross-eyed. Ethan misses a couple of easy shots, but I play so terribly that I don't feel qualified to ever watch *The Color of Money* again. Imagine a world class pool champion with a razor sharp understanding of angles deliberately trying to keep any of his balls from going in the pockets, and you'll get a pretty clear picture of how I humiliate myself in front of these women. Balls that lie with such short, unimpeded paths to the pockets that a strong wind could probably put them in are sent careening towards the far corners of the table by my cursed cue. Remember, Ethan claims not to be remotely competitive, so he doesn't comment or seem to mind losing horrifically, but I'm embarrassed enough to forego a rematch and get back to what I'm good at.

We head back to the bar.

8__all in the game

Before long, Ethan and I have settled back into the lounge area, onto one of those stylish white leather couches that look far more comfortable than they actually are. My head has begun to swirl, as I'm well on my way to blissful intoxication. We've been alternating rounds of beer with shots or Jameson on the rocks, and it's a rocks round, so we sip serenely, saying nothing for several moments, simply taking in the flurry of activity around us. The place is now teeming with people, and I feel lucky to have found a spot to give my unsteady legs a rest. I'm watching a tall guy with over-greased hair going through his audition with three girls who appear to be way too young for him seated on the couch opposite from us. Witt materializes and inquires about our interlude with the two girls playing pool.

I shrug. "We were just playing pool. I wasn't really thinking about it in those terms." I smile, because as soon as I make this statement, I realize that it's true.

Witt gives me the same quizzical look you'd give someone who stood up in a business meeting, stripped, and began speaking in tongues like they do at those Pentecostal churches, but before he can respond, we're interrupted.

"Hey, boys!" It's the skinny brunette and her tall blonde friend, the same two for whom Witt had constructed his monument of country music bullshit earlier.

"Hey! My line dancing partners," Witt exclaims, and clinks glasses with both of them. He begins chatting with them in his easygoing, radio-friendly style. The skinny brunette is making most of the responses, which inspires me to try to engage the blonde's attention. I can't think of anything witty or clever to say, which for some reason is what I always believe I must do when meeting a new person. Usually drinking improves my comedic acumen, but for the moment I'm sitting here mute, like a seventh grader at his first social mixer. I can't think of a blessed thing to say, funny or otherwise. Ethan asks her something about her necklace, which appears to be handmade. She tells him she got it at a Native American pow-wow last summer, which she attended with a friend. Not surprisingly, Ethan is well-informed about the tribe she mentions—his base of knowledge is indescribably varied and arbitrary—and immediately they've launched into a full-scale conversation. It all seemed so effortless, and my congenial mood starts to fade as I inwardly scold myself for not having the gumption to start a conversation of my own. A moment ago I'd hesitated to speak because I blanked when trying to come up with something clever or amusing, but now I'm flat-out abusing myself, declaring the cause of my silence to be a deficiency of courage. This is another thing that tends to happen when I drink: I become a brutal critic of my own neuroses.

I'm startled by the suddenness with which both girls turn toward each other with stifled shrieks and then look towards Witt, who's got a self-satisfied grin smeared across his face. It takes me a moment to realize that a new song has come on, and that it's the very song that Witt had previously claimed to have had a hand in producing. So that's what he was saying about Taylor Swift to the DJ. An extraordinarily clever move. He is the Bobby Fischer of picking up women.

The girls practically drag Witt onto the dance floor. Ethan and I are not invited.

"Unreal," I mutter. For a moment I feel sorry for these girls being sold such outlandish lies, but I suppose that if a woman is shallow enough to be impressed by flashy jobs and big money then she deserves to be misled by a guy like Witt.

Ethan doesn't reply, but the expression on his face is somewhat dour. I don't know what's going through his head, but I find myself pining for the days when I possessed the tenacity and creativity to pull off a stunt like Witt's just done. Then I skeptically question whether I *ever* really had that sort of mojo. The volume and collective throbbing of this place is starting to irk me.

Witt and the girls return to our spot immediately when the song ends. "It wasn't line-dancing, but fun nonetheless," Witt pronounces. Both girls are glowing. As Witt drains the last of his beer, the blonde checks her phone.

"We've gotta go meet our friends at Streets of London," the brunette says. She exchanges a glance with her friend. "You guys wanna come?"

Friends? I look over at Ethan, who shrugs in response. Normally I wouldn't even consider stepping foot into an English pub on a day like this, because that's the irrational bigotry with which I was raised, but I'm intrigued by a second chance to locate my mojo with friends of these girls. As I'm about to voice my endorsement of the idea, Witt explains that we can't, that we're waiting for friends to arrive here. (We aren't.) The girls' expressions look as deflated as I feel, until Witt reminds them that he's going to hold them to their offer for line-dancing. He extracts a business card—a business card!—and hands it to the brunette.

"If you're serious about it, you can give me a shout," he says. "But don't call between one and three p.m.; that's when my stories are on." The girls giggle. Witt turns and points to us. "Refills?"

We trade goodbyes with the girls and they head out. Instead of following Witt to the bar, I grab his shoulder. "Why did you do that, man?" I demand, with more irritation in my voice than I'd intended. "We could have met their friends!"

"Nah, not a good move, following them to a bar. Not yet."

"Shit, man," I grumble. "At least we could have gotten out of here."

Witt looks sincerely flabbergasted. "You want to get out of here? Why?"

I shrug and drop my gaze. "I don't know," I admit.

Witt asks Ethan, "What's the matter with him?"

"I don't know; ask him."

"Look, I'm sorry, Witt. I guess I'm just a little frustrated with myself, that's all."

"What's wrong?"

I look around the bar before I answer. "I don't know. I should have tried harder to talk to those chicks. I just feel like I'm losing my touch, you know?"

"You're not doing well lately?" Witt seems genuinely concerned.

I rationalize my pessimism by explaining how the only girl I had been excited about lately had turned out to be batshit crazy. I summarize my night with Ruth, and he cringes in empathy at the most gruesome highlights.

"Look, it's not you," Witt promises. "Lots of them are crazy; trust me."

"I think they all are," Ethan adds. "But so are most of us."

"For sure," Witt agrees. "You just need to meet more girls, that's all. If you cast a wider net, you'll find more of the sane ones." He looks over at Ethan, who nods. "Why don't you try Match dot com or something like that?"

I snort.

"Hey, it works, man," he says. "I got hella dates on that site."

This stuns me. "What? You've actually used online dating sites? *You*?"

He rolls his eyes, dismissing my insinuation. "Dude, there's no stigma about that stuff anymore. It's totally normal these days. Everyone tries them out. You just gotta know what you're doing, that's all."

"What do you mean?"

"You gotta check out the profiles very carefully and know who to avoid," he explains. "For example, no Christian chicks—they won't play."

Ah. Witt and his one track mind.

"And nobody who doesn't drink," he continues, "because what're you gonna do on a date? You can only play putt putt so many times."

"Makes sense," I say.

"I like putt putt," Ethan comments.

"Most importantly, avoid profiles that only have photos of the girl's face, no matter how hot she looks. Close up shots of faces only is a clear sign that she's fat."

"You should be writing this down," says Ethan, mocking Witt with a straight face.

Despite my mood, Witt amuses me. He puts a lot of thought into the strangest things. "What else?"

"Well, obviously, avoid chicks with kids. Planning a date with them is like trying to schedule face time with the President—they gotta get sitters and all that bullshit." What he really means is that he's terrified of being tied down into some sort of commitment. "Oh, and don't waste your time with Indian chicks; they only like other Indians."

"All right, I get the picture."

"You should write a brochure," Ethan says.

"Experience, man." Witt shrugs.

"I don't know; I just don't think I'm the online dating type." The whole thing just sounds exhausting.

"Listen, fuck it. Let's go to Streets and pick up those two girls. Get you back in the saddle, bro!" He playfully jabs my shoulder.

I search my thoughts for the desire I'd had a few minutes ago to do just that, but I'm surprised to come up empty. "I don't know, man. Maybe it's not such a good idea."

"It'll be fine, man. Come on!"

I look at Ethan, hoping he'll say no. I just don't want to experience another moment where I freeze up when trying to talk to a girl then spend the next five minutes beating myself up for it. "I'm fine with whatever," Ethan says. Big help.

"Nah," I say. "I'm just not feeling *on* tonight, I guess. I just want to chill and drink."

Surprisingly, Witt doesn't push. "Up to you."

Ethan pipes up. "Why don't we go to the Sheraton bar? It's probably a little more chill there."

"There's not gonna be any chicks there," Witt whines.

"That sounds pretty good," I say, immediately warming to the idea of lounging in an easy-chair with quiet piano music playing in the background. "I could go for something to eat." I turn to Witt. "You down?"

"I don't know; I think I'm gonna stay here," he says. "There's a blonde chick over there I was talking to earlier. Unfinished business. You know."

I smile and nod. "All right, man, I think we're out."

Witt drains the last sip of his beer and gives us both quick man hugs. "Match dot com," he reminds me.

"Yeah, yeah. Good luck with blondie," I say.

He spots her across the room and winks at me. "Like the dick said to the condom, 'Cover me, I'm going in!'" He pretends to straighten an imaginary tie and disappears into the crowd.

◎◎◎

Outside, Ethan and I pause for a moment to acclimate ourselves to the cooler temperature, the welcome silence, and the new sensation of not getting bumped into every few seconds. "He's a character," Ethan says.

"You're not that crazy about Witt, huh?"

"He can just get to be a bit much at times, that's all. Don't you think?"

I grin. "He makes me laugh. But I'll admit, sometimes it's like being around a horny sixteen-year-old."

"On speed." Ethan chuckles.

"Still, I kind of miss being like that."

"I don't think you were ever like *that*."

"I just mean the thrill of chasing girls around, the sense of adventure. You've got to admire someone who's that good at picking up women. It's like he has Jedi mind powers or something."

We begin the walk towards the Sheraton. Ethan peers at me curiously. "Is that what you want to be like? Running around trying to sleep with a different girl every night? Seems tedious to me."

"Nah, I'm not looking for a series of one night stands. I couldn't feed a girl a bunch of horseshit just to get her in bed; that's not me. But I'm not really looking to be tied down yet either. I don't know, I'm somewhere in the middle I guess. I want *something*; I just don't know what."

Ethan doesn't say anything for a moment. "You're just kind of lonely, that's all."

This sounds like an accusation to my Jameson-flavored brain, and I feel defensive. "Lonely? No. If anything, I get sick of being around people all the time."

"That's not what I mean."

I know that's not what he means, and I feel sheepish. There could be a shred of truth to what he's saying.

"Why don't you try Match, like Witt says?"

"Are you serious?"

"There are no problems the Internet can't solve," he declares solemnly.

I realize that he's joking, or at least half joking. But the seeds of an idea have been planted.

9__getting committed

What is my life's noble purpose?

This is what I'm pondering at the front desk while I'm pretending to work on my inventory list. I've always vaguely felt that I was meant to accomplish something important during my time on this planet, and I'm fairly certain that running a second rate motel isn't it. At thirty-three, I'm a year older than Alexander the Great was when he died, but by that time he had conquered the known world. Mick the Mediocre.

Angelina was unfulfilled.

The phone rings. The little Asian man in Room 17 who checked in alone last night seems to be describing some sort of problem with his toilet. At least that's what I think I decipher. He speaks extremely quietly and with a thick accent. I tell him I'll be up to check it out shortly. I wish I could hire a full time maintenance man. Ever since the one who worked for Remi inexplicably stopped showing up one day about a year ago, I've had to try—in my bumbling fashion—to handle maintenance issues myself. The thing is, I'm terrible at it. I don't know how to fix anything in the conventional way. What little I know I've learned by trying to fix things myself, screwing it up beyond recognition, calling in a professional, and watching what they do to correct my mistakes. Not very efficient, I'll grant you, but more economically feasible than hiring someone full time. The motel is generating steadily declining income ever since this damn recession hit. If things don't pick up, the next cut I'll probably have to make will be to shut down our laughable excuse for a café, although I may decide to fire the maid staff and do the cleaning myself rather than tell José he's out of a job. Another holdover from Remi's era, José is my no-nonsense one-man kitchen crew, and he is absolutely terrifying. My best guess is that he's somewhere between thirty-five and sixty years old, and I've never seen him smile. He's built like a tree stump, and he gives everyone this menacing look—kind of like a tree would probably look at a guy with a saw in his hands.

Which reminds me, I had asked for a BLT at least a half hour ago. Because he's forced to work out of a kitchen area that's roughly the size of a grand piano, José offers a very limited menu. Mostly sandwiches and pastries. Guests usually come into the lobby to order food, or they can call the front desk, but either way José resolutely refuses to interact with them. He'll leave the prepared food plates on a shelf situated in the short hallway between the front desk and the back part of the office, where the kitchen is. He apparently approaches this shelf with ninja-like stealth because I've never seen or heard him place a plate there. It's up to whomever is working the front desk to poke their head around the corner every few minutes to see if an order has appeared. He prefers that no one steps foot in his kitchen to check on an order, or for any other reason whatsoever. Most of us are happy to comply.

I have to head into the back to grab a plunger anyway, so when I pass by the empty shelf I decide to risk popping my head into the kitchen to check on my sandwich. José is already standing and facing the doorway in an unsettling, Hannibal Lecter style pose.

"José, how's it going?" I ask with as much cheerfulness as I can muster.

No answer. If I had to bet between José and one of the Presidents on Mt. Rushmore altering their facial expression first, I'm pretty sure I'd take Teddy Roosevelt.

"With my BLT?" I clarify.

He stares at me as if trying to settle upon which method he'll use to murder me, and then murmurs, "Is coming."

I glance around the kitchen. I can't spot any bacon, lettuce, or tomatoes. Not even bread. The counters appear to have just been cleaned. "Great," I say. "I have to look into a maintenance problem in seventeen, but I should be back soon."

No expression, no response. I back away from the doorway and hurry over to the utility closet, feeling like a jester who's narrowly escaped with his life after performing poorly for an ill-tempered king. I snatch the plunger and head back through the lobby so I can pretend to know what I'm doing in Room 17 while trying not to flood the place.

After speaking to the little Asian man for probably a full two minutes through the small sliver of doorway that appears when the chain lock is still engaged, I'm able to convince him that I'm the same guy he spoke to on the phone a few moments ago, and he lets me in.

I'm certain that he checked in alone, so I find the state of his room puzzling. Stacks of neatly folded clothes are piled everywhere—they cover the bed and the table, the top of the mini-fridge, the counter beside the closet. There are even some shirts balanced precariously atop the TV. Or are those blouses? The clothes appear to be a mixture of men's, women's, and children's—all different sizes. He had only checked in for two nights, yet he's brought enough outfits to clothe the entire Brady Bunch family for a week—including Alice! Hell, maybe even Oliver; who knows what he's got in the dresser drawers? On the bedside stand there are a package of crayons and a couple of coloring books; the top one is open to a page that's half colored.

The humans are a perplexing species.

He is chattering softly, and I pretend to hear and understand him as I proceed to the toilet. It's definitely close to overflowing, but at least it's filled only with clear water. Although if it had been otherwise, at least I would have probably lost my appetite for the BLT that I may never get. I turn off the water valve and commence plunging, but all I accomplish is splashing some water on the floor. I take the top off the tank and peer inside with the same expression of feigned understanding that I use when I check under the hood of my car. Everything looks like it's hooked up correctly. I try some more vigorous plunging. Nothing. My list of strategies for fixing a toilet is now pretty much exhausted. I furrow my brow for effect and turn to the little man. "Looks like I'm going to need a snake or something."

He backs away, his eyes growing larger and rounder than I'd have thought possible for an Asian.

"Not a *snake* snake," I try to reassure him. "I mean a ... look, I'm going to need tools that I don't have, so I'm going to have to call someone." He mutters something barely audible, and of course I don't catch it. One of the words sounded like *taco*. "Anyway," I continue, "I can get you set up in another room so we can get this fixed."

His shoulders sag as he scans the room. I don't blame him for feeling dejected; it probably took him all morning to lay out this peculiar assortment of clothes. I offer him free lunch to make it up to him, and he seems to like the idea. He pockets the package of crayons, picks up the coloring books, tucks them into the front of his pants, and stares expectantly at me. I have no idea how to interpret this gesture. I was about to offer to help him move his stuff to the new room, but now I just want to get away from him, so I tell him I'm going to grab a different room key, and I make my hasty exit.

Another typically bizarre day at The Shady Spot Motel. Unfortunately, it doesn't promise to get any better, because the "someone" I'm going to have to call to fix the toilet is Rollie, and Rollie is his own special brand of strange. I'm not sure I'm up for his shenanigans today, but I decide it's better not to put off fixing that toilet, so I head back to the office to find Mr. Clothing Hoarder a new room and look up Rollie's number.

At least my BLT is waiting for me on the shelf when I get back.

◎◎◎

After getting the Asian gentleman settled in Room 20, I give Rollie a ring, hoping that he won't be able to make it out for a day or two, but he tells me he can come right over. I'm certain that I hear the bleating of sheep in the background of wherever he's at.

About forty-five minutes later I see his truck pull up. I attempt to look as busy as possible so he doesn't try to trap me in a conversation. He strolls into the lobby, decked out in a navy blue workman's coverall that looks like it was purchased at a yard sale from Michael Myers. I've never seen him wearing anything else. It's got the name *Franklin* embroidered on it in cursive letters, which I asked him about once, but he just laughed at me and shook his head in something that resembled pity, so I never brought it up again. He's a bit taller than me, with pointy shoulders and a toothpick perpetually parked in the corner of his mouth. Like always, his jumpsuit is unbuttoned to an uncomfortably low spot, right above his paunch belly, revealing his pasty chest, sparsely covered with scraggly red hairs.

I delay letting him know that I've noticed his arrival, but I can feel him grinning at me. "Mick!" he announces at length in his booming baritone.

I look up. "Oh, hey, Rollie. Thanks for coming out. God, I'm swamped here; I didn't have time to give the toilet much of a look." We're both aware of my lack of ability to repair things, so I'm not sure why I always play this game.

"So your hairline's finally begun to recede, eh?"

I have unusually thick hair. As far as I can tell, I've never lost a single strand. "I don't think so, man."

"Hmm." This isn't the first time he's suggested that I'm going bald. I'm not sure what kind of agenda he's pushing with this. It could be that he's highly competitive and miffed that he's losing to me in this category. He's got a regular Jack Nicholson widow's peak going on. Or it could just be a byproduct of his latent insanity.

"Rollie, what were you doing hanging around with sheep?"

"What *wasn't* I doing?" he quips, laughing lasciviously.

"You're an odd dude," I say, to which he makes no response. "Here you go, Room 17." I toss him the key. "How much do you figure you'll overcharge me for this?"

He feigns offense. "I never cheat my friends, Mick."

"Yeah, right." It's borderline frightening that this sociopath thinks of me as a friend.

His eyes light up. "Any good lookin' babes staying?" Rollie is constantly in heat, kind of like Witt, only far creepier.

"Not your type, man. They're all over eighteen."

"Ha!" He paces across the lobby in the wrong direction and looks out the window. "How long since you've cleaned that pool?"

"Look, man, I'm swamped here. I really need that toilet fixed."

"Say no more." He's still looking out the window. He doesn't budge.

After a few more moments, I ask, "So you can't even give me a ballpark what it'll cost to unclog a toilet?"

He turns from the window. "Mick, I don't have time for all this chit chat. Fixing your shitter's not the only thing I have to do today." He starts ambling across the lobby, which for him counts as hurrying.

"Yeah, more sheep to shave?"

He pauses at the doorway and fixes me with an ambiguous smile before he walks out.

"I hope you're only shaving them!" I call after him.

I work on filling out my inventory sheet for about twenty minutes, but I need DaLisa's input in order to finish. DaLisa has worked here for over two decades and knows more about this place than I do. I spot her on the second floor balcony and holler that I need her in the lobby. She gives me one of her typically sassy responses before agreeing to come down in a few minutes. DaLisa is an overweight, Jamaican, grandmotherly sort who divides her time equally between treating me like a doting mother would and busting my balls. Even though she makes me feel like I'm an unqualified kid pretending to run a motel, she makes me laugh, and I trust her implicitly.

The little Asian man comes down to collect on my lunch offer. He spends an inordinate amount of time scrutinizing the menu—which consists of only eight items—and I'm tempted to ask him if he's got all his clothes laid out yet in his new room, but I bite my tongue. He makes a couple of comments, but I can't tell if he's talking to himself or to me. And of course I don't even come close to comprehending what he's saying. When he stops and looks at me imploringly, I realize that he's asked me a question. I have him point to what he wants on the menu and I write up the order for José. As this is happening, DaLisa waddles in, snags the inventory form, and puts on her reading glasses, which she keeps somewhere in the deep recesses of her bosom. I once saw her pull a roll of quarters out of there. It staggers the imagination.

"DaLisa, how's the search going for a new maid?"

"It's going."

I walk back and place the lunch order on the counter just inside the kitchen door for José, being careful not to actually step into his territory, and when I get back to the front desk the Asian man asks me something indecipherable. It's something about his food, but I can't make out what he's getting at, so I have him repeat it a couple of times.

DaLisa sighs loudly. Without taking her eyes off the form she's working on she says, "He wants to know does he have to eat at these tables, or can he have it in his room."

"Ah. No, you're welcome to have it in your room if you want. I'll bring it up when it's ready."

He thanks me and leaves. He nearly collides with Rollie on his way out the door, and does a little half jump to the side like a startled cat. Rollie's beaming, bearing a soaking wet, pinkish bra in his raised arm.

"What are you doing, man? That's dripping all over the carpet!"

He pays me no mind. "Here's your culprit, Mick."

DaLisa sighs again, louder. She makes no effort to hide her revulsion to Rollie. It takes me a minute to deduce what he's talking about. "Wait, that's what was clogging the toilet in seventeen?"

"Yes, sir. Thirty-two C cup." He's grinning proudly.

"What the ... who flushes a bra down a toilet?" I glance over at DaLisa; she rolls her eyes.

"Hey, Mick," Rollie says more quietly, "you mind if I keep this?"

"Rollie, what on earth would you want with a ... you know what? Never mind. Do whatever you want to with it, man." He stuffs it into the deep pocket of his jumpsuit. Doesn't even wring it out first.

"So it's working now?"

"Clean as a feather."

"I'm pretty sure that's not an expression, but thanks. So how much do I owe you?"

"I'll write you up a bill." He practically skips out the door to his truck.

What would possess a woman to flush her bra down the toilet? Then again, what possesses them to do any of the curious things they do? It's like they're blind to their own insanity. Take my last steady girlfriend, Clare, for instance. We'd met at a bar and had gone out a handful of times before she spent the night. When we woke up in the morning, I was pleased to note that I wasn't feeling a debilitatingly urgent desire to get her out of my place like I all too often do. It made me feel like I was getting into something real. I suggested we walk to a nearby café for breakfast, and in the middle of the small talk along the way she blurted out, "Yeah, I plan to be pregnant by the end of this year."

Obviously, that stopped me in my tracks. This was on a September morning, by the way. She seemed genuinely confused that I was reacting to the comment as if it were a big deal. "Well, that's kind of big news," I'd explained. "Probably something you should mention to someone that you're getting involved in a romantic relationship with."

"Oh, don't feel pressured. I'm not saying it has to be with you."

You're probably doubting that it actually happened this way, but I swear to God that's exactly what she said. The most inconceivable thing, however, was that I actually continued to date this girl for another few weeks. Luckily, she didn't persist with the pregnancy timetable, so I, being the pudding-brained moron that I am, decided to ignore the sheer lunacy of the entire situation and kept the relationship going. What eventually broke us up was when we tried to spend a weekend together in San Francisco. Saturday night I'd been too drunk for sex so we'd gone to bed, but she inexplicably got up and left the room for several hours. I don't know if she didn't think I'd notice or what, but I found this to be very irregular behavior and told her so when she finally returned and crawled back in bed. Her response was to claim that she hadn't gone anywhere, that she'd been in the bed beside me the entire time. Even when I pointed out that the freezing temperature of her skin could only mean she'd recently been outdoors, she stuck with her story. I decided not to press the issue any further and instead began planning the goodbye speech I planned to deliver on the drive home the next day.

That was a very deflating incident for me, because I had been legitimately entertaining thoughts of eventually settling down with Clare, which was a big deal for me because I typically tend to get frightened off by the thought of commitment. I'm not sure why. I don't have a past riddled with the types of heartbreaking events that lead characters in movies and books to fear commitment. I don't come from a broken home. It doesn't make sense, this aversion to serious relationships. Sometimes I worry that I'm too much like Witt, who doesn't want to be tied down because he's constantly on the lookout for an upgrade for whatever girl he's with. I don't want to be that superficial, and I don't think that's it, but I can't put my finger on exactly what the real reason is. I wonder at times if there's a connection between my irrational fear of marriage and the way I feel about this motel. Some days I wake up in a panic that I might be stuck here for the rest of my life. The Shady Spot seems to take up too much of the time and energy that I should be devoting to writing my book and becoming the person I always wanted to be. Sacramento is a long way from New York.

The ambivalence is what kills me. Once I'm in a relationship, I tend to get squeamish that it may turn into my last relationship, as long as we both shall live, but when I'm not in a relationship I'm just as miserable. The urge to find a girl and make her mine is overpowering. These contradictory impulses are frazzling to one's mind. This must be how Elvis felt towards the end, when every day he'd take a pile of uppers and a pile of downers and let them battle it out in his brain.

Despite my denials at the time, I suspect Ethan may have been on to something on Saint Patrick's Day when he suggested I might be lonely. There must be some reason I feel pangs of jealousy whenever I see a group of happy couples hanging out together. Maybe it's not even the fact that they're couples so much as the fact that they have a fun group of friends. Here I've been, assuming that getting a girlfriend is the only way to solve my loneliness problem, when maybe a solid group of good friends could also do the trick. I have friends, but they're not *good* friends, and they're definitely not a group. I consider Ethan to be a true friend, but Witt and Stacy are more like drinking buddies, and the three of them don't particularly like one another. So, obviously, we could never star in an Applebee's commercial. Also, I've noticed that those ads usually feature a mixture of the genders, and while I've often had girlfriends, I've never had girl friends. It's always been impossible for me to hang around girls without feeling at least a twinge of sexual tension. I'm always nervous that one of us will catch feelings and it'll get awkward. I mean, you don't go to the bar to watch a ballgame with a girl!

This loneliness situation has got to be dealt with.

10__make me a match

With the staunch resistance of a kleptomaniac wandering through a flea market, I had maintained my opposition to trying online dating for a good two-and-a-half hours after that moment of clarity when I'd realized how lonely I was. Since then I'd been navigating through Match.com profiles and at the present moment I'm revising my own profile—for about the twelfth time—which has been posted now for about two weeks. Of course, all this is being done under a shroud of secrecy. The thought that someone I know might find out I'm on Match petrifies me. Part of me is chagrined that a move like this reeks of desperation, but knowing that Witt has done it gives me some level of comfort. Another part doesn't want to admit to people like Maggie that there's any merit to her fraction of a person philosophy. And I'm damn sure not ready to admit that to myself yet, either.

If you've never been on an online dating website, trust me when I say it can be a jarring experience. I must have read a hundred profiles of women by now that live within fifteen miles of Sacramento, and I can attest to the fact that somehow it's even weirder than dating in real life. I was disconcerted to read CaliGurl_79's profile and realize I had apparently already done something to piss her off. The bitterness this woman harbored toward everyone with a penis was palpable in the scathing paragraphs she'd written, which I thought was an odd strategy to employ on a site that's designed to help you make positive first impressions upon strangers. Her diatribe concluded with the following sentence: "Good looking guys please do not contact me, I have my reasons." Despite the run-on, this struck me as hilarious, and I couldn't help emailing her to ask if by writing to her I had, in fact, owned up to my inherent unattractiveness. Shockingly, I never heard back from her, but the next day her paragraph had been completely rewritten.

Another interesting discovery: Some profiles are as authentic as Joan Rivers's smile. Yep, they purport to be local girls, but feature a professionally done photograph of some too-good-to-be-true model. They're only on the site to direct lonely mental midgets to other sites where they'll have to shell out some money to see lewd pictures of the dream girl. It didn't take me long to catch on to this trick; the written details on the profiles are dead giveaways. If it lists them as "searching for men between the ages of 18 and 80," who live within a thousand miles of their ZIP Code, chances are they're not really the girl next door searching for her soul mate. If their paragraph about what they're like and what they're looking for sounds like it was written by a man who knows nothing about how women think—and we can smell our own—you can rest assured it's a fake. You can tell a man wrote it if it's outrageously bland, positive, or unspecific. "I'm looking for a man who is strong, honest, and can make me laugh." In other words, all the things every man everywhere fancies apply to him. "I like spending time with friends and family, or just hanging out watching sports." Definitely written by a man. Surfing through all these profiles is kind of like being at an extravagant buffet where some of the food is made out of decorative plastic.

Another thing you notice is that a lot of the genuine profiles don't sound all that real either. There is a definite "type" of woman on this site who feels it necessary to only post photos of herself jumping out of airplanes or in front of famous European landmarks. I guess the idea is to present oneself as adventurous, cultured, and interesting, but it just seems pretentious and silly to me. Then there are the ones who only post photos of themselves with their group of girlfriends. First of all, they're all dolled up and dressed similarly, so it's hard to even tell which one she is in the photo. You can generally count on the prettiest one not being her though. I find these group photos off-putting, because I'm trying to meet one girl, not trying to be the sole male cast member of *Sex and the City*.

Being a writing enthusiast, I'm most interested in what they've written about themselves. A preposterous number of girls in this town seem to be cliché addicts. Seriously, how many people do you know in real life who "live every day like it's your last"? I'm betting one at most, right? But there's no shortage of these intrepid swashbucklers on Match. Personally, I like to spend a day every now and then unshaven, lying on the couch in my boxers all day watching *Scrubs* reruns. Living every day like it's my last just sounds too damn exhausting.

The other cliché that has begun to irritate the life out of me is the astounding number of girls who write glowingly about their "*amazing* group of friends." The overuse of this adjective never fails to grate on me. The Grand Canyon is amazing. Blake Griffin jumping over a car to dunk a basketball is amazing. Unless your group of friends happens to all be wizards or magicians, I highly doubt that they're *amazing*. I think this is just a phony way to compliment yourself. *You know what all these phenomenal people have in common—they're all crazy about me!* I thought about talking about my group of friends when writing my profile, but I didn't think the word "lackluster" would imply anything positive about me.

Other things I've found about the written profiles: Some ladies type in ALL CAPITAL LETTERS, which makes me feel like they're already yelling at me. No, thanks. And, of course, if the profile is riddled with grammatical errors—more than one, actually—I just can't muster any optimism that she and I will be able to enthrall each other with stimulating conversation. But that's just me.

Obviously, I'd wanted to play with my new toy, so I'd sent about a dozen emails within the first week. I received responses back from two of them. So really it's not a much different success ratio than you'd get while approaching women in public, but it's much easier for a woman to ignore an email than to physically turn her back to a person in a bar and pretend they didn't speak to her. So, if anything, online dating might turn out to be more difficult, because the same rules of politeness don't even apply.

The good news is, one of the girls who replied actually seems pretty cool. Her name is Sara, and we've written back and forth a couple of times now. She likes to be outdoors, loves the 49ers, and would rather avoid getting bumped into at super loud clubs. Also, she has beautiful green eyes. This time I noticed the color of her eyes.

My online experience thus far has taught me two major things. One is that most people are completely full of shit. Second, I was wrong in supposing that a tight group of friends could cure loneliness, because even the girls who have an *amazing* circle of friends are desperate enough to seek a boyfriend on a website with a monthly fee.

Actually, the third thing I've learned about a site like Match is what a colossal time waster it can be. I glance at the time on my laptop and am shocked to realize I'm supposed to meet my sister for lunch in exactly ten minutes.

◎◎◎

I'm meeting Maggie in a vegan bistro near the Imax theater on K Street. Her choice of venues has me fully expecting Maggie to announce she's become a vegan, because sometimes I suspect she stays up at night coming up with ways to repel me. I glance at my watch on the way in and cringe at how late I am. Again. Maggie is perusing a menu at a round table in the corner. There are two glasses of water already on the table, and, although it seems out of character for my sister to be thoughtful enough to order one for me, I appreciate it because I worked up a sweat hustling over here. It's unseasonably warm outside for the first week of April.

"Hey, Maggie," I say, sliding into the chair opposite her.

"Well, look who decided to finally show up."

"Yeah, I was afraid that if I was on time, we'd have to come up with a new way to begin our conversation," I say, while reaching for the second glass of water.

"Hold on, that's not yours!"

I freeze. My stomach drops as I realize I've been ambushed.

"My friend Alice is joining us for lunch. She's in the restroom."

As I suspected, an Improvised Romantic Device is lurking just out of sight. There's no other reason Maggie would have invited a friend to lunch with us. My mind races through dozens of scenarios—from sprinting out the door to lighting a stack of napkins on fire and leaping through a shattering window, but I realize etiquette dictates that there can be no escape. The Lunch Sequence has already been initiated. "Maggie," I whine.

"What?" she says in her classic feigned-ignorance tone.

"Come on, I know what you're doing here."

"Since when can I not bring along a friend— oh, quiet, here she comes!"

A rather stunning blonde woman takes the seat next to Maggie. I'm not sure, but I think my mouth actually drops open.

"Alice, this is my brother Mick."

Alice flashes a toothy smile and reaches across the table to shake my hand. "Hi, Mick, nice to meet you."

"Yes," I reply, because I like to come out of the gate galloping when trying to impress a hot woman. Her hand is cold and clammy.

"Sorry," Alice says. "My hands are kind of wet; I just washed them."

"No worries," I say. "I was just rummaging through the dumpster outside, so it all evens out." Both girls stare at me without expression. I may have forgotten to mention that sometimes when I unexpectedly meet an attractive woman, I morph into a mildly stupid character from a low-budget horror movie.

Maggie snatches her menu from the table. "So what do you recommend, Alice?"

As if snapping out of a trance, Alice examines her own menu. "Oh, uh, yeah. The veggie Panini is absolutely to die for."

Humiliated, I bury my head in my own menu and am momentarily flabbergasted to notice how many meal options contain tofu. As I'm reading, I'm distracted by the portly man at the next table. He's decked out in a smart-fitting suit—probably on lunch break from the nearby Capitol building—and he's begun carrying on a phone conversation with his phone lying on the table, set on speaker. "God I hate when people do that," I grumble.

"Do what?" Maggie asks.

I look up. Maggie and Alice don't seem to have noticed the suit, whose conversational volume is louder than the music from the overhead speakers. "Why do people think we want to hear both sides of their conversation?"

"I know," Alice whispers. "He's not eating or using his hands for anything. There's no reason for him to have it on speaker."

Nice. I've finally said something that's not completely stupid, and she's even agreed with me. I feel myself starting to relax.

"Maybe he has arthritis and it hurts him to hold his phone," Maggie offers.

Damn, whose side is she on? I hold my menu in front of my face to "read" it.

After we order, Alice leans toward me. "So, Mick, your sister tells me you own a hotel?"

"A motel, yeah." This sounds more self-deprecating than I'd intended, so I try to spin it. "It's a lot like a casino resort, except there's no casino, and it's not all that resorty." Not even a smile. "But it's got a pool," I add sheepishly.

"Cool," says Alice, sounding like she thinks it's anything but.

"Mick writes a blog," Maggie interjects. "He averages over two hundred readers a week."

This is not true. This is a number that she pulled out of the air. I don't know what the actual number is, but I'm sure it's nowhere near that. But the fact that my sister is trying to help me avoid continuing to make a fantastic fool of myself is somewhat comforting.

"Oh, really?" Alice brightens. "What about?"

"It's a ... kind of a satirical literary review type thing," I manage. Alice seems interested. "It's ... I do reviews of books. Like really bad reviews. Tearing the books to shreds in like a *way* exaggerated fashion." Alice stares at me blankly. I'm apparently not doing a good job explaining myself. Or communicating in my native tongue in general. "Like this week's post was a contemptuous review of *The Great Gatsby*."

She blinks. "You didn't like *The Great Gatsby*?"

"No, I did. It's—"

"It's not supposed to be a serious review," explains Maggie.

"Yeah, see it's more of a parody of those critics who never like anything and think it makes them sound smart to put everything down."

"Oh," Alice says, dragging the word out to indicate her relief that I've finally started to make some form of sense.

"Yeah, so I lambaste what are generally considered to be quality books, but in doing so I'm not actually making fun of the book. I'm making fun of other critics. It's ... you know, it's just to make people laugh."

"Oh, I get it. That's kind of an interesting idea," Alice says with profound indifference.

I make one more attempt. "Like a couple of weeks ago I reviewed

Grapes of Wrath, and I furiously accused Steinbeck of stereotyping people in rural communities as having no business savvy, because of that shopkeeper that tells the Joad kids the wrong price on the penny candy. You know, as if I didn't actually understand that scene at all."

"Cool," says Alice.

The frustrating thing about vegan bistros is they don't provide steak knives for you to shove into your trachea.

◎◎◎

Later that afternoon it's quiet at the motel, so I decide to work on my blog, but I keep repeating my feeble explanation of it in my head, trying to imagine how it must have sounded to Alice. I didn't even attempt to get her number, so it's not like I'll get a chance to ask her. I enjoy writing my blog, but I hate it at the same time. For one reason, I suspect it's nothing more than a stalling mechanism to distract me from working on my novel. But mostly it's the idea of blogs in general that bothers me. Putting your writing out there for the world to see feels a little conceited, or at least presumptuous, to me. It's like announcing, "Hey world, I'm so clever and important that I've done you a favor and given you access to my personal ideas and opinions!" That is why I could never even consider writing posts that are genuine or personal in any way. I justify my blog by telling myself I'm merely providing people with harmless entertainment if they feel like slacking off at work. That way it doesn't seem too audacious to be putting it out there. Still, part of me thinks that any sort of writing is on some level a cry for acceptance and corroboration, and if I think of it that way, it does start to sound as pathetic as it probably seemed to Alice.

Then wouldn't releasing a novel be even more arrogant? I decide to put that thought out of my mind.

I shake my head and try to console myself by considering that maybe today's lunch debacle will at least deter Maggie from trying to set me up for another couple of weeks. I don't have time to consider the situation any further because the phone rings and I find out the toilet in 42 seems to have exploded on a poor old woman from Tennessee. If you ever feel embarrassed over having blown your chance with an attractive potential date, I recommend putting yourself in a situation where you'll most likely get sued. Takes your mind right off it.

11__the new maid

DaLisa had finally come to me two days ago with the name and information of a new maid she wanted me to hire. Like I've said, I trust DaLisa's judgment so I went ahead and filed the paperwork and made it official without even meeting her. An hour ago I got to meet her in person, and I've been able to think of little else since. Her name is Abonice—pronounced like the Swedish disco group and the city in France—her skin is the color of licorice, she is slender and tall, and the smile that splits her face nearly in half is capable of rendering a man amnesiac for up to a half hour. Or, at least, that's what I feel like has happened to me.

Don't get me wrong, I haven't for a moment considered the possibility of anything happening between Abonice and me. The first reason is that she works for me. With the sexual harassment lawsuits and general unpleasantness that would undoubtedly ensue once the relationship was over, it wouldn't be worth the risk to even start it, so I've made myself adopt a strict policy of not dating coworkers. Luckily, the policy does not prohibit my ogling them from safe distances. Second, her information lists her age as twenty-two, and it has become abundantly clear to me over the past few years that girls within this age bracket—if they register my existence at all—identify me as an irrelevant piece of background scenery rather than as a sexual being. I've reacted to this new categorization with mixed emotions. As attracted as I am physically to girls in their early twenties, I'm equally repulsed by their immaturities. Even as recently as a few years ago I could easily overlook a vapid personality if it came in a pretty, shiny package, but these days I can't seem to get past it. Society has been ganging up on me in its attempts to make me feel creepy for still being physically attracted to girls who are more than a decade my junior, but I don't buy it. If the average man didn't find young women desirable, *Playboy* would've stopped publishing college issues a long time ago. The only thing that would make me feel creepy is if I were pretending to enjoy a conversation about *The Voice* with some airhead just because I thought it would get me closer to undressing her. Still, if my brain decided to go ahead and stop being so powerfully drawn to the eighteen-to-twenty-four demographic, it would be just fine with me. Then I wouldn't have to feel like a guy with a severe peanut allergy who wakes up every day with a voracious craving for Reese's Pieces.

Although I pose no predatory threat to Abonice, I cannot say the same for Rollie, who is currently replacing the toilet up in Room 42. I'm still cursing myself for calling him back in here. Considering that it only took him a matter of minutes to solve the bra-clogging problem in my previous toilet saga, the bill he gave me would suggest he makes more money per minute than I make in three or four days. I had even looked up the names of other plumbers online before I decided I wasn't up to running the risk of encountering an even bigger swindler. With Rollie, at least I know what I'm getting. One thing I know for sure is that if he catches sight of Abonice, he'll find an excuse to be here every day, relentlessly trying to scheme his way into her bed. This is the thought that has kept me stealing nervous glances out the window every few minutes, dreading the moment when Rollie emerges from 42 and spots DaLisa showing our new ebony angel the ropes. For some reason, I feel protective toward this young lady, at least where Rollie's concerned, and this disgruntles me because I never wanted to be a knight. I also can't say I'm enthused about the fact that I'm apparently going to lose control of my mental faculties for ten to thirty minutes every time she smiles at me. Right now I'm angry at Reena for leaving me, and furious at the ghosts who scared her off.

To distract myself, I check Match. Not surprisingly, there are no messages waiting from Sara. Things had been going smoothly in our email conversations, and in my next message I was going to suggest we meet in real life, but it doesn't look like I'll get that chance. In her last email she asked what my career goals were. I guess I didn't stop to think what a loaded question that was, and I made the rookie mistake of responding truthfully, telling her about my plans to write a novel and wow the critics. The rest of my email was friendly and funny, and that's all I'd said about my goals. I haven't heard a peep from her since. After several days, I sent another short message asking if everything was okay and expressing concern that I hadn't heard from her. Still nothing. I've been racking my brain for explanations for her disappearance from cyberspace and the only thing I can come up with is that maybe my response to her question about goals hadn't sounded lucrative enough, monetarily speaking. I hate to immediately jump to such cynical conclusions about a relative stranger, but here's how I arrived there. Everything else in the email had been about safe topics—the Niners, some photos she'd posted from Yosemite, movies we wanted to see—so I know I couldn't have offended her with any of that. When I talked about the book I planned to write, I'd mentioned something about the critical acclaim being more important than sales figures. I know that a lot of women who have crossed the threshold into their thirties are focused solely on starting a family, and therefore they regularly scrutinize suitors' potentials as earners/providers. I hope I'm wrong about the reason she's decided to ignore me, and that it's something less shallow and horrible, but maybe too many negative experiences with women have finally jaded me toward their true intentions.

Of course, there's always the possibility that she met a guy with a boy band face and a four-pound penis. Somehow, this thought doesn't console me.

There is, however, a surprise waiting in my inbox. It's from 5thBorough347, and the beautiful girl in the picture looks vaguely familiar. The message simply reads:

Didn't I kick your ass at pool on St. Patrick's Day? - Brooklyn

Ah, yes. That's where she seems familiar from. I can't tell if she's just talking smack, or if this message is an invitation to begin a conversation. I decide to rebel against the cynicism, so I send her a short, friendly note in response:

Madame, I believe you are sorely mistaken. I am known far and wide for my prowess at billiards, and I seem to recall thrilling the assembled crowd that evening with my display of near-perfection. Also, I seem to recall being taller. — Mick

I hit Send, figuring that I'll be able to tell whether or not she's cool by how—or if—she responds to a facetious message like that. I take a few minutes to check out Brooklyn's page. I remember her being pretty, but the photos she has posted make her look absolutely stunning. Under Interests she lists hiking, basketball, movies, air guitar, and attending public hangings. Interesting. Under About Her, she merely goes on a diatribe about how many *Seinfeld* episodes feature problems that wouldn't have existed if the gang had all owned cell phones. I dig this girl's sense of humor. Now I *really* hope she writes back.

I glance out the window and am relieved that I don't spot anything untoward, such as Rollie dry-humping Abonice's leg. What I do see is an older couple emerging from a monstrously oversized Chrysler and primly approaching the office. As they enter through the glass door and head towards my counter, I close my laptop and shove it off to the side.

"Good afternoon," I greet them warmly. "Welcome to The Shady Spot Motel. How can I help you?"

The couple has a distinguished air. The man appears to be in his late fifties, and, despite the spring-like weather, he's wearing a sport coat, a sweater, and a silk scarf tied around his neck beneath his gleaming white collared shirt. I believe this is the first time I've seen a man wear one of those in real life; I thought it only happened with occasional passengers on *The Love Boat*. He adjusts his wire-framed glasses and looks at me earnestly. "Yes, we do not have reservations, but I noticed a vacancy sign illuminated outside."

"Sure, no problem. I've got some rooms available," I say, pulling up the information on the desktop computer. "I've got one queen size bed or two queens, whichever you'd prefer."

The man exchanges a glance with his wife. Her lips purse so tightly that I worry she's about to spit at me. "Are the rooms with king-sized beds currently occupied?" the man asks.

"Uh, we don't actually have kings. Just queens and doubles." I drop my gaze, feeling guilty for somehow having let him down.

The woman smooths the front of her lavender dress. "Layton, ask him what the rates are."

"The rates are—" I begin, but the man cuts me off.

"What are your nightly rates?"

This throws me for a second. Does he think I didn't hear her question? "Uh, it's sixty-five for weeknights and eighty-five for Friday through Sunday."

They exchange another glance, but neither's expression changes.

"How many nights were you interested in?"

"Layton, ask him if there are smoking and non-smoking facilities."

This time I can barely suppress a smile. "Ma'am, I'd be happy to answer your questions directly if—"

"Is smoking permitted in the rooms?" the man asks.

How perplexing. "No, sir, this, uh, this is a non-smoking building."

"Not even cigars?"

"No, but you'd be welcome to smoke cigars on the balconies or common areas outside, if you'd like."

"Good heavens, no," the man replies. "I never touch them."

"Oh," I reply dumbly. I'm literally lost for words.

"My wife cannot stand the lingering smell of cigars."

"Oh, I see. Yeah, well, I don't think there's anything to worry about," I assure them. "The rooms don't smell like smoke. I know it does some places, but not here. It doesn't, uh, it doesn't smell like smoke here." They stare at me, expressionless. "Free continental breakfast," I add.

"What can you tell me about the bulbs?" the man asks.

"The bulbs?"

"The light bulbs. I dislike anything over sixty watts; they give off a harsh, unpleasant glare."

Is this guy serious? I have no clue how many watts the damn light bulbs have. "Oh, no, sir, they're all sixty watts or below."

"Excellent. I'll need a seven o'clock wakeup call."

"A.m.," his wife chimes in.

"Well, there are alarm clocks in all the rooms that you can set."

He frowns. "So you don't provide wakeup call services."

"I ... yeah, we can give you a wakeup call in the morning if you'd like,

I guess. Sure."

"Excellent."

This conversation has confused me to the point where I don't know if that means he wants the room, or if he's just expressing his fondness for wakeup calls.

"How many towels are the rooms situated with?" A direct question from the woman. I'm taken aback.

"Uh, there are two sets of towels in each bathroom, and usually an extra set as well."

"Layton, tell him we'll need a minimum of four sets nightly."

"We can set you up with as many towels as you'd like, ma'am," I blurt quickly, before Layton has a chance to further annoy me by repeating the request.

They agree to take a room for three nights. I won't bore you by sharing the other seventy questions they asked during the check-in process, but I will tell you that by the time I'd helped them carry an absurd number of suitcases from their car to their first floor room, I was ready to move to L.A. and clean carpets for a living. Oh, and of course their luggage didn't have wheels. Seriously, who still buys luggage without wheels? I didn't even know they still made it.

Moving to Los Angeles is something that has crossed my mind a few times lately. The stories I've been told about New York City winters are a little daunting. Plus I've been considering the possibility of writing a screenplay version of my first novel so that in case I run into bad luck trying to get the book published I can try to sell the screenplay instead. Once it's turned into a movie, it should be easy to get the actual book published. And, anyway, aren't movies the new novels? These days, film is how you reach a mass audience. That's what I'm going for. For one thing, I want to have a greater impact on the world than those whose only contributions are a couple of spoiled kids running around irritating people. And second, reaching a huge audience is where the money will come from that will allow me to finally escape the daily grind of answering the inane questions of pesky old people who have apparently never stepped foot inside a motel before.

Sometimes this place starts to feel like a prison. I jump back on my laptop to distract myself. I check my regular email and am absolutely shocked at what I find. A girl named Alice Cummins has contacted me through my blog site and is telling me how great it was to meet me the other day and how she'd love to hang out again. I can come to no other conclusion than to assume this has to be my sister's friend Alice, in front of whom I'd imagined I'd made a total ass of myself. I reread the email three times to be sure I'm not hallucinating. I was certain that she'd thought I was an idiot, but now she wants to see me again. Something like this might give a rational man pause, at least long enough to wonder if perhaps something might be slightly off with the girl herself. But as for me, I remember her beautiful blonde hair and gorgeous body, and my penis basically types up the response email for me.

I know you'll find this shocking, but when I actually take Alice out to dinner a few days later, it doesn't go very well. We eat at a table beside the window in a downtown pub grill, and Alice completely loses her mind every time a dog walks past the window. She says things like, "Oh my god, Labs are so cute! I can't even deal!" She repeats this last phrase often. I miss a great portion of what she says during the meal because in my head I am trying to work out why someone would use a phrase like this, ever. I assume she means "I can't even deal with it," but what does that even mean? I hate when people use meaningless phrases. If you literally can't emotionally deal with something because it's cute, you need serious psychiatric therapy. What bothers me even more is that she leaves off the words "with it." Why? I don't like pointless abbreviations either, like when people say "vacay" instead of "vacation." What, you don't have the time to pronounce that extra syllable? It all seems a little pretentious and silly to me. Which makes sense, because she is a friend of Maggie's, after all.

What seals the deal, however, is when I drive her home after dinner. She invites me in for a nightcap, and when we walk in she pays and says goodnight to a babysitter named Tammy. All through dinner, Alice had not mentioned she had a child. It's late so little Bethany is asleep and I don't get to meet her, but the proud mama educates me for several minutes how wonderful she is. She's almost two, and the photos plastered all over the living room reveal her to be an adorable-looking child. I check them out while Alice goes into the kitchen to open a bottle of wine. During my snooping, I come across a small hand-stitched pillow sitting on the shelf that features a picture of a baby cradle, along with the name Kaylie Marie and a date from roughly two years ago.

"How many kids do you have?" I ask Alice when she appears with two overfull glasses of wine.

"Just the one." She hands me a glass and smiles up at me coquettishly.

I gesture toward the pillow. "What's that all about? Kaylie?"

"Oh, yeah, that's Bethany's real name."

We clink glasses, and Alice takes an enormous couple of gulps. I am confused. "Oh," I say. "Wait, so why do you call her Bethany?"

"Oh. Her dad and I divorced like eight months ago."

This doesn't appear to even resemble an answer to my question. "Uh-huh."

"He's a dick. Anyway, I was never all that crazy about the name

Kaylie," she goes on. "So I call her Bethany. I figure on the two weekends a month that she's with him, it will make it incredibly awkward if he calls her by a name she doesn't even know as her own." She titters at this point, rather casually, as if it's a harmless prank.

"What? Why?"

Her face gets serious. "Because fuck him, that's why."

Angelina was ... psychotic.

12__the fifth borough

After having reaffirmed my sacred vow to never date someone my sister recommends, I'd gone the Match route again and developed a nice little correspondence with Brooklyn. She seems really down to earth, and she's pretty much hilarious, too. I'm on my way to meet her for coffee, and I'm as nervous as an actor auditioning for James Cameron.

This coffee shop is one I frequent. When I walk in four minutes late, I scan the place and see no sign of Brooklyn yet. Molly is perched behind the counter and greets me brightly.

"What's up, stranger?"

"Stranger?" I say. "I was here yesterday."

"You were? Were you wearing your invisible Harry Potter cloak?"

"Unless you morphed into a tall, gangly dude with a goatee, I don't think you were here."

"Ah, that's the new guy, Scott." She rolls her eyes and makes a face like she just bit into a rotted ham sandwich.

"So when I come to buy my beans, I can say 'Bean me up, Scotty'?"

She grins. "You're such a dork."

I doubt she even gets the reference. Molly is a college student and one of the main reasons I come here so often. She's effortlessly beautiful, and she never fails to brighten my day. Some women exude this unexplainable aura, equal parts hope and possibility, validation and redemption, and their magnetism is as undeniable as it is mysterious. Age seems to be an irrelevant factor in possessing this power, but outward beauty is one of its telltale signs. All men immediately recognize when they're in the vicinity of one of these miracles, in the same way you walk down the sidewalk and your olfactory sense doesn't need your eyes to verify that there's a bakery nearby. We feel this powerful urge to just be close to a creature like this, and not for any deviant or sexual purposes necessarily. It's more of a parasitical desire to subsist for a while off the mystical vivacity they emit into the atmosphere around them. Molly is just such a being.

The tin bell over the door jingles, and Brooklyn walks in. Suddenly I'm surrounded by such beauty I fear I might pass out. The first thing I notice about Brooklyn is something that I'd noticed in a couple of her photos. The way she dresses seems to perfectly reflect her personality. Both buttons on her white pullover are unfastened, a lightweight multicolored scarf hangs loosely around her neck, and she's wearing ridiculous-looking striped shorts that closely resemble men's boxers. Most thirty-year-old women in this town wouldn't be seen in public dressed like that, but Brooklyn seems to be immune to the self-conscious doubts that plague most of us. It's obvious that this is her look—because she likes it, and not because she's driven by a compulsion to intentionally look different, like so many hipsters do in a contrived effort to project an image of differentness.

We order lattes and take a seat on one of the sofas. "I like the vibe of this place," she says, looking around.

"Yeah, I come here a lot." My nerves have calmed, but not enough; I'm trying desperately to hide this fact.

She smirks. "I'm surprised you invited me for coffee instead of shooting pool."

"Well, I know how delicate a woman's self-esteem is, and I didn't want to shatter what you have left."

She giggles. "How chivalrous of you."

My mouth is on auto-pilot at this point, because inwardly I'm busy marveling at how much prettier she is in person that her online photos indicate. She appears to be wearing little or no makeup, and her light brown hair is tied back in a simple ponytail, suggesting the same type of effortless beauty Molly possesses.

By the time we get our coffees and are halfway through the first cup, I've relaxed and am enjoying being able to actually listen to what she's saying. Brooklyn talks excitedly about the new baseball season and how she's got tickets to several upcoming Giants games. I tell her a highly-embellished story about how I comically failed in try-outs for my college basketball team. We both talk about how loathsome ESPN is this time of year, when we're forced to look at Mel Kiper's hair as he blathers on endlessly about his NFL draft conjectures.

Before I finish my first cup I've decided not to try to rush into sex with Brooklyn. This is one of the tests I've developed for myself. If I'm inclined to put off sex and let it happen naturally, it's a sign that I'm thinking of the girl as a possible keeper. I'm excited by this realization because I've dated several women since Clare over the past seven months, but I've tended to think of them all as nothing more than a dating relationship that might last a couple of months at best. I'm very optimistic about Brooklyn.

During our second cup of coffee, a girl who vaguely resembles Jan Brady comes in, and I mention my childhood affinity for The Brady Bunch reruns. Brooklyn says she was more of a Partridge Family fan.

"Are you serious?" I demand. "The Brady Bunch was by far the best and most culturally relevant fake family band in the history of television."

"No way, dude. The Bradys were campy. Everybody knows that."

"And the Partridges weren't? They all look campy now, but at the time they were enormously popular worldwide. They sold millions of records!"

"So did the Partridge Family," she retorts. ""I Think I Love You' was a massive hit."

I set my coffee mug on the table and lean back, pressing my fingertips together in a tent shape like the psychiatrists on TV do. "I daresay there are more people on the planet even today that know the words to The Brady Bunch theme song than even remember *that* song!"

She doesn't miss a beat. "'I Think I Love You' was adopted as the national anthem of Ecuador in 1997."

I stare blankly.

"Okay, just kidding," she says with a smile. "But that song made an international sex symbol out of David Cassidy."

Now it's my turn to roll my eyes. "David Cassidy was merely the Jonas Brothers of his time. The Brady Bunch had not one but two teen heartthrobs—Barry Williams *and* Christopher Knight. Not only that, but Marcia Brady was the lightening rod of the sexual awakening of generations of young boys, yours truly included."

She shakes her head sadly. "I hate to tell you, but Barry Williams was ugly. And The Brady Bunch clan featured no one who even approached the precocious charm of Danny Bonaduce."

I stare at her glumly. "I don't think this relationship is going to work out."

She nearly spews latte when she laughs. "And I thought you had such potential."

I laugh, and one sentence continues running through my head: *Hey, I think I love you!*

When we part ways after that second cup I lean in for an awkward attempt at a kiss out on the sidewalk, but she dodges smoothly and embraces me tightly. Was that a deliberate dodge or just a normal first date miscommunication? I'm shaken, just slightly, but I venture, "See you again soon?"

She flashes me a glorious smile. "For sure."

©©©

I really should get new phones for the motel. The ones we have are appalling; they look like they were installed about the same time the building was constructed. They're the same dingy off-white color that all the early Apple computers were, except the handsets are a little more yellowed from the oily handprints of generations of bargain vacationers.

They're about ten inches in length, although the four rows of the keypad numbers only occupy a small square in the middle of the right half; the receiver takes up the left half. Above the keypad numbers are four rows of holes where buttons have been yanked out, leaving only dust-craving cavities. There are two rows of these cavities below the keypad as well, possibly the remnants of Hold or Conference options that Remi deemed too expensive to provide to guests. All the crevices where panels fit together are riddled with dust growing in mold patterns, like the first goatee of a high school boy, as if the maids through the years made a collaborative decision to abstain from cleaning them and instead see what developed in some sort of a collective science project designed to gross out the public.

I'm pondering all this the next day while I'm in and out of the unoccupied rooms testing the toilets. It's probably the ghosts who are causing all these flushing problems. My phone's text alert sound sends my heart plummeting into my lower abdomen as I immediately think—hope—it might be Brooklyn. It's only Stacy, asking if I want to grab a beer soon. I sit down on the bed to calm myself, and the squeaking sound the springs make reminds me of someone stepping on a Smurf. I contemplate texting Brooklyn. I know one of the cardinal rules of dating is to avoid coming on too strong at first. You're supposed to wait a minimum of two days before contacting someone for the next date. Under this rationale I have already talked myself out of texting her twice this morning. But now I'm thinking that Brooklyn is not like most girls— she seems to behave more genuinely and feel unusually comfortable with herself. I can't imagine her being scared off by a sincere text from me expressing my interest in her.

Also, when you're single for a long period of time, and everyone else in the world seems to be in a relationship, it's hard to feel completely comfortable. A subtle nervousness is constantly there, like when you're winding a jack-in-the-box and trying to steel yourself not to jump once it pops. I'm kind of in a hurry to be in a relationship again, but the middle part, after all the pursuit, awkwardness, and getting-to-know-each-other nonsense is over and you're just comfortable with one another. In my haste to fast forward to this state of existence, I decide to flip the bird to the rules of dating and send Brooklyn a text.

Had a great time. U R awesome! Dinner?

Sincere, short, positive, to the point. Brilliant, I think, as I hit Send.

Over the next hour I finish checking toilets and basic room inspections and have to frequently remind myself to continue inhaling and exhaling. Every time something obnoxiously loud happens—like a motorcycle passing by the motel, or one of Midtown's ubiquitous leaf blowers—I pull out my phone and check for a text to make sure I didn't happen to miss the text alert sound.

When the response does finally come, it says:

Me 2. Ur fun. Not sure about the romantic thing but love to kick it again just friends. Do u play pub trivia?

So this is what it feels like when a skyscraper collapses on top of you.

13__a monkey in the time of chimpanzees

Much like Frank Gehry and his architecture, I am generally considered to be a master artist, and my trademark medium is self-pity. Last night I got Irish drunk with Stacy, expounding on the heartlessness of women, and like a true friend he kept repeating, "Bitches ain't shit but hos and tricks."

I'd woken up on my sofa, fully dressed, when it was just starting to get light outside. My head felt like a couple of the contestants from *The Biggest Loser* were sitting on it, and my mouth was so dry it was probably a fire hazard. The TV screen was paused on a scene from a Will Ferrell movie. The coffee table was strewn with the remains of what appeared to be a junk food feast that could have served four people. It had been a struggle to get myself into a sitting position, and I'd say a good five minutes elapsed before I attempted to make it to my feet. A lamp in the corner of the room was knocked over, and, upon closer inspection, I deduced that its new location on the floor was the result of my having hurled several items at it, among them my keys and wallet. I was not able to locate my phone, but the severity of my hangover left me unable to muster the concern that this fact would normally produce in me. I tend to get panicky without my phone, and I must confess that I do not have a single phone number committed to memory. Not my sister, not my parents, no one. I realize that this is irresponsible, but I decided to put off berating myself for it until I'd arrived at the motel to make sure it wasn't here.

It's not. I'd sat in the office staring blankly at my desk for a period of time that I'm unable to even guess at, failing to come up with a plan to locate my phone when the motel's phone rang and nearly burst my eardrums.

It was Stacy. It turns out I'd forgotten my phone in his car, and now I'm leaning heavily against the front desk counter at the motel, halfway through my second Gatorade, waiting for him to come drop it off. It's probably good that I didn't have access to my phone last night, as I'm prone to sending the occasionally less-than-genteel drunk text to unfortunate women who have raised my ire. For reasons I can't explain, I tend to get irrationally furious at women who reject me. Fuel my brain with a little alcohol, and it entertains theories of conspiracies, of clandestine late night meetings wearing shrouded hoods, at which collusions among the single women population of the entire state are agreed upon in order to exclude me from their inner circle.

In my right mind I know it's just a coincidence, but it's hard to ignore the uncanny track record I've had over the past couple of years. Every girl that I'm genuinely interested in either reveals herself to be a psycho or — more often — never likes me in the first place. It's hard to believe that there aren't darker forces at work.

I realize that I just don't enjoy dating anymore. These days it just seems to be a hassle, an elaborate exercise that never really goes anywhere, full of sound and fury and all that. I used to enjoy the hunt itself, not caring whether it was headed anywhere or not. But now that I do want it to go somewhere and it never seems to, the whole experience just tends to repel me. When I spot a beautiful woman across a crowded bar, I'm no longer filled with excitement, but dread. Coming up with an opening line starts to become intolerable, because it feels too much like drawing up the first play in yet another game when your record is oh and two hundred something.

All morning my mind has been see-sawing between forlornly wondering what I'd said or done wrong to turn Brooklyn off, and incredulously questioning what's wrong with her to think I'm not good enough for her. Now I've moved on to contemplating whether I'll respond to her text or not. I don't know why I'm even considering it. Maybe a pathetic part of me is convinced that I can still win her over if given another chance. So maybe if I see her again under the guise of friendly hanging out my incredible charm and magnetism will lead her to realize and fix her mistake. Although I realize that it's me we're talking about here, and not Ryan Gosling, so chances are pretty solid that I'll never speak to her again.

It never occurs to me to simply take her up on her offer of hanging out as friends in a sincere fashion, because that concept is as foreign to me as not wishing for Clayton Kershaw's gruesome death. I know that some guys establish strong and lasting friendships with women they once dated, and kudos to them, but I don't have the faintest idea how they do it. My policy has always been to stay as far away from exes as possible and do my best to forget about their existence. Spending time with Brooklyn would be a constant reminder of my not being good enough for her, and whose self-esteem needs that kind of abuse? There's no switch I can flip in my brain that will make me suddenly stop being attracted to her and just view her as a friend. I can't imagine the level of maturity it would take to consciously force one's mind to keep that in check. As I mentioned before, I'm pretty terrible at being a grownup.

I spot Abonice coming in through the front door. I look up in the opposite direction, as if surprised, and say, "Wow, did it suddenly get prettier in here?" I turn toward her. "Oh, hi, Abonice. Didn't see you come in."

Her slightly turned lips suggest the faintest trace of what may be a smile, although I may be reaching. "Hi, Mr. Collins," she says. I love her voice. It's soft and velvety, with a hint of an accent that I'm guessing is Caribbean. I'll never ask her, because I learned my lesson after I'd been here about a year and asked DaLisa what part of Africa she hailed from. She had looked at me like I was puppy who'd once again chewed her favorite slipper and informed me that Jamaica is nowhere near Africa.

"Call me Mick," I say. "You make me feel old."

She has a habit of not looking at you straight on, but instead turning her head slightly to one side and looking from the corner of her eyes, which emphasizes their bountiful size and almond shape. "DaLisa wants me to ask if the soap has arrived."

"Ah, yes!" I scurry to the back room and grab the box that arrived this morning. It's about the size and weight of a toaster oven, but I offer to carry it for her anyway.

"I can get it."

"Okay, there you go. We like to keep things clean around here!" I turn my head slightly to the side and lower my voice. "Most of the time."

She makes no expression. "Thank you, Mr. Collins."

What a cretin. She must think I'm an absolutely wretched excuse for a life form. I can't help but agree. As I watch her disappear through the front door and around the corner, I replay this encounter in my head about forty times, and each time it grows more tragic, pathetic, and unwatchable. What was I thinking, trying to come off as sounding charming and flirtatious? Especially in my presently disheveled physical and mental state. I suddenly feel like throwing up, and I don't think it's from last night's alcohol.

I lay my head face down on the counter and close my eyes. I highly recommend this posture next time you have to do some serious self-loathing. Beautiful young creatures like Abonice are into the latest technology; they have no use for an outdated model like me. I need to dismantle the part of my brain that compels me to try to impress that age bracket, because the repeated spectacular failures only bring my glaring mediocrity into clearer focus. It's not fair, this transition I've made into the wasteland of the over-thirty crowd. At some point in my existence, I might have had a shot at a girl like Abonice, but it pains me to realize that such moments have vanished, and they're never coming back. I know I'm no longer appealing to the young and beautiful, but whatever happened to letting a guy down easy? Would it kill one of them to at least play along once in a while and allow me to retain a shred of my delusion of being still somewhat appealing?

Forehead on counter, waist deep in mental self-flagellation, I make no attempt to move when I hear the front door open again. Then I hear Stacy's laugh.

"Yo, I feel the same way, dog!" He smacks my phone down on the counter, which jars my head so badly I briefly consider murdering him. "Shit was cray cray last night."

I stand up and squint at my phone. "Thanks, man," I mutter, scrolling through three text messages.

"No worries, yo. I know how you get without your phone." Grabbing the remote from beside my Gatorade, he turns on the lobby's TV in the far corner.

"Not too loud, man."

"Yeah, I hear you." He motions at my phone. "Anything good? Shorties hitting you up?"

"Don't even get me started."

"Aw, come on, man, you still on about last night? Fuck that bitch, man."

I squeeze my forehead between my palms. "No, it's not that. I just made a total ass of myself."

"What? When?"

"Just now. Right before you arrived. With that super hot new maid I was telling you about."

"For real? What happened?"

"Never mind, it's too embarrassing. I'm just a gross old man."

DaLisa marches into the lobby and fixes me with a disapproving look. I don't even want to guess whether it's because Abonice told her about my creeping her out or whether it's because I look like I woke up in a dumpster. She doesn't even acknowledge Stacy's presence. "Carpet's just about worn through in twenty-three," she says.

I sigh loudly and look back at my phone, pretending to read. "Find a throw rug to cover it," I respond. "I can't afford new carpeting right now."

"Mm-hmm," she says, and I can feel her holding me in her glare for another few seconds before she disappears into the back.

Stacy leans toward me. "You must be getting desperate, bruh."

"Not *that* maid," I whisper harshly. "There's a new one; she's like ... look, just never mind, okay?"

He grabs a pastry from the case. "Yo, can I get up on this?"

I wave my hand dismissively, dialing my voicemail. "Shit, I'm supposed to go to my parents' today," I groan.

"Thank god I don't have to work today," Stacy says, stuffing the entire pastry in his mouth at once.

"Yeah, lucky you."

Stacy wipes his hands on his low-hanging basketball shorts and holds out a fist for me to bump. "Yo, I gotta hit it. Terry's making me go shopping."

"Thanks for bringing my phone, dude."

"Word," he says, pausing for a moment to glance at the TV. A commercial comes on that's playing "I Think I Love You" by The Partridge Family. "Hate that fuckin' song," Stacy says on his way out.

"Yeah," I say, and then realize Stacy has been gone for probably two or three minutes at least. "Me, too!" I say aloud anyway. Fuck the Partridge Family, Brooklyn! I look around the lobby, nodding with what I hope is an expression of grandeur, like a general surveying his well-stocked arsenal. I blame my childhood habit of watching forty or so hours of TV a week for my tendency to do theatrical nonsense like this, even when nobody's around to see me. It's like I see portions of my everyday life like they're scenes from a movie, and I tend to replay them over and over in my head, imagining a more clever line I should have said, or a more grandiose way I could have delivered the line. Sometimes—like right now—I even find myself posing dramatically, with my hands on my hips, trying to arrange my face to exude something akin to fortitude. Gary Cooper wouldn't wallow in self-pity in a situation like this. By god, I'm not going to let one little rejection shake my unflappable confidence. I've got more than one email conversation going on at the moment on Match, so it's on to the next fish. The next fish in the sea. No, too obvious. Just "to the next fish." See? I'm doing it again. Dammit.

Then, in a stroke of madness or inspiration, I decide to force myself out of my comfort zone and into the Friend Zone. Brooklyn wants to offer me the olive branch of friendship? Fine, I accept. I can do this. She's not going to force me to shy away and pine for her in the shadows somewhere. I pull up her last text and type my response:

Now you want to lose to me in pub trivia too? Might as well embrace your defeat now.

She responds almost immediately:

Death first!

Damn. Why does she have to be so relentlessly cool?

◎◎◎

Later that day, after I suck down my third Gatorade and Quinn comes in to relieve me at the front desk, I stop by to say hello to my parents. My mother usually maintains a spotless house—no small feat considering my father leaves an average of three whiskey glasses per day condensating in arbitrary spots throughout the first two floors. He forgets where he leaves them, so in lieu of searching for them he simply makes himself a fresh one instead.

But, anyway, the fact that it's usually so neat and orderly in their house draws my eyes immediately upon entering the kitchen to the dozens of rectangular cards with varying shades of color swatches spread haphazardly across the table. "What's all this?" I ask.

"We're having the paint stripped and getting the house repainted," Mom says, picking up exactly two of the cards and stacking them neatly at the edge of the table.

"What, the whole house?"

"The whole interior. Dr. Swanberg says all the lead paint might be causing your father's memory problems."

I'm unable to prevent a scoffing sound from escaping my lips. "What?"

"I read an article on the computer," she explains. "Lead paint can cause all sorts of health problems, and now they think it can affect mental capacity, too."

My father and his steadfast ally John Jameson have waged an ongoing war with his mental capacity for as long as I can remember. "An article, huh? What website? Snopes dot com?"

"I can't remember what the website was."

"And Dr. Swanberg went along with this?"

My mother looks off to the side. She's a horrible liar. "Yes, he said it was certainly possible."

"Possible? How long did you have him under the lights until he finally agreed with that?"

My dad looks up from his paper and squints off into the corner of the adjoining den. "Under the lights," he repeats softly, nodding.

"Mom," I continue, "when he said the word *possible* did he follow it up with the word *but*?"

"Michael, don't be vulgar."

"No, Mom, I mean .... look, *possible* doesn't mean likely, or even feasible. It just means that it's not *impossible*."

"You're so good with words, Michael. That's why you're such a wonderful writer!"

My dad chimes in. "Peter Tosh was a wonderful writer, that's for sure."

My father, a seventy-year-old perpetually-drunken Irishman who, to my knowledge, has never even smelled marijuana, has in the past year become a devoted fan of classic reggae. I know. It's the weirdest and most hilarious thing I'm aware of in my present life.

This whole thing sounds like a scam to me, but I can't spot the angle. Does Dr. Swanberg have a brother I don't know about in the painting business? "Mom, I think you have to, like, eat the paint. I've never heard of any airborne-related complications, at least not until you're actually stripping the paint."

"Well, we're not stripping it," she says, as if breaking down something complicated for a stupid person. "We're having professionals do it."

My dad chuckles. "Flashdance," he mutters to himself.

"Either way, you can't be hanging around here while the job is being done. Da, are you on board with this malarkey?"

"Your mother read an article." He shrugs.

"Michael, of course we're not staying here while the job is being done. We're staying in a motel."

Unbelievable. It takes me longer than normal to make my lips form the words. "You booked a motel? I *own* a motel! Why didn't you ask me?"

"We didn't want to impose," she says. She holds a cardboard strip up to me and points out a beige swath. "What do you think of this one?"

"Mom, I don't *live* at the motel. How is it an imposition? It's not like you'd be using my bathroom. I've always got empty rooms."

"We don't want you going to any trouble."

"That's what I'm trying to explain to you. It's like the opposite of going to any trouble!" I say, exasperated. "You're not wasting your money on some other motel. You're staying at The Shady Spot, and that's final."

That was not final. We spent another fifteen minutes verbally square dancing until I got Dad to force my mother to relent. I had a few days until they had to be out of the house, so I told them I'd make all the arrangements tomorrow when I went into work, and drive them over when it was time. Then I went home, caught up on a couple of Match emails, showered again, and collapsed into a sleep I didn't awake from until the next morning.

14__arriving with certainty

The next morning, I'm feeling much better. It's a beautiful day, and I've convinced Quinn to come in and cover for me again so I can go play golf with Ethan. While I'm waiting for him to arrive, I notice two teenage girls walk in from the pool area to check out the vending machine over in the corner. They arrived yesterday with their parents and younger brother. Both blonde with deep tans, one is wearing cutoff jean shorts and a bikini top, the other a tight T-shirt and bikini bottoms. Girls certainly do develop much earlier than they did back in my childhood, I think gloomily. Rhianna Gladsen was pretty much the only girl in my high school that had breasts substantial enough to actually qualify as breasts. She still holds a special place in my heart — a few notches behind Princess Leia, of course. But these girls look like college girls already. They're probably not quite that old yet, but it won't be long before they join that dreaded demographic of eighteen-to-twenty-four-year-old beauties that will no longer register my existence when I pass on the street. Just like Abonice. Some wistful impulse — probably my compulsive wish to still be thought of as *cool* by children — makes me call out to them and ask if they need some change for the machine.

"Oh, no we're good," the taller one says cheerily. The shorter one smiles brightly at me; then they go back to scrutinizing the rows of junk food. Those were the days — to be able to eat that garbage with impunity, no traces of it daring to show up on your resilient body. Another thing I miss.

"I'd like to eat tapioca pudding offa their bare asses."

I spin. "Rollie!" I hadn't realized he'd come in and was standing next to me. "Jeez, man, you can't say stuff like that."

"Relax, they didn't hear me."

"Still," I stammer, red-faced, "that's gross, just …." And I grasp for a way to convey why one doesn't *say* things like that, but then I realize who I'm talking to. "Look, never mind. What do you need?"

"I checked out the toilets in forty-two and thirty."

I try not to cringe. "And?"

"And what was the other one?"

I roll my eyes. "The other two. Twenty-one and eighteen, right above us. But what about the two you looked at? Why did the one in forty-two explode?"

He grins, the toothpick in his mouth nodding skyward. "They say patience is a virtue, Mick."

"Yeah, well, they also say 'Ask and ye shall receive,' so I'm asking for functional toilets."

"Wait, and thou shalt prosper."

"Okay, that's definitely not a real expression." The door jingles.

"Scarecrow," Rollie declares, looking past me.

"Rollie." Scarecrow is what he calls Quinn, my assistant manager. I'll never admit it to Rollie, but as nicknames go, Scarecrow is a home run. Quinn, bumbling through his early twenties, is a couple of inches north of six feet tall, but with only enough pounds on his hockey stick-like frame to barely cast a shadow on a sunny day. His skin appears to have never made contact with sunlight, however, and his face perpetually registers an expression of nervous surprise, as if every time I see him I've suddenly walked in on him breaking the law. I gave him the fictional title of assistant manager a couple of months ago in an attempt to calm him down and indicate my confidence in him so that every damn conversation between us wouldn't seem like a professor catching a student cheating.

"Hey, Quinn, thanks so much for covering for me, man."

"Yeah, everything's fine," he blurts breathlessly. "I mean, no problem. Or, you're welcome." His eyes dart around the room as if he spots bats.

"You eating enough beets?" Rollie says, squinting at him.

"Rollie, the toilets?"

"Right." He heads off, but fixes Quinn with another skeptical glare on his way out.

As I trade places with Quinn behind the counter I lean over to him. "Look, do me a favor. Abonice is supposed to get here pretty soon. Make sure Rollie only uses the back staircase. Know what I mean?"

"Yes." He holds my stare for a few seconds. "Wait, what do you mean, exactly?"

"If he sees Abonice, he'll be all over her. You know how he is. He won't get any work done, and besides, she's ... she's just a ... well, she doesn't deserve to have to deal with that. You know?"

He starts shaking his head no, corrects himself, and spits out, "Yes! Okay. Back staircase. Got it. No problem."

I suppress a smile. "So, *are* you getting enough beets in your diet?"

Panic clouds his features. "What?"

"Yeah, I don't know what that means either. Maybe you should look it up; leave me a report in the office for the morning."

"Absolutely!"

"Kidding, Quinn," I call on my way out the door.

◎◎◎

Ethan and I are playing nine holes at William Land Park. It's a public golf course, but it winds in, through, and around a sprawling city park, which means there's no shortage of oblivious picnickers strolling aimlessly through the fairways at any given time, which is quite stressful for someone with no firmer a grasp on how to aim a golf ball than how to figure out a woman. On the fifth hole, Ethan grooves it about three hundred yards off the tee. With a five iron, I might add. He has a disgustingly beautiful swing, while mine tends to resemble a drunken lumberjack who hopes his ax makes contact with the middle of the three trees he's seeing. As I am lining up my tee shot, a small boy wanders onto the fairway. I yell as loudly as I can for him to move, but he can't hear me. Discovering Ethan's ball lying there, he snatches it up and runs off, holding the ball triumphantly above his head, like he's at an Easter egg hunt.

"Damn," I say to Ethan. "That was a good shot, too."

He frowns. "My lucky ball."

I, on the other hand, am in no danger of ball thieves. Clutching my driver, which feels as cumbersome and awkward in my hands as a jousting pole, I swing as hard as I can and watch my shot fly straight and true, but it only travels about twenty yards into the fairway. Not the ball, mind you, but a sizable chunk of earth and grass. The insolent Titleist remains squatting serenely on its tee, unperturbed, mocking me.

"Wow, that one traveled the whole way around the world and happened to land back on the tee. That doesn't happen very often."

"Shut up, Ethan." On my second swing I make solid contact—with the top half of the ball at least—and it easily clears forty feet in the air before bounding along the ground like a spooked jackrabbit for another sixty or so yards. "At least it went straight," I say meekly. It might sound like I'm being sarcastic, but this fact is actually an accomplishment of which I'm proud. Basketball has always been my game, and I was a pretty good third baseman back in high school, but when it comes to golf I've always been less of a Greg Norman and more of a Norman Bates. I once hit a shot at the driving range at Haggin Oaks that defied the laws of physics and flew straight up, nearly taking one of my eyebrows along with it, curving in midair and managing somehow to land behind me. Luckily everyone was focused on their own shots, and no one witnessed it, or I might have ended up the subject of an ongoing scientific investigation.

I don't know why I keep playing. Maybe it's the pristine beauty of golf courses and being out in the delicious California sun. Maybe it's the occasional nice drive or amazing chip shot I happen to pull off that gives me false hope that I'm about to turn a corner. Or maybe I'm just a glutton for punishment. Golf is my favorite way to be miserable.

The rest of our nine hole round this day plays out in typical Keystone Cop fashion for me. I only lose three balls, which for me is not too shabby at all. Whenever there are woods nearby, my ball behaves like a petrified woodland creature that's been held in captivity and has been waiting to make a break for home at the first opportunity. Two of my balls disappear this way. On the seventh hole, my tee shot takes a miraculous bounce off a palm tree and lands back in the fairway, coming to rest amid a group of geese that are engaged in some serious R and R and barely seem to perceive its arrival among their number. When I approach the group for my second shot, I'm expecting them to waddle away from me in an offended kerfuffle. That is not what happens. When I'm about five yards away, three of them simultaneously charge toward me, stomping webbed feet, flapping furious wings, and shrieking war whoops. I'm so startled that I stumble backwards a few steps, nearly dropping my golf bag. I cast a dumfounded look at Ethan, who's standing about thirty yards away waiting to continue his walk toward the spot where his textbook tee shot landed. His gently bouncing torso betrays the laughs he's trying to stifle.

I shake my head, also somewhat amused, imagining what that little scene would've looked like on YouTube. I approach the ball again, this time marching confidently, swinging my six iron like I'm ready to fence with them, and commanding "Shoo!" in my best authoritative tone. Since they're Canadian, you'd think they'd be well mannered. What I haven't counted on is the possibility that this could be the most badass flock of geese in the Western Hemisphere. This time, the original three attackers are joined by two more, vigorously protesting my encroachment with flying feathers and a deafening resonance of unrestrained rage. I retreat again, and now Ethan is doubled over, hands on knees, hooting delightedly. I'll have you know these are not small birds, and their attempts to frighten me are more successful than I'd rather let on. Their behavior makes no sense. There are no baby birds in their midst that they appear to be defending. As far as I know, geese are not territorial. This just happens to be the most ill-tempered, pugnacious group of winged creatures that have existed since the days of the pterodactyl. I shout my own threats, swing my club wildly, pretending I'm about to fling it at them, but my actions only manage to incite the ire of the ones who had stayed out of the scrum up to this point. All seven of them now present a united front, furiously defying my intrusion upon their turf. And that's how I lose my third ball of the day. I'm no animal expert, but I know better than to tangle with the Hell's Angels of the fowl community.

After our round, we're having a beer back at the clubhouse, and

Ethan keeps breaking out in sporadic chuckles, repeatedly providing me with vivid descriptions of what the geese attack looked like from his perspective. It's getting old.

"Yeah, all right man. Can we talk about something else now?"

Ethan is nearly spasmodic with laughter. "How about when you hit that ball into the tree on three, and it bounced back at you and almost took off your head?"

"I really thought I could get around that damn tree."

By the time we're on our second beer, Ethan is making a genuine effort to discuss different topics. "So who's this chick you're going out with tonight?"

"I met her on Match. She seems pretty cool. Single mom. Black girl. Super hot." I don't mention that with heels on she is taller than me, a detail I'm trying not to let bother me.

"A mom, huh?" Ethan studies my face.

"Yeah, so?"

"You're always giving me shit about Georgelle having kids."

"That's because they're not even her kids, man! It's completely different. This girl, Jen, has one kid, a little girl. Hell, I like kids."

Ethan's eyebrows raise as he swallows a gulp of beer thoughtfully. "I thought you didn't want kids."

That is a loaded question. You may remember me describing my mixed emotions about my niece and nephew. I do like kids, in *theory*. I explain to Ethan how I'm not eager to pass along my own DNA, which includes bonuses like a family history of heart disease and cancer, and quite possibly alcoholism, but I am not opposed to ending up with someone who already has kids of her own. What I leave out is my nagging suspicion that my aversion to the idea might have more to do with a hesitance to take on the inherent responsibilities involved with bringing a life into existence. It's probable that I have a very real fear of commitment, but it's a topic I'm not ready to confront myself with at the moment. I add, "My hypothesis is that if a woman already has kids of her own, she'll most likely be in less of a hurry to want more."

Ethan nods, "Could be." Then he scowls. "Do you hear that?" He motions with his head toward the speaker in the ceiling.

"I Love Rock 'N Roll?"

"That's the second Joan Jett song they've played since we've been sitting here, but not a single Pat Benatar song? Really?"

"Heathens."

"Damn right," he says, without a trace of irony. "So is that what you seek out on this website, single moms?"

"Let's not give me credit for putting that much thought into it. She's also got that insanely hot black woman appearance." He doesn't nod or anything, so I add, "I know you know what I'm talking about."

He shakes his head piously. "I don't see color, Mick."

I can't stand it when people say that. "That must make traffic lights a challenge."

He looks at me blankly.

"Come on, Ethan, you know what I mean: those oversized eyes, wide set, the shape of almonds. You know, like Georgelle's?"

"Ah. Yeah, she does have beautiful eyes."

"And you know, those bodies that only black girls seem able to pull off. Comic book dimensions, asses shaped like ...." I fumble for a simile. "Well, like fictional things I've conjured in my dreams." Once again, the verisimilitude of my incredible talent as a writer presents itself.

"Comic book dimensions?" Ethan doesn't have the affinity for comic books that I do, but I think he's just being obtuse. His girlfriend has comic book dimensions.

"Like Serena Williams."

He sputters, almost spits his beer. "Serena Williams?" he says incredulously. "What comic book are you talking about, *The Incredible Hulk*?"

"Well, young Serena anyway. I'll grant you she has gotten a little muscular late in her career, but she's still hella sexy."

"Are you sure you wouldn't rather date Lou Ferrigno? He's probably free tonight."

"Yeah, hardy fucking har, man." I tell him that we've got to head out so I can shower and get ready for my date, but mostly I'm getting mildly annoyed with him. I'm grateful I didn't mention to him that Jen works as a correctional officer, or it would've surely spawned a whole new series of Serena Williams/manly women jokes. All my friends are such witty bastards.

◎◎◎

My date with Jen that evening turns out to be one of my most memorable, but not for any positive reason. The motel hasn't been doing all that well lately, but I always make sure that my employees receive their full paychecks. From what little is left, after paying bills, I can pretty much keep the rest. This whole plumbing situation has sent me home with empty pockets the past couple of weeks. Of course, I would never mention circumstances like this on a first date, so I meet Jen at a somewhat upscale steak and seafood spot on J Street. I know the manager, Jason, and he's saved one of the best tables for us—secluded from most of the foot traffic, dimly lit, a nice romantic ambience.

When Jen walks up to me on the sidewalk, I'm pleased to notice that she's a dead ringer for her photos on her Match profile. Most of the time, the girls you meet up with in real life are like swollen, paler versions of their online photos. Jen's face, featuring only subtle makeup and her natural eyelashes, is possibly prettier than her Match photos would've had me believe. When we make our way to our table and she takes off her coat I can tell her brickhouse body from the photos is intact, not covered with two more dress sizes worth of fat, like I was expecting. I'm a little intimidated by her towering over me in her black high heels, but I try to swallow those thoughts away.

We eat lobster and gradually make our way through a bottle of expensive Chardonnay, and the conversation flows smoothly and easily over the next hour. I tell her about some of my misadventures lately at the motel, and she has a lovely laugh. She tells me stories about working at the women's correctional facility and shows me her "hard" face. I agree that it's a pretty menacing stare and ask her to give me a running start if I ever offend her. I cannot get over the fact that her last name is Paup. A prison guard named Jen Paup. The following line occurs to me: *I'd rather be in Jen Paup tonight than in solitary*, but you'll be pleased to know I don't say it out loud.

We talk about her little daughter Kiesha for a while—the star of the second grade, if her mom's account is to be believed. A soccer player, of course. Why do so many kids play soccer these days? Kiesha does sound like a darling little kid, though, and I casually mention that I'd like to meet her someday. I tell her a couple of related stories about my niece Maddy.

In the middle of our affable back-and-forth about children, Jen whips out the kind of non sequitur that tends to irk the crap out me, but the subject matter is even worse. "So is this kind of an experiment for you?" she asks.

I'm at a loss. "What do you mean?"

"This whole dating a black woman thing."

Encountering a question like this—mid-conversation—is akin to spending all day on cruise control down the 5 and then suddenly having to stop for a passing herd of camels—equal parts irritating and baffling. I just find it bizarre that in this time in our history race is still such a big deal when it comes to picking out who you want to go out with. But bearing in mind that this is the first real snag we've hit during our conversation, I shrug it off and answer honestly. "Nah, I've dated girls of all different races. I don't really have a preference. It just depends on the personality of the individual, I guess."

She squints slightly and nods, like a visitor at a seminar who's not quite sold on the keynote speaker.

"And good looks don't hurt, either," I say, trying to manage an impish wink.

She smiles, but it's clear to me why she asked the question, and why she reacted the way she did to my answer. This *is* an experiment to her, and nothing more. The optimism I'd felt moments ago that maybe this could develop into a real relationship is beginning to ebb. But that doesn't stop me from continuing to shove my best foot forward. My refusing her offer to help pay for the hundred and thirty-ish dollar meal is intended to project the image of a financially independent, responsible man.

By the time we exit the restaurant, I'm hoping I've impressed her enough with my funny stories, enthusiasm toward her daughter, and mostly-made-up anecdotes about what it's like to be a writer that she will agree to a second date. After my third glass of wine, I've found it difficult to stop picturing what she must look like naked. But, even more importantly, she seems like a real grownup, a woman who's emotionally stable and has her shit together.

The ghosts of all my recent catastrophic interactions with women are jockeying for position in the front of my brain and quickly convince me to chicken out from trying a goodnight kiss as we stand facing one another under the awning, J Street traffic zooming past us. Instead I shoot for old school charm: I take hold of her hand and kiss it, telling her I had a wonderful time.

She is all smiles—seductive, sexy smiles, although that might be my imagination. She asks if I need a lift home.

"Oh, that's okay," I say, attempting a sheepish, Clooney-esque grin. "I only live a few blocks from here." This is the truth, but the real truth is that it's unseasonably chilly for a spring night, and I kind of do want a lift. However, at present I'm feeling there's a strong possibility that I need to pass gas, so I'm eager to maintain the hopefully positive impression I've made on Jen by getting as far away from her as rapidly as possible.

She tilts her head slightly to the left and smiles again. "Oh, come on, I'm right over here. I'll give you a ride."

The ghosts in my head seem divided as to how to interpret her insistence. Several of them try to convince me that her use of the phrase "give you a ride" holds significant metaphorical promise. I tighten my abdominal muscles and agree, walking with her toward the left corner of the building.

And this is when things take an unfortunate turn.

You may remember what comes next. God knows I'm trying to forget it. Instead of walking around the car to the driver's side, Jen accompanies me to my side. She's going to unlock my door for me, I think, how chivalrous. But she stops two feet before the car, spins around, and starts patting down my pockets, like I've seen cops do on TV. For a second, I think she's joking, and my voice box prepares to emit a congenial laugh. But then she gruffly raises my arms, pats them down, along with my torso—front, back, and sides.

Folks, I pride myself on having a pretty creative imagination. When I'm about to embark on a first date, I sometimes mentally run through how it might turn out. I can visualize all kinds of outcomes, from the G-rated ones to the NC 17 variety. And with as many illogical and unpleasant incidents that have occurred unexpectedly on my recent dates, I would feel pretty confident saying I'm not fazed by much.

However, what is happening to me at this moment is so far from the realm of possibilities that I'd dared to consider that for a moment my brain refuses to acknowledge that it is actually happening. Standing there, with my arms held above my head, I stare numbly around at what I'm no longer convinced is the real world. I only loosely register the puzzled looks that spread across the faces of passing pedestrians as they slow their gait down the sidewalk in order to get a clearer glimpse of what's being done to me.

When Jen pops back up and says, "Okay, you're good," and she opens the passenger side door, I find that I lack the ability to form a coherent thought to vocalize, so I mindlessly crawl into the car, like I'm under a hypnotist's spell.

I literally do only live a few blocks away, so the car ride is far too brief for my flustered mind to arrive at a single rational explanation for the pat-down. We had sat together and talked for almost ninety minutes, probing conversational topics far beyond the normal first date chit chat, yet it had apparently not been enough to convince her that I wasn't armed in some way, diabolically waiting for my moment to strike. And *she* had insisted on giving *me* a ride—I had even refused her initial offer! I think during the ride she had said thanks or given me a compliment on the meal, but as we turn on to my street I realize that nothing she has said during the short drive has penetrated past my outer ear.

Her brakes gently squeal as she idles the car outside my building. She looks at me with an ambiguous expression that I couldn't even hope to interpret at present. It's possible that she wants me to kiss her, but it's equally possible that she wants me to blow up a playground, or to sell me some luggage. I hesitate. It's as if all the little ghosts working in my head crumble up the pieces of paper they'd been working on, shrug, and say, "You're on your own, pal."

I don't know how the decision is arrived at, but I lean toward Jen.

And this is when, from her mysterious bag of tricks, she produces Stupefying Surprise #2 of the evening. She recoils so quickly from my leaning face that she audibly bumps the back of her head against the window. "What are you doing?" she practically shrieks.

"What?"

"I don't know where those lips have been!"

I'm going to give you a moment to reread that last sentence, and bear in mind that she is definitely not joking. I'm sure the expression on my face at this point resembles someone who has just undergone shock therapy as I fumble to make my way out of the car.

I think I manage to say goodnight before she drives off, but I can't tell you for sure. As I watch her car disappear around the corner I let out a fart so devastating it could make a coyote faint.

So much for the black woman experiment.

15__the breaking point

My conversation with Witt abruptly cuts out. I usually have excellent coverage, and I never experience the dropped call problems that plague some of my friends, so it makes much more sense several minutes later when Witt calls me from a land line and explains that he was at the bathroom sink when I was telling him about getting frisked, and he started convulsing so hard with laughter that he dropped his phone in the toilet.

In time, I may be able to laugh about this incident, but right now it's pretty fresh, and it stings. Bad. I am starting to seriously question the existence of single women who are still in touch with their uncrazy side enough to be able to make it through more than one date with me. It's pretty depressing, to be honest, this encroaching certainty about my destiny to grow old alone and die miserable. I wonder when—if ever— I'll be able to make peace with the probability that finding someone is simply not in the cards for me. That I'll remain a fraction of a person forever. I'm so lost in self-pity that I haven't heard a thing Witt's been saying.

"You still there?" he asks.

"Oh, yeah. Sorry. I spaced out for a minute. What did you say?"

"I said that you're simply not meeting the right kind of girls on Match. You need to find some kindred spirits, man."

I roll my eyes. "Witt, if I knew how to do that—"

"I have a plan."

"Of course you do."

"Look, just hear me out," he says, and his tone has changed from amusement to what I might call actual concern.

"Yeah, okay, what?"

"Sensitive writer types."

So much for actual concern. "Yeah, laugh it up."

"No, dude, I'm serious! That's what you are. You're a super intelligent guy, you actually care about things enough to think them through. You're deep like that."

Wait, maybe he's not just making fun of me. "Okay," I say. "So?"

"So where do you meet girls like that?"

"I have no fucking idea." I'd spent the majority of last night lying awake in my bed, failing to come to an understanding of what the hell had happened with Jen Paup. I've been bordering on anger ever since about the third hour of lost sleep.

"Writing classes, man," Witt says in the kind of voice cops use to talk people off ledges.

"Writing classes?"

"Yes. Kindred spirits."

"I don't know. What kind of—"

He says, "Sac State, dude. Evening classes. I've got it all figured out. I'm gonna help you."

As he makes this pronouncement, I spot my mother through the glass, making her way towards the lobby. My parents have settled in here at the motel while their house is being repainted. "Look, Witt, someone's coming in. I gotta call you back." It's not just that I don't want to be talking about this in the presence of my mother; it sounds like another one of Witt's sophomoric schemes, and I honestly don't think I'm up to it. At this point, going on another date is right up there on my wish list with getting an IRS audit or talking politics with my sister. Right now what sounds good is smothering my sleep deprivation headache with a cold compress and taking a nap on my couch for about three years. Witt makes me promise to call him back soon, and my mother—god bless her—pretends to be perusing the pamphlet rack with great interest until I hang up the phone.

"Hey, Mom, what's up?"

"Oh, hello, Michael. I'm going to the grocery store to get some milk. Do you need anything?"

"What do you need milk for?"

"Oh, you know your father and his cereal."

"Why doesn't he just come down here to the lobby? We've got tons of cereal." Sometimes my mother's habit of being too polite to ask for anything, ever, really rubs me the wrong way. But I remind myself that I'm overtired and add, "What's he eating these days?"

Mom's face flattens into the forced smile she uses when she's attempting to hide her annoyance or dislike about something. Which is every time. My mother would have the world believe that nothing has ever rattled or frustrated her, which is quite a feat to attempt when you live with my dad. "Your father doesn't want to leave the room. He found a channel on the TV that plays that reggae music nonstop."

Like my mother, I've learned to pick my battles with my dad. There will be no talking him out of this until he tires of the Music Choice channels on his own. "Hold on," I say, shaking my head and stomping back toward the kitchen. I'm prepared to meet José's steely glare with one of my own, but he's inexplicably nowhere in sight. I snatch two pint cartons of milk from the fridge and bring them to my mother. "Here," I say, more gruffly than I'd intended.

"You seem upset, Michael," she says, her brow knitting in concern. "Are you getting enough fiber?"

According to my parents, constipation causes the overwhelming majority of crises in people's lives. You can imagine how frustrating it is to defend your system regularity as often as one of them brings it up. As I hand her the milk, I spot Rollie past her shoulder, outside by the pool, standing and staring. This cannot be good.

"I'm just tired, Ma," I say. "I'm sorry, but I have to deal with this." I scamper around the counter and out to the deck. Rollie's absently scratching at his exposed chest hair with a dazed expression on his face and his toothpick aiming toward the sky. I follow his gaze, and, sure enough, on the opposite side of the pool the two teenage girls are reclining face down on loungers, their pert butts sunny side up and their bikini tops unfastened.

"Rollie!" I hiss.

He turns. "Mick! Hey I hope you're not coming out here without sunblock on that receding hairline. That skin can be sensitive—"

I yank him by the arm toward the lobby. "Hey, man, I really need to talk to you inside, like now."

He allows me to lead him inside, and before the door swings shut behind us he innocently asks, "Something wrong, Mick? You seem perturbed."

"First of all, do *not* stand around the pool ogling the guests!"

"Ogling?"

"I'm dead serious man, you can't *do* that shit." He seems to recognize the seriousness of my reproachful look and doesn't respond. "And, second, you haven't even given me the status of the toilets. You've been looking at them for two days; now what's the fucking story?"

"Oh, that." He casts his eyes downward for a second, then puts his hands on his hips, looks out toward the pool, and sighs dramatically.

"Oh, Jesus."

"Well, there's some good news and some bad news," he drawls. "Bad news is I think we're gonna need to replace some pipes."

I blink, not comprehending.

"That means we're gonna need to tear up the floor over in that area," he explains, nodding toward the dining section of the lobby, opposite the counter.

"Good god almighty," I mutter, experiencing a sinking feeling in my chest.

"Yeah, I'm pretty sure that's what needs to happen."

"Pretty sure!" I sputter, too loudly, quickly darting my eyes around the lobby to make sure no one heard me.

"Well, Mick, you can't be a hundred percent sure until you check the pipes."

I sink onto the sofa next to me. Earlier this morning I didn't think I could feel any worse, but now I realize that all that was merely mental calisthenics to prepare me for the professional grade gloom I'm slipping into now. "I can't afford this," I mumble.

"That's the good news," Rollie says brightly, perching against the armrest of the sofa perpendicular to mine. "See this is a more-than-one-man job. With an assistant, I bet I could knock her out in a week or so."

My eyes involuntarily close at the thought of Rollie hanging around on a daily basis. I rub my closed eyelids to try to alleviate some pressure. "How is that good news?" I blurt. "Now I gotta pay for you *and* an assistant! Are you insane?"

"That's the thing," he says, grinning like a simpleton. "You could help me. We'll get 'er done in half the time, and it saves you a chunk of cash!"

"Oh, wow, what a great deal, Rollie! Except I don't know the first goddamned thing about plumbing." I get up and kick the sofa, emitting a small puff of dust into the room's tension.

"Look, I'll show you what to do. There's nothin' to it."

"Oh, you'd do that for me?"

He doesn't seem to catch the sarcasm, because he shrugs and says, "What are friends for?"

I've had enough. Enough of wasting my time with women who are either heartless bitches or complete psychos. Enough of my so-called friends clowning on me. Enough of not being able to write anything worth a damn. Enough of hemorrhaging all my money trying to keep the roof on this piece of shit motel that I never wanted to own in the first place!

"We're not friends," I scream, feeling my cheeks suddenly flushing. "This is the first time you haven't openly tried to cheat me, and even this is probably some kind of a scheme that I just haven't figured out yet!"

Rollie slowly rises to his feet and faces me. I feel my muscles tighten; I prepare for the worst. He's either going to storm out, or get right up in my face and tell me to go screw myself. I'm not a violent guy, but I'm ready to give him all he can handle if he makes a move on me.

Instead of hurt or rage, a wholly perplexed expression appears across his face. "Of course we're friends, Mick," he says simply.

I deflate. Collapsing back onto the couch, I cover my face with my hands and let out a sound that's somewhere between a hopeless sigh and an angry grunt. The thought of apologizing to a guy like Rollie galls me, but somehow I feel like he deserves one. "I'm sorry, man, it's just a lot of shitty things have been piling up, and I feel like this place is in such lousy shape I'll never be able to get rid of it."

"Get rid of it?" The toothpick nearly drops out of his gaping mouth. "Mick, why on earth would you want to get rid of this place?"

I shake my head, looking around at the lobby walls that have come to feel like prison bars. "Man, do you think I want to be running this dilapidated old barn for the rest of my life?"

Rollie looks around the place in what appears to be disbelief. "Why the hell not?"

I almost laugh—more from weariness, I suppose, than for any good reason. "I want to do something important, man. I don't want to be stuck in this place forever."

Rollie whistles. "Shit, Mick, I don't know what you're talking about. You're living the *good* life here! Your own boss, set your own hours, hang out with friends—and all the while you're doing something good for people, man. Givin' them a nice place to stay while they're traveling, taking care of 'em."

This time I do laugh, a long, barely controlled, giddy, overtired cackle. Only a space cadet like Rollie would look at me and think I'm living the good life. There's no point in trying to explain what the hell I'm talking about. I *am* sorry I yelled at him, though. In his own way, the guy's harmless enough, I guess. Collecting myself, I say, "Maybe you're right, Rollie. Look, can I just give you a call tomorrow and we'll talk about it then? I'm really not up for it today."

He shrugs. "Yeah, sure, Mick. You get some rest, and I'll lay it all out for you tomorrow."

"Cool. Thanks."

He ambles over to the front door, but he stops when he grasps the handle and turns back toward me. "Hey, are you gettin' enough fiber in your diet?"

More uncontrollable laughter escapes from me.

"I'm just saying, Cracklin' Oat Bran—it's the *shit*." He waggles his eyebrows. "If you know what I mean."

"Goodbye, Rollie."

◎◎◎

That evening I get home around six thirty, after having stopped for some wings and gator bites at Sandra Dee's. I almost never feel up to the task of attempting to cook, or even to shop for ingredients with which to cook. I'm not sure the right words exist to express my ineptitude in the kitchen. If you give me a piece of bread and a toaster, I can give you back either a warm, dry piece of bread or a charred object with such indistinguishable features that only a fire inspector would be able to identify its original form. Instead of courting disaster, I tend to subsist on sandwiches at work, pub fare, and fast food. It's a much more genteel and socially acceptable way to slowly kill oneself, with none of the social stigmas that come along with smoking cigarettes or abusing narcotics.

My intention is to finish a damning review of *The Catcher in the Rye* that I've been working on for my blog and go to bed early, but then I receive a text from Brooklyn reminding me about the pub trivia that I'd agreed to attend with her tonight at The Fox & Goose. It starts in about a half hour. I curse loudly. Trying to decide upon an age-appropriate temper tantrum to act out, I almost throw my phone across the room, but a quick assessment of my current finances convinces me that I can't afford to replace it at the moment, so I settle for some more high decibel cursing.

I hear my neighbor Thelma cackling through the wall. This is not necessarily related to her possibly having overheard my cursing. Thelma is crazy, but in the legitimate, clinical sense. She must be an undiagnosed schizophrenic or something, because that ear piercing cackle will erupt at arbitrary intervals day and night. It sounds like the noise giddy cartoon witches make when discussing their diabolical plans, and it's enough to send shivers up your back. Thelma will stay inside her apartment for weeks at a time; she never has visitors, but that doesn't stop her from the occasional animated conversation that I can clearly hear through the thin walls of my apartment. I know that it's a sad commentary on our country's deplorable mental healthcare system, and I know it's not Thelma's fault, but it gets extremely annoying nonetheless. The other day I was standing at our mail boxes chatting about the Giants with my other neighbor Ross, when Thelma emerged from her apartment in a nightgown and thick wool socks. She just stood grinning ambiguously at us, and we both gave her a polite nod in greeting. As I was grousing about Matt Cain's grim deterioration from a once dominant pitcher, Thelma piped up with, "It's like the fox lady!"

We paused, and I politely asked, "What's that, Thelma?"

"Do you guys remember the show about the lady with all the foxes? You guys remember."

"Uh, not really, no," Ross replied.

Thelma chuckled. "Yeah," she said. "I also remember *Thundercats*." With that, she waddled over, took the incoming mail out of her box, stuffed it all in the outgoing mail slot without looking at it, and disappeared back into her apartment. A strong scent of curry lingered in the air. Ross and I immediately retreated to our own apartments.

Presently, with Thelma's muffled giggling in the background, I start three different times to text an excuse to Brooklyn why I'm not coming, but each time I delete before sending. My sluggish mind seems unable to come up with a story that doesn't sound like a pathetic and far-fetched excuse. Another part of my brain—a little voice I don't recognize—seems to be trying to compel me to grow up and go hang out with this lovely girl and her friends, that it's silly and impetuous to want to withhold my company from her simply because she had the audacity to *not* be attracted to me. My natural impulse is to skip trivia and hope Brooklyn doesn't bother trying to contact me again. But it occurs to me that steadily following my natural impulses so far has led me to a state of existence that I don't find very satisfying. Logically it seems that I'm going to need to start acting against my normal instincts if I'm going to find a way to transform my life into something more tolerable.

So I go. Brooklyn's two friends—one guy and one girl, both single—are funny and smart, and although I'm not sure how many correct answers I have contributed, our team places fourth out of eleven. When I finally make it to my bed, I feel proud to have for the first time in my life hung out platonically with a girl I'm attracted to and still enjoyed myself.

Okay, okay. In truth, every time Brooklyn said something funny or flashed her adorable smile my heart ached with the peculiarly rueful sensation of having lost something you never actually possessed. But it's also true that there were moments interspersed with all the agony in which I found myself genuinely having fun and managing to somewhat enjoy my time in the dreaded Friend Zone.

16__big fish

The next morning, I sleep in until 10:30. I swing by the coffee shop—because I don't trust myself making coffee any more than toast—and finish up my latest blog post. Last week's book review got an unusually high number of comments, so I'm feeling pleased with myself, and that's probably why my immediate reaction when I see an incoming call from Brooklyn is to answer eagerly, expecting it to be something positive—such as her admission that she was wrong about not being crazy about me.

Sometimes life likes to yank the old carpet out from under you like that. Apparently last night at trivia I had made a gross miscalculation and let it be known that, unlike Brooklyn's other two friends, I did not have to work this morning.

"I'm in a real pickle here, Mick," she says.

"What kind? Because if it's not dill, this conversation is over." This joke lands about as well as you'd expect that it would.

Brooklyn's tone is urgent. "Look, I hate to even ask you this because I know we barely know one another and all, but I remembered you saying last night that you're not working today, right?"

"Right."

"The thing is, my ride to the airport just bagged on me, and it's too late to get a Blue Van, and a cab ride is so expensive ...."

She prattles on, and I am literally shaking my head in incredulity.

Angelina was presumptuous.

Just like Dante's hell, there are multiple levels of The Friend Zone, and my descent has been dizzyingly fast. Being asked to give someone a lift to the airport is only slightly above being asked to help them move, and generally is a level that should take months—if not years—to achieve. Who the hell does Brooklyn think she is? And just *what* the hell does she think I am? Surely she must know how brutally insulting this seems to me. There have got to be rules written down someplace about just how much you are allowed to ask of a guy you've rejected!

I am still fuming, yet about thirty minutes later I'm on my way to pick her up at her apartment. There was simply no way to turn her down without coming across as a monumental prick, and besides, this gives me the moral high ground with her. She asked something completely inappropriate of me, but I did not return insult for insult. I may be the only one keeping score here, but this definitely puts me ahead.

Brooklyn is going to visit a friend in Hawaii. This too pisses me off. In my early twenties I used to travel a lot. Random road trips. Backpacking trips to Europe. Visits to relatives in Ireland. But no more. As my thirtieth birthday approached, my traveling partners began to disappear. Derek, Manuel, and Nick all got married, and apparently there are laws I was unaware of that state that a married man is no longer allowed to go anywhere further than the grocery store without his spouse. Stacy and I once enjoyed a memorable trip to Vegas together, but he never goes anywhere without Terry anymore. Ethan spends all his free time with Georgelle.

I'm too offended and frustrated to keep these depressing feelings to myself once Brooklyn gets in the car, so it all comes pouring out of me like wine from the spigot in Colin Farrell's kitchen sink. "And I won't even mention the ones who had kids," I vent, "because once your friends have kids, that's the last you'll see of them. And it's just as well, because for some reason being a parent and being fun are two things that don't seem to coexist."

"So I take it you don't want to have kids someday?" Brooklyn says.

"Not really. I mean, if I meet the right woman and she has kids of her own, it's not a deal-breaker or anything, but I'm just not in a hurry to have kids of my own." I explain to her my theory about how everyone wants to have a legacy, but most people chicken out of creating one themselves, so they substitute having kids in place of accomplishing anything big.

"Is that why you think people have kids?" she asks, one of her eyebrows arched skeptically.

"A lot of times, yeah. You don't?" I'm still feeling somewhat hostile toward her, which is why I'm almost begging her for an argument.

"I don't know," she says, squinting across the empty fields along the 5. "I guess that could be true for some people, but I think others just want that special bond that only exists between a parent and a child, you know?"

I shrug.

"There's like this unconditional love a small child has for its parents, and I've always thought some people are so eager to have kids because they've never felt unconditional love from anyone."

"Yeah, maybe," I mumble, thinking of a couple of girls who got pregnant in my high school class who probably had pretty lackluster home lives. Who knows, Brooklyn could have a point.

She continues, "I also think a lot of people just have an innate desire to nurture; they want to share their lives with children, and to try to bring them up and mold them into strong, independent people of their own."

A lot of this makes sense. Dammit, why does this girl have to be so smart on top of everything else? I grudgingly admit that maybe I just don't understand people with kids as well as I think I do. I don't know if I really believe that, or if I just want to shut her up. I opt not to tell her the story about my most recent date with a mother. Partly because it's still a little too fresh for me to find the humor in it, but mostly because that incident has convinced me that women in general are crazy, and it doesn't matter whether they have kids or not. Instead I tell her about a date I had a couple of months ago with a single mom. We met for dinner, and we hit it off immediately. At least, I thought we did.

"We closed the place down—the very last ones in the restaurant. That's how good our conversation was going," I explain. "I walked her to her car, and she said she would definitely be interested in going out again. She kissed me goodnight."

"Really?" Brooklyn says, making it sound like she's not much of a first date kisser herself.

"Yeah. So the next day I text her and ask if she's still up for going out again, and when. Instead of answering the question, she responds, 'I forgot to ask you last night, how long was your longest relationship?'"

Brooklyn looks at me askance. "That's odd."

"That's what I'm saying! I responded by asking if her answer about another date depended on my answer to that question. But jokingly. You know, I put a smiley face at the end of it."

"Right, so what did she say to that?"

"She just writes back, 'So?'" I look over at Brooklyn, and she shrugs. "So I tell her. And she doesn't respond at all."

"What? Have you never been in a long term relationship or something?"

"I dated my college girlfriend for over three years."

"That's as long as my longest. So you never heard from this girl again?"

"I ended up emailing her a day later and said I guessed she didn't want to see me anymore, and that sucked because I thought she'd had a good time. She writes back and tells me it was the most fun she'd had on a date in at least a year, but that she didn't think we had enough in common to get into a long term relationship."

"Whoa," Brooklyn says, whistling. "She sounds hard core."

"Yeah, I asked her what she was basing that on, but I never heard from her again." I realize that I have been laying down the foundation of my argument that will unequivocally prove to Brooklyn that all women are crazy, but we are already pulling up to the terminal by this time. She thanks me profusely for the ride, and before she gets out she squeezes my shoulder and tells me what a good guy I am. As far as consolation prizes go, that one is right up there with a bouquet of flowers made out of dog shit.

◎◎◎

The next day at the motel, it happens. I knew it would, and it's every bit as disconcerting as I had feared. I look up from the desk and spot Rollie at the base of the stairs out front, chatting with Abonice. She has a look of suspended judgment on her face, like she's waiting for a punchline that isn't coming. I nearly lose my balance sprinting from behind the counter out through the front door.

"Yeah, the bench press gets all the press, so to speak," Rollie is saying. "But it's the military press that tells the truest tale. I'm a veteran, by the way." He's puffing out his chest like he's making up a fake yoga pose. He's not a veteran, by the way.

"Rollie!" I say, practically skidding to a stop beside him and laying a heavy arm around his shoulder. "I need to see you inside. Abonice, I'm sure you have something you need to be, uh, attending to."

She does that thing again where she turns her head and looks at me from the corner of her eyes. "Yes, Mr. Collins."

It's difficult to drag Rollie into the lobby, as he seems intent upon watching Abonice walk up the stairs. "Mmm, that little one is a Sit and Spin candidate. You know what that means, Mick?"

"I'm sure I don't. Look Rollie, just stay away from her, all right man?"

He scrutinizes my face for a moment, then grins. "Ah," he says, "it musta been the breeze out there. I didn't pick up the alpha dog's scent on her. Say no more, say no more."

It's easier to let him believe I have designs on Abonice than it would be to explain my irrational devotion to protecting her virtue from sleazeballs like him, so I change the subject. "Are we all set to get started on the floor?"

"I have to pick up a couple more things this afternoon, then we'll get at it tomorrow mornin' at eight sharp."

"Okay, I'll—"

"Sharp, Mick. Eight sharp." He nods solemnly, like he's admonishing me.

"Yeah, fine. Rollie, my shift starts at seven. I'm not gonna be late. I was just going to say my friend Stacy is going to come by and help."

"Oh?" Rollie seems concerned.

"Yeah, I mentioned what we were doing, and he seemed really excited at the prospect of getting to bust stuff up, so I said he could help."

"Wait, this is a dude?"

"Yeah, Stacy is a guy."

"Whew," he declares, shaking his head. "Well, the more the merrier!"

The desk phone rings. "I gotta get that," I say.

Rollie waves, and heads out the front door, calling out, "All rright, see ya at eight thirty sharp!"

It doesn't occur to me until after the door closes behind him that he said eight thirty instead of eight. What a weird guy. I pick up the phone, and it's my father, calling from two rooms away. I'm taken a little bit aback. My dad tends to actively avoid phone calls rather than initiate them. "Hey, Pop, everything okay?"

"Champ, I need your mailing address," he says far too loudly.

"Do you need my first name, too?" I joke, holding the receiver away from my ear.

"Hold on, I don't have a pen." I hear the phone clank down on a table, and I'm pretty sure I can hear Toots and the Maytals playing in the background. I'm not going to try to estimate how long it takes my father to return to the phone, because you wouldn't believe it anyway. Finally, he announces, "I'm back."

"What do you need it for, Da?"

"What's that, sport?"

Stunning. "My address. You said you need my address. Why do you need it?"

"Something for you came to the house. In the mail."

"Well, why do you—"

"It's an invitation to your fifteenth high school reunion."

I roll my eyes. "Why do you need my address? Can't you just give it to ... wait a minute. You guys don't know my address? I've lived in the same apartment for like eight years."

"We have it written in the address book back at the house, but we're not allowed to go over there. They're fumigating."

"They're painting. At any rate, my point is you don't have to mail it; you can just—"

"I had to open it so I could put it in a new envelope to mail it. You see, they cancel out the stamps once something's been mailed."

"Yeah, Pop, I get it. But why don't you just give me the invitation, instead of mailing it?"

"Oh. You don't want me to mail it?"

"You can throw it away, for all I care."

"What do you mean, throw it your way?"

Enunciating my words slowly and clearly, I say, "Why don't you just come to the lobby and hand it to me?"

"Oh, I see what you mean." He pauses, and I listen to the reggae in the background for several seconds. "I don't know if I'll be able to get to that today, son."

DaLisa shuffles into the lobby and heads past me to the back. I nod in greeting, but I can't perceive any response from her. "That's fine, Da. I don't need it anyway. There's no way—"

"I'll be over in a few minutes," he says, cutting me off yet again. "I have to put on some pants."

"Look, don't worry about—" I begin, but he has hung up. Despite the fact that I don't think I completed a single sentence, this has been the longest conversation between my dad and me in probably five years.

"Hey, DaLisa," I call, heading to the back. I find her staring into one of the supply cabinets.

"Mm-hmm," she says disinterestedly. She extracts her reading glasses and some sort of list from the infinite luggage compartment that is her ample bosom.

"Listen, do me a favor. Keep Abonice away from Rollie, okay?"

She turns and tilts her head down so she can study me over the tops of her glasses. When she does this, I feel like I'm in a TV movie being reproached by a prickly school teacher. At length she responds, "She's too young for you."

"That's not what I mean!" I say. "It's just Rollie, you know? He's just so ... gross."

"Mm-hmm."

"Come on, don't pretend you don't hate Rollie. You know exactly what I mean."

She stares back into the cabinet. "Abonice is a big girl. She can take care of herself."

"Yet she's too young for me, huh? Exactly how old do you think I am?"

"Not as young as you think you are," she says, studying the label on a bottle of wood polish.

"I know what you're doing. You're trying to get under my skin, but it's not going to work. I know you agree with me about this."

"I could care less about young Abonice and that Bumbaclot."

"Bullshit. You think he's as gross as I do. And don't use that phrase *I could care less*. It doesn't make any sense."

She looks at me over the top of her glasses again.

"If you *could* care less," I explain, "that implies you *do* care somewhat. If you say I *couldn't* care less it implies that you don't care at all. I hate it when people misuse that expression."

"Mm-hmm."

The bell from the front desk dings. It's a shame, because I was prepared to hold her stare this time until I won. "Look, just do it, okay?"

My father is standing at the front counter, smiling. He sees me approach, but he rings the bell again anyway. He's wearing a bathrobe over his shirt. I'm glad there is a counter between us, because I'd be mortified if he doesn't happen to be wearing pants. "Oh, hey, Pop. You didn't need to bring that over, really."

He produces an empty coffee cup and sets it down on the counter.

I point to his right. "The coffee station is over there." He looks over, but not far enough for his gaze to have possibly reached the coffee station. He turns back to me. He seems confused, which is to say, he seems like his normal self. "Did you bring the invitation?"

"Ah," he says, reaching into his pocket. He hands me the invitation, still in its torn-open envelope.

"Yeah, thanks. Not that there's any way I'd go to this thing," I say, pulling it out to read it. I glance up and see my dad staring at me with the expression one makes when struggling to remember what they were about to say. "Da, if you want more coffee, feel free to help yourself." I indicate the coffee station again. "There's regular and decaf over there."

He takes his coffee mug and approaches the station tentatively.

"Fifteen years," I grumble, reading. "Sweet Jesus."

DaLisa reappears, toting two bottles toward the sliding door that leads to the pool. "Hey," I call. "Don't forget what we talked about." I try to achieve an authoritative manner when I say this, but I'm pretty certain I have failed laughably.

"Keep the girl away from the man," she says.

"Right," I say.

My father turns toward DaLisa and brightens. "That accent. Are you from Kingston?" he asks. "Trenchtown?"

She ignores him. "One question, young Mick."

I nod.

"Why do you care?"

I'm not sure why, but this question riles me. "Just do it, all right?"

DaLisa sighs and heads out the back.

My dad has turned back to face the coffee station, but he's standing still, his coffee cup in one hand and his other arm at his side.

"You just push the button."

Still no movement. "What button? Do I have to put in beans?"

Understand, they are just typical coffee thermos dispensers, with the push buttons on top—the kind everyone you know has encountered at least a hundred times in their lives. Bordering on exasperation, I walk over and fill his cup, leaving a little space. I don't bother to point out the sweeteners, cream, or cinnamon because I know he doesn't like anything in his coffee. At least not anything he'd find here. I return to the counter and finish reading the invitation. "God, this sounds like torture," I mutter.

"What's that, bud?" Da says. He's holding the coffee near his face and blowing gently. I wonder if he realizes he's not blowing anywhere near the direction of his cup.

"Fifteen years, Pop. Does that make you feel as old as it does me?"

"I remember being fifteen," he says wistfully, a gentle smile lighting up his face. "Mary Jo Baker." He squints down at the envelope in my hands. "Is that the invitation?"

"Yeah, that's the invitation that you just handed me."

"Ah, you'll have a grand time."

"There's no way I'm going to this mess."

His smile drops. "Why not?"

"God, I don't want to see these people. What am I going to say? Hey guys, I live in a shitty apartment and run a shittier motel?"

"I love this place, boy-o!" he says, looking around. Then he fixes me with a serious look. "You're a small business owner. You're an important part of this community."

I stifle a laugh. "Yeah, right. There are three other motels on this street alone."

My dad seems ready to say something, but he turns and brightens. "José! Hula."

I take a moment to assure myself that I'm not hallucinating. José is indeed walking out from the back, in full sight of the public. He's carrying a Styrofoam carry-out box, and I swear the look on his face in some ways resembles a human smile.

"Is *hola*, my frien'," he says. He approaches my father, and the two actually embrace. I kid you not, they hug! "Here your san'wich."

"Oh, thank you! I got some coffee too," Da says, holding up his mug.

"Is wonderful," José says. "I walk you out." The two of them walk out the front door, practically arm in arm, like long lost friends.

I have now officially seen everything.

I look back at the invitation. I had forgotten that my school colors were blue and yellow. I keep in touch with very few people from my high school, at least intentionally. I do run into them around town every now and then, which is why I stay home so often. Just last week I ran into Wendy Reynolds, who I used to work with on the yearbook staff. She's got triplets, and she still managed to get made a partner at her law firm. The week before that when I was at the coffee shop I saw a guy that I think was named Dave something; he said he works at the Capitol, and he was driving a Mercedes. Danny Santini—the clown who drunkenly crashed his Camaro into the goal post on our football field—moved to L.A. and is supposed to be in a movie with Matt Damon next summer. I see my old baseball teammate Charlie pretty much every time I walk into the Torch Club. The guy practically gets his mail there, but he still somehow scored a pretty little blonde wife who looks like a swimsuit model. Statistically speaking, at least half of my graduating class has to be divorced and miserable by now, but I don't ever seem to bump into them. I hate having to smile politely as I meet everyone's attractive, successful spouse, which is why there's no way I'll be attending my reunion.

It's amazing how certain we all were back in high school that we'd be successful one day. I wrote a pretty popular humor column in the school paper, and everyone knew I was going off to get an English degree from Davis and planned to be a writer. How am I supposed to stand around wearing a tie and tell two hundred people that in the fifteen years since they've seen me all I've been able to accomplish has been writing a blog that barely makes me enough money to hit the McDonald's Value Menu once a week and running a two-star motel with third-world-quality plumbing? Just thinking about it makes me want to steal my dad's bottle of whiskey and pass out under a table somewhere.

DaLisa walks back through the lobby, giving me the stink eye. What bothers me most about her "Why?" question is that I don't know the answer to it. Why *do* I care whether or not Rollie gets his grimy paws on Abonice? I have no intention of getting involved with or even pursuing an employee, but I suppose some small part of my vanity likes to think that it's at least a possibility. I'd hate to think that I'm one of those guys whose entire self-esteem is based on the number of attractive women that want to sleep with me, but it's strangely comforting to think that if I were to attempt to woo Abonice it would end in success. As narcissistic and immature as that sounds, it's the truth. And although it's not a competition I plan on entering, if someone I consider to be less appealing than myself—like Rollie—were to end up in bed with her, I'm fairly certain that I'd feel like I had lost.

If you don't find yourself engaged in this level of neurotic thinking on a regular basis, count your blessings. Not only are women crazy, they're driving me there as well.

The phone rings.

"Shady Spot Motel," I answer lifelessly.

A woman's voice says, "Is Mr. Michael Collins available?"

Instinctively, I adopt a richer, more sensual tone, because it's a woman, and because I'm an idiot. "Speaking. How can I help you?"

"Mr. Collins, I'm calling from the offices of Richard Cromwell, CEO and president of Knight's Lodge Incorporated in San Jose. You are the owner and operator of the Shady Spot Motel in downtown Sacramento; am I correct?"

The way she says it makes me feel like someone of great consequence. "Uh, yes, that's correct."

"Mr. Cromwell would like to know if you'd be interested in meeting with some of our representatives to discuss the possibility of a corporate acquisition process."

I've been distracted by the confident sexiness of her voice, so I'm not sure I caught what she is asking. "I'm sorry, a meeting about what now?"

"Mr. Collins, there's interest on our side of possibly expanding our brand into the Sacramento region. Would you be open to meeting with us on a very informal basis, just to sort of exchange ideas and talk about the possibility of entering into a more formal discussion about our acquiring the Shady Spot Motel?"

My breath catches in my throat. It has not occurred to me that anyone would be interested in actually giving me money to take this rundown old shack off my hands. Especially not someone as rich as the Knight's Lodge chain. My mind immediately races through dozens of numbers — possibilities of what they might offer me for it. Wild guesses really, but each of them looks remarkably similar to a down payment on a New York City apartment.

17__getting some class

I had been so excited about meeting with Cromwell's people that I'd nearly agreed to the day that Liz—the woman I spoke to on the phone— suggested for early next week. Then, midsentence, I'd visualized them coming to tour the place and seeing Rollie and his toothpick popping out of a gaping cavity in the lobby floor. I pushed them back another week, so now I've got just under a fortnight to get the plumbing situation sorted out and the lobby's floor rebuilt.

The following afternoon, I've managed to gather the whole staff—all half dozen of them, plus Rollie—and I'm explaining my goal of having this place looking and functioning perfectly by June 29th in time for the visit from the Knight's Lodge execs.

"She said Mr. Cromwell himself might even be here, so we need to make this place look better than it's ever looked," I say. "If all goes well, there's a chance they might make an offer to buy." My smile is not returned by any of the faces around me. I'm not a dreamer; I wasn't expecting exuberance—or even full cooperation—from this lot, but I was expecting at least a little enthusiasm at such an announcement. Of course, Quinn looks nervous, his eyes darting around the room as if he expects rotten tomatoes to be hurled at him from multiple directions at any moment. Rollie's face betrays no emotion; he knew this was coming. But everyone else wears expressions that vary between surprise and concern.

"You're selling the motel?" DaLisa asks, eyeing me over the tops of her glasses.

"It's not even a sure thing that they'll make an offer. They just want to come by and have a look. Very informal. But everyone's gonna be on their best behavior. Rollie will be done with the plumbing by then, so we don't have to worry about him being here. No offense, Rollie." He shrugs. "So, yeah, if they like what they see, hopefully they'll decide to buy it, yeah."

DaLisa exchanges a look that I can't interpret with Abonice and the other maid, Maria.

"Guys, Richard Cromwell is, like, a billionaire," I explain. "He owns all the Knight's Lodge hotels, all over the West Coast and Midwest. This is exciting news. Be happy!"

DaLisa clears her throat and fixes me with a reproachful look. "If the rich man buys the motel, what's goin' to happen to us?"

The bottom of my stomach drops like there was a trap door beneath it. What a fool I am. This had not even remotely crossed my mind. "Well," I stammer, "I—I'm sure they'll keep all of you on."

José is attempting to bore through my skull with his stare. DaLisa looks at the other maids and rolls her eyes. Chynna, the girl who works the front desk part time, is texting, and it appears her thumbs are punching the screen rather angrily. I have to say something to calm this brewing storm. "Look, guys, don't worry about it, okay? If I do end up selling—and it's nowhere near a sure thing at this point—I'll make sure your jobs are safe with the new owner." Since I'm pulling this directly out of my ass, I decide to add, "And this Cromwell guy is so rich that—if anything—you'll probably get raises." I force a reassuring smile, hoping they buy it.

I feel like such a heel, making an announcement like that without even considering how unnerving it might sound to my staff. Cromwell might very well bring in his own people. The thought of this overwhelms me with guilt. What would Remi think of me? But, on the other hand, these are adults, able to take care of themselves. They're not my responsibility. Once in a while one has to look out for oneself. This could be my ticket out of this life that I'm trapped in, my one chance to get back on track towards what I should have been doing all along. But even these rationalizations, true as they may be, ring hollow when I think of that look DaLisa gave me.

After the meeting breaks up, everyone is fairly quiet for the rest of the day. Except Rollie, of course. I'm not convinced that even death could shut that guy up. I smile, imagining his corpse peppering the mortician with embalming advice until the exasperated old guy finally sews his mouth shut. He's jabbering away as we pick up where we left off this morning. Rollie had arrived at eight fifty-two sharp, and we'd gotten started on the lobby floor. With Stacy's enthusiastic help, we had finished tearing up the floor, and now the pipes are exposed. Rollie is tapping on the main pipe in various spots with a screwdriver, listening, and uncannily resembling someone with no clue what the hell they're doing. He stops talking for a moment and looks over at me, squinting. "What are you doing with clay pipe sections?" he says at length, in a suspicious tone.

"How the hell should I know? I didn't build this place."

He eyes me for another long moment, then shrugs and goes back to his diatribe about aging. A few minutes ago I had made the mistake of mentioning that I have a birthday coming up soon, and Rollie had insisted on guessing my age. I bristled, feeling offended when he guessed forty, but he explained his rationale that most guys don't start losing their hair until their late thirties. What a guy.

As enjoyable as that conversation had been, it doesn't compare to how much I'm relishing the current topic. I had tried to steer Rollie away from the subject of birthdays by telling him I'd received an invitation to my high school reunion. As I've mentioned before, I'm an idiot. Now he's sitting with his legs dangling into the abyss we've created in the lobby floor, looking off to the distance wistfully—accomplishing zero, work-wise—describing his experiences at his twenty-year reunion. As surprised as I am to hear he had actually graduated from high school, I'm more concerned about his lack of progress at the moment.

"Rollie?" I interrupt. "What should we be doing next? Remember, we're on kind of a tight timeline here."

"Yeah, boy, I coulda had my pick of three different chicks to bang that night," he continues, ignoring me. "None of 'em paid me any nevermind back in school, you understand. But when they seen what I'd become, they sure changed their tune."

"What you'd become?" I ask, holding back a smirk.

"Hell, yes. Run my own business, set my own hours. Don't hafta answer to nobody."

"Well, technically you should kind of answer to me, since I'm paying you."

He points at me. "And I'll tell you somethin' else, Mick. I'm helpin' people too."

"At an incredibly slow rate."

"Hoo-ey! Chicks eat that shit up," he says, grinning broadly. "Helpin' people, providing one of life's basic necessities. That's how come I can go to bed at night feelin' such confidence in my station in life. The ladies pick up on that, you know; they love a confident man."

"They do, huh? Are you sure it's not just the jumpsuit with some other dude's name on it?"

"Mick, there ain't no cause to be jealous. You're in the same situation as me." He winks at me.

"No, man, the situation I'm in is I've got prospective buyers coming in here to look the place over in eleven days, and right now I've got a giant goddamn sinkhole in the lobby of my motel!"

"Mick, you need to relax. There's not much more we can do today. I told you we'd be done in plenty of time. Then my flooring guy will be in and out of here faster than you can believe. Now, you trust me, don't you?"

My eyes widen. "What in our history together would suggest that I trust you, even a little bit?"

"That's the stress talkin', Mick. That's why you lose your hair. Gonna get bags under your eyes next."

The phone rings, and I jog over to the front desk, thankful for an excuse to get away from Rollie. I swear he stays up at night, concocting new ways to get under my skin. I jot down a reservation for two nights for a guy coming in on Sunday night for business. When I hang up, I spot Chynna drifting in through the front door, both thumbs and eyes glued to her phone, as usual.

"Chynna, what are you doing here already?"

She doesn't look up from her phone. In her trademark bored voice she says, "You told me to come in at five thirty today, remember? You have a class or something like that."

With all the excitement, I had forgotten. Tonight is the first session of the class Witt and I had signed up for at Sac State: Introduction to Creative Writing. Witt's latest brainchild. It's supposed to be an opportunity for me to meet the kinds of girls I'm into—the smart, creative, sensitive types—and a chance for Witt to meet the kinds of girls he's into—those with a vagina. You may be thinking that it sounds like a ridiculous scheme, and that I'm a fool to go along with it, and I'd be hard pressed to argue. Especially now that I'm hopefully going to be moving away from this town soon, it seems pointless to try to meet someone. But I'm still going through with it. For one, I'm thinking a creative writing class might be the prompt I need to get over the debilitating writer's block that's had me stuck at one sentence for the past few months. And secondly, I have to admit that my male pride has been severely wounded of late. Between Brooklyn's flat out rejection of me, and Abonice's failure to recognize me as a member of the male gender, I could use a little confidence boost. Sure, it would be great to find a compatible girlfriend, but at this point, mere attention from someone I find attractive would suffice. Of course, if I do meet someone at this class, I wouldn't have to mention the possibility that I'll be moving soon; that would only weed out the girls who are looking for more than a short term fling. In this circumstance, I don't want to eliminate any potential suitors. A part of my conscience tells me it's morally reprehensible to withhold information like that, but I find that part can be pacified if I ply it with enough alcohol. Desperate times call for desperate measures, and all that. Playing the game this way doesn't seem to bother Witt, so maybe I'm just being too uptight, as he often suggests.

◎◎◎

We arrive a few minutes early for class and select seats near the back of the lecture hall. "Prime scouting location," Witt calls it. There are about forty other students in the room, ranging from traditional college age to a couple of gray-hairs. It doesn't start well. The syllabus uses "who's" where it should say "whose" in the second line, which makes me indignantly cynical about how much I'll actually be able to learn from this class. I am absolutely appalled that two young girls in the front row are wearing pajama bottoms. I'm not much of a fashion snob, but, damn, put some effort into it when you're going to be out in public!

At first I'm inconspicuously scoping out all the females in the room, but I soon get drawn in by the professor's lecture about creating compelling characters. I take copious notes during the next ninety minutes, but Witt's arms remain folded across his chest as his eyes wander carefully around the room. By the time the professor dismisses class, I've excitedly scribbled a few lines of ideas about Angelina's character.

I'm kind of lost in my thoughts as we exit the building so I'm not quite sure how it comes about, but soon Witt and I are engaged in a conversation with a couple of young ladies on the sidewalk, under a bright street lamp. Both girls have long brown hair and glasses, and both look to be in their mid-twenties. The one that's doing most of the talking, Annemarie, is wearing two hemp necklaces and what appears to be a homemade skirt, adorned with colorful patches made from various materials. She seems confrontational with Witt, but, of course, he handles it all expertly, and she never seems to get pissed off. Her friend, Sue, smiles a lot and offers as little to the conversation as I do. Witt keeps trying to involve her, but she responds mostly with nervous laughter and a bunch of "I-don't-knows." Every now and then she'll offer a vapid "Totally" when her friend makes a point. Annemarie's forceful demeanor kind of turns me off as she's lecturing Witt on the necessity of only buying organic produce. She's what I call a *hyperactivist*, someone who purports to be passionate about most of the trendy underdog causes, excitable, quick to anger, tending to seek out confrontations, always eager to convince others to see things their way. I find most such people disingenuous and tiresome, but she is quite striking, and it's clear she has a hella nice body, which is no doubt why Witt has continued to nurse the dialogue between them.

Soon Witt has suggested that we all go out for a drink, and the girls seem up for it. He turns to me. "What do you say?"

I'm not sure I can endure another hour's worth of conversation with these two. "Wow, it's already after nine," I say, checking my phone. "On a Wednesday?"

"Come on," Annemarie offers, "Wednesday is the new Thursday!"

I'm not a hundred percent sure what she means by this, so I say, "Or the new Friday, I guess you could say."

Blank stares.

In a voice that sounds like he's embarrassed for me, Witt says, "Mick, Thursday has been Friday for ... god, since forever."

"Totally," agrees Sue.

18__roots and finances

Witt and I meet Annemarie and Sue for drinks at Ink, on N and 28th. The best part of the experience—by far—is the plate of chicken wings I order. Trying to feign interest in Annemarie's myriad extreme leftist views rapidly becomes as tedious as trying to pry any sort of meaningful conversation out of Sue. After about forty-five minutes, I make up an excuse and extricate myself from the situation. Witt gives me a dark look, indicating his disapproval of my breaking etiquette by abandoning my wingman, but I ignore him. I would much rather go home and work on my book while the ideas generated during class are still fresh. Actually, when it comes to spending time with these two girls, I'd prefer stuffing my pockets with candy, hanging from a tree branch, and letting blindfolded kids pummel me with a stick.

Of course, when I get home I pull my usual trick and procrastinate on the book, choosing to check my Match email first. I've not been receiving responses to any of the emails I've sent out lately, and it's becoming frustrating. It's also made me pretty pessimistic about contacting anyone new. It seems like a waste of creative energy since the odds are that they won't write back anyway, so what I'd done a couple of days ago was to copy and paste the same unspecific, friendly email and send it to roughly a dozen women. Casting a wider net, you understand. However, none of them took the bait. None. Only one new message in my inbox, and it's from Jen Paup.

I'm surprised to see it, because a few days after our infamous date/frisking session she had emailed me to ask why I hadn't contacted her. Rather than going into specifics, I had replied that I just thought we weren't a very good match, and that I wasn't interested in going out again. When I read her latest message, I'm not sure whether to laugh or board up the doors and windows.

Mick,

I don't accept that. I do not feel that you are in a position to be qualified to make such a decision at this time, as you do not know me well enough yet to know whether we are "a good match." You are jumping to conclusions, and that's not a healthy way to approach a dating relationship. I feel that we should meet to discuss this. What is your schedule like this coming week?

Jen

As if I'm not under enough pressure with readying the motel for Cromwell's visit, now I have to consider the possibility that I'm going to be stalked by a woman with firearms training. Perfect.

◎◎◎

The next day, when I arrive a couple of minutes late to the school auditorium for Maddy's kindergarten graduation, I note with interest that Marc is sitting on the aisle, next to Keegan, then my parents, and then Maggie. I smell trouble in matrimonial paradise, and I can't wait to lord it over her. I nearly trip twice as I make my way past everyone's knees down the row to the empty seat beside my sister.

"Not sitting next to hubby?" I whisper with mock innocence.

Maggie rolls her eyes. "Shh, it's about to start." Evasion. Not usually her tactic. Maybe there's something to this. "Nice of you to show up on time," she adds.

I smile, but decide not to press the issue. The ceremony starts, and I can sort of make out the stage as I crane my neck to find a gap between iPhones and iPads being held up to videotape the festivities. Of course Maddy looks ridiculously adorable in her little cap and gown, and so do many of the other kids. The occasional moments of unrehearsed behavior elicit chuckles from the crowd. The biggest laugh comes for a boy who jumps up and down—constantly—during his time on the stage, until a teacher comes over and leads him off. Other than that, it all tends to blur together after the first fifty or so graduates, and I find myself distracted by thoughts of the upcoming motel visit. I'm brought back to the present when my father withdraws a flask from his blazer pocket and my mother, her face crimson, nearly swats it out of his hand.

After the ceremony, we're all mulling around in the twisted-crepe-paper-adorned cafeteria, sipping punch and munching on tasteless cookies as about a million photos are snapped. The snacks have enabled the children to locate another gear of energy, and many of them are streaking around the room bouncing off each other like heated molecules. My dad's grin is wide as Keegan and Maddy use his body like a jungle gym. Mom helps tend to them while Marc stands in their general vicinity, checking his smart phone.

Maggie and I are standing about thirty feet away, near the punch table, and I ask her if anything is going on between her and Marc. I'm taken aback when she responds that she's not up for talking about it, displaying a rare glimpse of genuine vulnerability. It sucks the desire to bust her chops right out of me, so instead I tell her about the miserable time I had last night trying to enjoy the company of girls in their early twenties.

"That's what happens as you get into your thirties. Your door of opportunity is closing, as far as being compatible with them."

I cringe. "Window, dammit! It's window of opportunity. How does everybody know that expression except you?"

"Whatever, Captain Semantics," she says. "My point is that this is a positive thing. People in their twenties don't *get* people in their thirties. What you need is someone closer to your age that will get you."

I drain the last of the punch from my cup. "Yeah, maybe so. I just wish girls in their thirties looked as good as girls in their twenties."

"Mick, that's ageism. And it's inaccurate. My friend Denise just celebrated her thirtieth birthday, and she is absolutely gorgeous."

"No!"

"What?"

"You know what," I say, wagging a finger at her.

Maggie smiles and returns the wave of another mother, who's being dragged toward the cookie line by a very hyper five-year-old. "Ugh, Doreen McCormick," she says under her breath. "She is literally the *worst* person on earth."

"Really, Maggie? Is she literally the worst person on the planet? Including Middle Eastern dictators and Justin Bieber?"

Maggie snorts. "Let's just say that if I ever get a cancerous tumor, I'll know what to name it."

"You've got a lot of anger stored up, don't you?"

My sister rolls her eyes. "Mick, talking to you can be overwhelmingly exhausting," she says.

A five-year-old boy with a red punch mustache charges toward me and stops mere inches away. He pokes my thigh, looks up at me, and declares, "Your pants are weird."

Placing my hands on my knees, I bend down to his face level and beam. "They're made from the skins of little boys that go around poking people."

He stares. Maggie rushes to say, "He's just kidding, sweetheart." He regards her for a moment, then resumes his stare at me.

Still face to face with him, I hiss like an irate cat. His eyes grow to lakes of petrified blue, and he retreats, shrieking across the cafeteria and disappearing into the crowd.

Maggie slaps my shoulder as I straighten up. "Mick, you can't talk to children like that. It can cause psychological damage!"

"He goes around poking strangers, Mags. I'm pretty sure the psychological damage has already happened."

She sighs and shakes her head. Suddenly she turns to me, and her eyes brighten. "Speaking of birthdays, what are the plans? Less than two weeks away."

I had forgotten that we were even talking about birthdays. "Ugh. There are no plans. I don't need any more reminders that I'm getting old."

"Well, that makes sense. Because ignoring the passage of time is sure to make it stop."

"It's a theory that hasn't been disproven yet, so I'm clinging to it, all right?"

"Speaking of time passing," she continues, not missing a beat, "I heard your high school reunion's coming up."

"Is there anything about my life Mom doesn't tell you?"

"Are you going to take a date?"

"Good lord, Mags, you think I'd actually go to that disaster? Not a chance."

She regards me closely, her eyes narrowing. "That's a mistake."

Maddy gallops into me, her arms thrown around me, and her head missing smashing my testicles by mere inches. "Uncle Mick," she shrieks, "I'm a flying rainbow pony!"

"The best one, too. Everybody knows that, kiddo."

She giggles excitedly and tears off in another direction.

"Don't run, Madeline," my sister warns half-heartedly. Maddy is running too fast to hear her. "I remember my high school reunion," she says, a faint smile appearing on her face. "Everyone got fat. It was fantastic."

My sister views nearly everything as a competition. "Yeah, well, I have no interest in seeing those people, fat or not," I say.

"Mick, it's your roots. Don't pretend it's not important."

"My roots? Hey, if you feel tied to this area, good for you, but I don't. I can't wait to move away from here."

"You always talk about that," she says, "but I hope you're not seriously considering it. Mom and Da need you close by."

Which is a ridiculous thing to say. My relationship with my parents is basically telephone-based. All my mom needs, besides a phone, is my dad. And all my father needs, besides a liquor store, is my mother. Maggie is just trying to guilt-trip me out of following through on my New York dream, but it's not going to work.

◎◎◎

After I leave Maddy's school, I stop by the motel to check on Rollie and Stacy. Yep, Stacy had so much fun tearing up that floor that he took the day off work today to come help Rollie again.

"This shit's the bomb, yo!" he says with unrestrained exhilaration when I walk in. "I shoulda been a plumber."

Rollie beams like a proud parent.

"Next I get to smash up a pipe!" Stacy chirps.

"Wait, what do you mean 'smash a pipe'?"

"Well," Rollie says, hoisting himself out of the hole and standing to face me, "I figured out the problem. It's like this." He fishes through the pockets of his coveralls. I'm expecting him to produce a part or a sketch or something, but eventually his right hand reemerges clutching only a fresh toothpick, which he pops into his mouth before he continues. "The slope of your main drain pipe here is off." He looks at me expectantly.

I shake my head. "Which means what?"

"Well, the drain pipe is supposed to slope a quarter inch per foot or more. Yours isn't sloping enough; it's too level, which is why the toilets and drains are getting backed up. See, you're not allowing ol' gravity to do its work."

"So you know how to fix this, then?"

Stacy asks me, "Is this a recent problem, or did the toilets always overflow?"

Rollie doesn't give me a chance to answer. "Oh, no, the pipe used to be at the right slope. County codes wouldn't have allowed the builders to get away with anything less than a quarter inch per foot. Strict sons of bitches. No, I'd say over time the building has settled. Probably these old clay pipes are sweating, which weakens the foundation." He turns to me and puts a hand on my shoulder. "That's why I'm just gonna go ahead and replace this main section of pipe with a plastic one. Seein' as how we got to fix that slope anyhow. Anyway, it gives your boy here a chance to go to work on this here one with a hammer. He's pretty excited about that."

"Fuckin' A," says Stacy.

"So you think this will be done in time, right?"

"Of course the slope could be off because that floor joist that it's attached to might have bowed over time."

"Rollie, will this be fixed in time?"

"In which case you'd technically need to replace the floor joist. And if it's one, chances are it's gonna be more than one needs replaced." He looks at me and shakes his head.

"What does that mean? Why are you shaking your head?" I'm getting nervous.

"So how do we replace those?" Stacy asks.

"We don't."

"What the hell is a floor joist?" I demand.

"Why not?" From Stacy.

Rollie laughs. "Shit, I'm not a framer. What the hell do I know about floor joists?"

"Rollie, you're not listening to me," I say, grabbing him by the shoulders. "What does this mean, time-wise? We've got ten days here."

"Mick, this is what I'm tryin' to explain to you. If you gotta do framing work, technically you'd need to get building permits." I stare at him, uncomprehending. He continues, "Hell, you'd be lucky to get a permit in ten *weeks*, forget days."

I feel lightheaded. "Shit," I mutter, moving over to fall into one of the lobby chairs. I can just imagine the face of Richard Cromwell when he sees a giant hole in the middle of the lobby. He doesn't strike me as someone who'd be interested in purchasing a "fixer-upper." I feel like I've been punched in the stomach.

"Fuck the permit, yo," Stacy says.

I blink at him, not comprehending.

"I mean, fix the floor anyway. Without the permit. Who gonna find out?"

I look at Rollie. He shrugs. "It happens. Hell, from Johnny Law's point of view I'd need a permit to replace this pipe here I'm fixin' to replace. But I figured you wouldn't want to wait around for that. It's just between the three of us here."

I had no idea you needed a permit to get plumbing work done. As I mentioned, I'm pretty awful at being a grownup. This seems like a pretty serious gamble, though. "What happens if the county finds out?"

"Mick you're gettin' ahead of yourself here," Rollie says. "I don't even know if the joists need to be replaced or not. Most likely they do, but who knows?"

"You said you know how to fix the plumbing part, right? What happens if we don't bother fixing the joists or whatever they're called?"

"If you attach a new pipe to an unstable joist, the same problem's just going to happen again a few years down the line."

"In a few years, it's someone else's problem though," says Stacy.

"*If* I'm able to sell."

"The problem is," Rollie explains, "when we find a flooring guy to come in and replace the floor after we're done with the pipes, he's obviously going to spot a joist that needs replaced. We'd need to find someone who's willing to play ball. And that'll cost you."

"What do you mean, find someone? I thought you had a flooring guy all lined up."

Rollie looks surprised. "Johnny Rice? Oh. I didn't realize you had decided for sure to go with him."

"What?"

"Plus, he got nabbed for indecent exposure. Drank half a bottle of whiskey and walked through a playground with no pants on."

"Damn!" says Stacy.

"Shit, Rollie! You said you had a guy! What are we gonna do now? We've got ten days!"

"Relax, Mick. I got me some connections. I'll find someone," Rollie assures me. "But I'm warning you, a rush job like this? It'll cost you."

I have loosely been planning on putting all of this on the credit card, and then using the money I'd get from the sale to Cromwell to pay off the credit card debts. It had seemed simple enough, but Rollie's tone is frightening me. "How much are we talking here?" I say.

"I'll get on the phone this afternoon, and then you and I can talk numbers. For now, though, I'd say it's lunch time."

"El Pollo Loco?" Stacy asks brightly.

"Now you're talkin'," says Rollie.

Stacy jumps up out of the hole. "You rollin' with us, Mick?"

"Nah, I'm good." They shrug, and hustle out to the truck. Actually, I am pretty far from good. I am counting on money I don't know for sure that I'll get to pay for repairs that I can't afford.

19_tricycle

The ballpark figure for the repair work, sans permits, is just over five grand, which is roughly three above what will max out my credit card. I'm afraid to go to my bank for a loan because I'm sure I'd have to admit that I need the money for a construction project and then it would be easier for the city to find out that I'd proceeded without permits. It's hard out here for a pimp.

Three thousand bucks doesn't seem like an obscene amount of money to borrow from someone, but my choices are rather limited. My sister and Marc are out, obviously. I can't show any measure of vulnerability around Maggie. She already thinks of me as a failure, and if I had to ask her for a favor in any form she'd treat me like an indentured servant for the rest of my life or until I finally murdered her to shut her up. My parents are out, not only because they'd be sure to tell Maggie, but because they've basically plunked down most of their cash on hand for the painting project and the down payment on the pool.

Yes, the pool.

A couple of days ago I found out that my parents—who are both pushing seventy—had decided it would be a good idea to spend their golden years luxuriating in the area that used to be their backyard beside a pool that will probably need to maintain itself, if I know my father. Despite the glaring facts that neither one of them can swim, and that my mother's skin is so fair that even sitting in the shade she can get sunburned from the reflection off the shiny wrapper of a nearby piece of Juicy Fruit, this is what they decided. And they simply cannot be talked out of it. So I think it's fair to say that it's only a matter of time until I, too, inherit the family trait of pronounced mental illness.

I decide to call Witt and hit him up for a loan. After enduring a short chastisement over bailing on him last night, I ask him how it went with Annemarie and Sue.

"Not bad," he says. It sounds like he's eating an apple. "We ended up at the Mix. At one point all three of us were kissing."

"Really?" This guy's life is like an episode of VH1's *Behind the Music.* "Holy crap."

More chewing. "Yeah, I blitzed it up, though."

"Really? Captain Smooth? What happened?"

He chuckles. "I drank more than I should. I started talking to this other chick with one of those tiny skirts that look like they're painted on, and I asked her what her ass's name was so that I could Friend it on Facebook." He chuckles again.

"Hmm."

"Yeah, they didn't find it funny either."

"Imagine that."

More chewing. "So what's up, man?"

I plow right in. "I hate to do it, but I'm in a bind here. I've got this repair job started at the motel, and I'm short on cash to finish the job."

Just chewing.

"So," I continue, "I was wondering if you'd be able to spot me some dough."

"Um," he says, drawing out the word as if he has to think about it. "Yeah, man, probably. How much we talking?"

"About three thousand."

"Oh." He stops chewing. Complete silence. "I could probably scrape together maybe five hundred by the weekend."

"Five hundred?" I sputter. "That's it?"

"Mick, what do you think I am?"

"A radio star!"

He laughs. "I wish I made as much as you think I do. I'm cash poor, dude. You know how much I have to pay each month for the Z4?" Witt and his damn Beemer. "Shit, I never even paid for the writing class we're taking."

"Wait, what? How are you going to it then?"

"I don't know. I just showed up. The guy didn't take attendance."

Unreal. Sometimes I'm shaken by the possibility that since my friends are cartoon characters, maybe I am, too, and I just haven't realized it yet.

I thank Witt for the offer but tell him I'm going to check with Ethan instead to see about a bank loan. He says he'll see me next week for class. I ask him if he's going to write the narrative essay we were assigned, and he just laughs and eats his apple.

◎◎◎

Almost a week later, the Recchi brothers have begun patching the hole in the lobby floor, and I'm breathing easier than I have for over a week. My mood has brightened, and it's because I'm already thinking of living as a writer in New York as the future that is coming up soon, instead of just one possibility. Usually I try to prevent myself from getting my hopes up, which is really just an attempt to build insulation against a crushing disappointment, but for some reason, when I see that ugly hole in the floor slowly disappearing, I can't help myself. This sale is going to go through. I just know it will. And then I'll be free to finally be the version of myself I always wanted to be.

Where Rollie found the Recchi brothers I can't fathom. They are twins from British Columbia, sporting matching Jewfros and irregular facial hair patterns, and they seem to communicate with one another mainly through grunts and shrugs. They've done good work, though, and should be finished tomorrow. They either can't or won't—I can't tell for sure—replace the carpeting, but I figure how hard could that be to do it myself? I'm sure Rollie will offer to help; he's been here every day, even after he finished the plumbing job, despite my heavy hints that he's no longer needed. I assume he's playing some long con game in an effort to bed Abonice, but he hasn't made any obvious moves, so part of me thinks he simply has no other place to be. Maybe the plumbing business has dried up more than he cares to let on. If his plan is to hang around the place most likely to next have a plumbing emergency pop up, there are certainly worse bets than the Shady Spot Motel.

Ethan helped walk me through securing a quick loan from his bank, which went smoother than I'd thought it would. When Ethan introduced me at the bank as Michael Collins, the loan officer asked, "Like the whiskey?" which is something I've heard about ten thousand times by now. I guess people just don't know their contemporary Irish history. Right now Ethan's in the lobby dropping off some more paperwork. He surveys the construction taking place and whispers to me, "Dude, did you hire the Coen brothers to replace the floor?"

"I know, right?"

"Listen, tomorrow night after Sean's football game Georgelle and I are going to get dinner and check out this comedy show in Old Sac. Why don't you come along?"

Sean is Georgelle's husband's son from a previous marriage, and I feel the familiar urge to point out to Ethan how unnatural it is for him to do parent stuff with a complete stranger's child, but I'm too tired to get into it. "I don't know, man, I have that writing class tomorrow night," I say, but in truth I am leaning towards dropping that class while I can still get my money back.

"Oh, man, you can't skip it? You'd really dig this guy."

I can't remember the name of the comedian Ethan is referring to, but I read an article about him in the SNR and would actually love to see him. I don't mention this, because the real reason I'm turning down Ethan is that I am so tired of being a third wheel when one of my friend couples brings me along on one of their field trips.

One of the things I miss most about having a girlfriend is the companionship aspect. If you read about something cool happening in town, you automatically have a partner to go with you to check it out. But not me. Every time I want to go anywhere, it's a monumental hassle to find someone to go with. I scroll through the names in my phone, and realize that now nearly all of them are part of a couple. So if I want to attend an event, I'm reduced to flying solo, finding a date, or joining a couple and effectively making their sleek bicycle into a pathetic, awkward tricycle. It's humiliating. "This is our friend Mick. He doesn't have anyone in his life, so we felt obligated to bring him along to barge into our lives."

I tell Ethan that I'll let him know tomorrow about the comedy show. "By the way," I say casually, "have you ever put down carpet?"

"Well, not to its face."

"Hilarious. But for real, when those guys are finished with the flooring, I'm gonna need to replace the carpeting. I've never done it before, and I could use some help."

"When?" Ethan asks.

"I'm not sure," I say, shifting my glance to the fabulous Recchi brothers over in the corner shrugging at each other. "Hold on. Hey guys," I call to them, "when do you figure you'll finish up?"

The scrawnier one squints at me. The other one cocks his head slightly to the side like a dog trying to interpret what its master is saying.

"Will it be done today, you think?"

The scrawnier one bares his teeth and sucks air through them, looking off to one corner of the ceiling. The other one cocks his head the other way and grunts a sound that could most closely be translated as "Hmm."

"Tomorrow?"

At this the brothers look at one another and exchange a series of shrugs and noncommittal head waves. The first one looks my way and sort of bobs his head like a dropped basketball bouncing away. He says something that sounds like "Ah, marracon mebby," which I interpret as an affirmative.

Ethan agrees to help me lay the carpet tomorrow after he gets off work, shows me which form to sign and mail back to the bank, and departs. The visit from Cromwell's people is fast approaching, and I've still got a lot to do. DaLisa and her girls are scrubbing down the rooms from ceiling to floor, and right now I've got Quinn outside power washing the exterior. I told José to prepare a special menu, on the off chance that the Cromwell people will want a snack or even lunch here at the motel. The lobby's ceiling has some discoloration from water damage, and I've decided the best quick fix is to simply paint over it, so I've got to run over to Ace and pick up some paint and painting supplies, along with everything we'll need to install the carpeting. I watch a few YouTube videos on how to install carpeting and create my shopping list. It doesn't look too arduous, even for someone as generally clumsy as me.

And I'll have Ethan and Rollie helping me, which gives me confidence, however illogical that sounds.

As usually happens when I don't have any time to waste, I soon find myself checking Match. My intention is to find a date so I can join Ethan and Georgelle for the comedy show tomorrow night, but I'm also checking to see if I've gotten a response from Sara.

Sara with the incredible green eyes. She had mysteriously stopped responding to my emails, and I'd purposefully forgotten about her. Let me preface this next part by saying that I *never* keep chasing someone who's tried to give me the slip. I don't know why I just phrased that in '70s cop movie jargon, but you get the point. At the first sign of the slightest dis, I usually adopt a defensive posture and try to purge their existence from my mind. Kind of a "if I'm not good enough for you, you can go fuck yourself" attitude, which probably stems from either my goofy male sense of pride or from a deeply nestled fear of rejection. Either way, it seems to me that pursuing someone who doesn't seem interested gives the impression that they're better than me and I must jump through hoops to deem myself worthy of them, and that just doesn't seem like a desirable position from which to commence a relationship.

Anyway, there are new people joining Match all the time, and since I haven't had a date since the disastrous Jen Paup episode, I'd run a ZIP code search for fresh faces yesterday, and guess who comes up in the search results. 49erGurl herself, Sara. I had clicked on her photo because it was a new one and I hadn't recognized her right off. She had posted a bunch of new photos from a two-week camping trip she'd just completed at Yellowstone National Park. I've always wanted to visit there, and the photos were so gorgeous I couldn't help but drop her a quick email just to compliment the photography. I hadn't expected her to reply, but she did, late last night. It was very friendly; she said she was glad to hear from me. Speculating that perhaps she's only *playing* hard to get—like Princess Leia—I act against instinct and shoot her a quick email to see if she wants to go to the comedy show tomorrow night with me and the first two wheels. Although I'm not expecting her to say yes, I know myself well enough to know that I'll be mired in suspended nervousness until I hear back from her.

There is also a message from a girl named Marie that I've exchanged a few brief, innocuous emails with over the past few days. This one merely contains her phone number. Her Match profile is so sparse and unspecific that it gives one the impression she may be on the lam from the Feds or something. I basically know next to nothing about her, but I must have put forth a good impression if she's giving me her number already. With the same amount of forethought I put into most major life decisions, I decide to double my chances of scoring a date to the comedy show by asking her via text if she'd like to go with me. Odds are that neither girl will accept the invitation, but on the off chance that Marie wants to go, let's be honest, there's no way it can go worse than my most recent date.

Less than forty-five minutes later I'm at Ace Hardware in Midtown, and I get a text message from Marie saying she'd love to go to the comedy show tomorrow night. Suspicion tickles the back of my brain stem. This seems too easy. I decide to hold off on confirming with her, to give Sara time to reply, but I can at least text Ethan and tell him I will be coming along with him and Georgelle tomorrow night. "With a date," I type proudly.

Despite my best efforts at the hardware store, the paint I'd bought doesn't match the ceiling very exactly. I only realize this after it starts to dry. So—long story short—Rollie, Quinn, and I repaint the entire lobby ceiling, which turns out to be much bigger than any of us could have fathomed. The Recchis had left all the carpet they'd torn up, so we laid it as a drip cloth before we moved to each new section of the ceiling. If you're ever looking for a way to destroy your back and simultaneously make all the muscles in your body sore, I'd highly recommend painting a ceiling. Michelangelo must have ended up a cripple.

When I hobble into my apartment that night I tumble into bed without changing out of my paint-splotched clothes. As soon as I close my eyes my phone alerts me that I've received a new email. Seeing it's from Sara revives my brain like a shot of espresso. She can't go to the comedy show tomorrow—which I expected—but she would like to see me again, maybe Friday—which I hadn't had the audacity to expect. Thrilled, I make three attempts until I compose a response which seems to strike the correct balance between enthusiasm and nonchalance. After hitting Send, I also text Marie to confirm with her for tomorrow night. I fall quickly to sleep after that, feeling satisfied. And sore. Very, very sore.

20__la vida loca

My bed was pulling one of those Death Star Tractor Beam tricks on me this morning, so by the time I get to the motel the hole in the lobby floor is gone. One Recchi brother, clutching some tools and clipboards, is chatting with Rollie by the vending machines. The other is sweeping up the subfloor.

"Yeah, man, fuckin' Peruvians," Rollie is saying.

I don't even want to know. "All finished, eh, guys?" I ask, smiling. Despite all my muscles feeling like they've been worked over by Conan the Masseuse I'm in a magnificent mood this morning. A full night's sleep and having set up two dates in the same week will do that.

The Recchi brothers nod and shrug at one another, and one of them hands me an invoice. No surprises here; they've stuck to the price we agreed upon. "Thanks, guys," I say, and I shake the hand of the one, then the other. Then the first one extends his hand again and I shake it once more. Whatever. I guess we've bonded.

Rollie walks them out to their van, and I greet Chynna as I pass the front desk. I stop. Retreating a few steps, I take a second look at her, just to make sure I'm not imagining things.

"What?" she asks, seeming embarrassed.

I was right. She is not looking at it. It is not even in sight. Strange things are afoot. "Did you lose your phone?"

It materializes in her right hand, like she's a gunfighter in a quick-draw duel. Reassured, I head back to the office and take care of some paperwork. About five minutes later I hear someone jingling change in their pocket behind me.

"Rollie, don't come back here, man."

He grins. "Whatcha up to? Somethin' untoward?"

"You're supposed to stay in the lobby. This is like my sanctuary back here. Don't invade my sanctuary, man!" I immediately feel guilty about sniping at him like this. After all, he didn't have to stick around and help us paint last night. Although I'm sure he'll probably charge me for his time somehow. "Look, what do you need, Rollie?"

He points to his grin.

Why don't I know anyone that's *normal*, for Pete's sake? "What is that supposed to mean?"

He heaves a deep sigh as he's not-too-subtly scanning the paperwork on my desk. "You got any toothpicks around here?"

"Why the fuck would I—listen man, why are you here so early, anyway?"

"I go where I'm needed, Mick. Like that one president always used to say. So you ain't got any toothpicks?"

"José probably has some."

Rollie's half-smirk fades. As if on cue, a sharp rattling sound emanates from the kitchen. It probably originated from the refrigerator, which lately has been producing unsettling sounds that only add to the insidious terror that pervades that room for most of us.

"Uh, never mind about that," Rollie sputters. "We should get going on that carpet, though."

"I just have to finish some stuff up real quick. If you're in such a hurry you can start putting down those new tack strips. I know how you like to *nail* stuff."

Ethan only works half-days on Wednesdays, so he arrives soon. Rollie has brought along plastic knee pads for us all to use, so after testing them out by repeatedly kicking each other, the carpet project is underway. A portable CD player on the shelf plays Pat Benatar's *Precious Time*, which Ethan insists is an essential part of any home repair task. Once we've stuck the padding onto the subfloor, we begin securing the seams with duct tape. As the three of us are espousing our shared admiration of duct tape's multi-faceted capabilities, Ethan asks who I'm bringing on our double date tonight. I tell him what little I know about Marie, but I explain that I'm more excited about having reconnected with Sara. Naturally, Rollie demands to see photos of both girls before our project can continue, so that he can offer incisive critiques of their physical characteristics. He is impressed by Marie's "rackola." Yes, that's the actual word he used in reference to her breasts.

Ethan agrees that Marie is a looker. "So why did you say you're more into the other one?" he asks.

"Both of 'em look too young for you," Rollie says.

"Well, mainly because I don't know hardly anything about Marie," I explain. "But Sara seems like she could really be a special one."

"The most special one is the one that opens her legs the widest and quickest!" Rollie laughs so hard at his remark that he actually has to stop and wipe his eyes with his shirt sleeve.

"What's with this guy?" Ethan murmurs.

"She likes all the same things I do: reading, sports, hiking, skiing. She seems incredibly intelligent." I look over at Rollie. "And she's super hot."

Rollie shrugs. "Meh."

I glance over at the desk area to make sure Chynna is still in the back. I still haven't told most people I know that I've been online dating, but Ethan already knows, and I don't care if Rollie knows or not. On the planet he's from the custom seems to be that all information is regarded arbitrarily, and facts and fiction have no distinction. "Anyway," I continue. "I hope this girl tonight is great, and we really hit it off. But my recent track record makes me a little doubtful. The girls on that site ... I mean, *most* girls in general are basically nuts." Both men make concurring sounds. "But online dating is starting to seem like a haven for the looniest of the loony."

"You ever tried Craigslist personals?" Rollie.

"Isn't that basically a bunch of hookers?"

Rollie winks. "Sometimes they post pictures."

It's time to spread the new carpet I bought. As Ethan and I heft the cumbersome roll, I am immediately reminded how sore my muscles are. Rolling it out is the easy part. It almost fits the space perfectly, which is lucky, because the trimming is the part I was most convinced I'd screw up.

"This is the color you picked?" asks Rollie.

"So anyway," I continue to Ethan, "Sara's one of the good ones, and now I understand just how rare that breed is, so I gotta be careful not to screw it up like I almost did before."

"How did you almost screw it up?"

I convey my theory about having not seemed ambitious enough when it came to money and not projecting myself as a capable enough provider. Rollie lectures me about how to think like a success and present myself that way.

"Yeah, I was probably a bit too forthcoming," I admit.

"Hmm," Ethan says, sitting back and closing his cutter. "I don't know about that. Is there really such a thing as being 'too forthcoming'? Sounds like you were just being honest to me."

"Too much honesty can scare off a little chickadee," Rollie comments.

"Exactly." Wait, did I just agree with Rollie? What kinds of chemicals do they use in this seam sealer?

Ethan shakes his head. "I'm not sure I'm following."

"I just think this time I need to be more strategic about how much honesty I disclose, that's all. I mean, if I'm right about having put her off about my salary ambitions it probably means she's looking for the stable provider sort, right? So it would be stupid of me to come off sounding like a guy who's not interested in making enough money to support a family."

"I thought you didn't want kids."

This trips me up. Ever notice how difficult it is to explain something to someone that you haven't quite fully figured out yourself? "Well, I don't. Not now, but who knows about the future? I might change my mind someday."

Ethan and Rollie exchange a perplexed look, making me fear that what I'd just said sounded even less logical than it had in my head. "So," Ethan says, dragging out the word, "you think it would be better to lead this girl to believe that you are a certain type of person that you're not, just on the off chance that someday you may decide to become that type of person?"

When he puts it that way it sounds ridiculous. "Ah, you just don't get it," I say, not taking my eyes off the straight line I'm trying to trim. "You've forgotten what it's like to be single."

"Maybe so, but it sounds to me like you're trying to pretend to be someone you're not, when you're already good the way you are."

"If it ain't broke," Rollie chimes in, "don't fix it."

"Yeah, if only you regarded plumbing that way, too," I point out.

"Look, Mick," Ethan continues, "don't try to change the way you are just to impress some chick. What would you want with some girl who doesn't like you for what you are anyhow? Change isn't always necessary, you know."

"Smart man right there," Rollie says. "That's what I keep tellin' you about gettin' rid of this place. Seems foolish to mess with a good thing."

"Getting rid of this place?" Ethan asks.

"Shit, yeah," Rollie says. "Your boy here wants to give up this place and move his dumb ass to New York City. You didn't know that?"

Damn. It occurs to me that Ethan did not know that. When I'd asked him for help getting a loan I'd just said the motel needed work done. I never told him about the potential buyers coming to town. After this information slips, Ethan is oddly quiet. Or maybe it's just my imagination. The guilty feeling is real, though. How can a person forget to tell one of his only real friends that he might be moving across the continent? Ethan doesn't bring it up again, and before long he takes off to get ready for the football game, but I feel like a jerk nonetheless. If Ethan had a big, life-changing event planned, and an ass clown like Rollie knew about it before me, I know I'd feel pretty low. Maybe subconsciously I've deliberately neglected to tell Ethan because Stacy was so bummed when I told him. Or maybe it's because I knew Ethan would try to talk me out of it. I don't know why he might be against the idea, but he'd come up with some reason, and it would make a lot of damn sense, and I'd start to think he was right. It's what always happens, whenever Ethan gives me advice about anything.

But this time he's not right. He and Stacy and Rollie may not see a problem with the rut I'm in, but if I don't change something soon my head is gonna explode all over 16th Street.

◎◎◎

It turns out that Marie can't make it for dinner, so I get to be a third wheel once again, but she is waiting outside the comedy venue when we arrive. Even wearing heels, she only comes up to my shoulder, and she's wearing one of those shapeless dresses that women wear to confound us guys when we're trying to get an accurate assessment of their body type. Her skin is that beautiful Pacific Islanderish hue, and I soon find out she's of Filipino descent. She has straight black hair that falls over her shoulders and plump, lightly glossed lips that look like they'd be a lot of fun to kiss. We all greet and introduce one another, then head inside.

This club has a well-lit and spacious bar room area outside of the actual room where the comedians perform, so we all order a pre-show drink. Georgelle orders something pink and ostentatious, and Marie copies the order. Ethan and I stick with beers. Marie seems kind of shy and quiet, and she has a tendency to repeatedly scope out the rest of the room, as if she's waiting for someone else to arrive. I make some small talk to put her at ease, but we don't have much of a chance to chat before it's time to hand over our tickets and be escorted to our seats near the stage.

It seems like the girls don't find the comedian quite as hysterical as do Ethan and I, but Marie laughs at all the appropriate places, and we exchange flirty looks and hushed comments throughout the performance. Ethan and I order another drink during the show, but both girls decline, and, after a rousing encore where the opener joined our boy onstage and basically shredded two blonde girls in miniskirts sitting in the front row, we all go back out into the bar room. Using our advance telepathic powers, I let Ethan know that it's time to split the party in half, and he and Georgelle depart. Marie agrees to stay for another drink and a bite to eat. We're standing at the bar, and Marie asks, "Are we going to sit at the bar or at a booth?"

"Doesn't matter to me. Whatever you like."

She scrutinizes the room while the bartender waits awkwardly close to us. "It doesn't matter to me, either," she finally decides. I start to pull out a bar stool for her, when she adds, "But let's get a booth. It's more private."

"Sure." The bartender hands us two menus and tells us to seat ourselves. About half the tables are occupied, so we choose an empty booth in the corner. I sit with my back to the connected booth, and she sits with her back to the door to the kitchen.

As I scan the menu, Marie says, "We're not going to be able hear each other unless we talk really loud. Can I sit with you on your side?"

"Yeah, for sure." I slide over, and she squeezes next to me. I'm not sure if she's making a move by this or not.

We order drinks and a couple of appetizers. When the server walks away, Marie says, "Now I have to tell you my story."

"Oh? Okay."

She casts a couple of anxious glances at the back of the guy's head who's sitting in the booth behind us. "Um," she hesitates, "I don't really want people to hear this. Can we sit on the other side?"

My heartbeat quavers with a twinge of premonition. We scoot over to the side of the booth where she originally sat, and I notice she waits for me to slide in first. Trapping me? In a half-muted but lighthearted tone, I ask, "Are you on the lam from the feds or something?"

Thankfully, she smiles in response to this. "No, nothing like that." With that, she launches into an extremely detailed account of how she arrived at this present incarnation of herself. How she immigrated here with her parents late in high school and had to learn English. How she was shy at first, and sought out the company of other Pacific Islanders. How she lost her virginity as a college freshman to an older Filipino guy named Joe.

Joe becomes the main character in Act 2 of her story, which commences once the server has dropped off our drinks. It is Joe that she ended up marrying while still a college student, after she got him to promise her he'd enroll in night classes to earn his GED. When she describes how Joe had a study partner named Denise, at whose house he sometimes spent the night after "studying," I think I know where the story is headed. But this tale defies expectations.

"Wait, you didn't figure out that he was cheating on you?"

"Not at that time, no. But, anyway, then I got pregnant."

Hold the fucking phone here. If it had mentioned on her Match profile that she was a mom, I'd have noticed. "Wait, you have a kid?" I ask, trying to sound casual.

"I have three. But I'll get to that."

Holy mother of god.

The account continues, depicting Joe as an ever more sinister character: a serial cheater, an unenthusiastic job seeker, a compulsive liar. How he offered to drive Marie's friend Tia home one night—ordinarily a ten minute trip—and didn't return for another two hours. He'd claimed he had a headache and had sat at Tia's place until he felt better. I'm thinking that this guy wasn't even a creative or plausible liar, but what concerns me most of all is how Marie didn't catch on to any of his shenanigans. I mean, how dim of a bulb do you have to be not to be able to nab him in a single one of these ridiculous lies?

Halfway through the plate of quesadillas, I can't help but ask why she stayed with this creep for so many years. "Well," she says, blushing slightly, "he had a pretty incredible body."

Come again? I could envision my friend Witt saying something this stupid, but ....

"But he was on steroids." She shrugs. "He still is, I think."

And this is when it starts to get weird.

Marie takes out her phone and begins scrolling through what appears to be roughly a million photos. "This is Joe," she says, displaying a photo of a greasy, shirtless, bald man flexing his muscles for the camera. Then she proceeds to scroll through over a dozen more photos of the man, in various stages of modesty.

"Yeah, I get the idea," I comment, just to make her stop.

At this point, I'd like to directly address the females among my readership. Ladies, it is a teensy bit of a red flag to even discuss your ex during a first date. Giving a twenty-minute lecture about the guy, illustrated with photographic visual aids is kind of like said red flag catching fire and incinerating in front of your date's offended eyes.

But it gets better. "This is him with that chick Denise." Yep, she's got a photo of him with the girl he cheated on her with. Then she shows me four more photos of Denise by herself, attractive photos that she must have pulled off a Facebook page or something.

I decide to order a Jack and Coke and strap in for the duration of this ride through Crazyville. The overall arc of the narrative seems to be that Marie has been through a lot, yet she's a better, stronger person because of it. But it's the supporting details that make this tale so damn engrossing. Joe ended up moving in with Tia for a few weeks, after which Marie took him back in. *She took him back in*! Of course, there are photos to supplement this chapter as well. One of them is Tia by herself, wearing only lingerie. This one she couldn't have gotten from Facebook, so I ask about its origins. "Joe sent it to me," she replies.

"And you kept it. Awesome." I am beginning to really enjoy myself.

The next fifteen or so photos are of Vanessa, the girl Joe is with currently. Apparently when Vanessa feels she's looking really good in a particular outfit, she takes a selfie and sends it to Marie, to brag about how much prettier she is. And, naturally, Marie keeps them all.

My third drink makes things a bit hazy, but what I put together is that Marie is a proud single mom, glad to finally be rid of Joe. And in response to my gentle inquiry, no she is definitely *not* still hung up on Joe, and she's totally prepared to move on to a new relationship. At one point she's showing me endless photos of her children; they're pretty adorable and I tell her so. Repeatedly. Yet the photos keep coming.

"I'll tell you one thing, though," she says in a serious fashion, "I'm still super tight down there."

I swear to god this is exactly what she says, apropos of nothing. "What?" I blurt.

She nods her head solemnly. "Most women after three kids, not so much. But I'm way tighter than any of them."

"How do you come by this information?"

"Trust me," she says, smiling. "Oops," she says after *accidentally* scrolling to a picture she obviously took of herself, her backside tilted toward the camera, not wearing a shred of clothing.

"Whoa," I say, not meaning to vocalize the word.

"I forgot those were still on here," she says, as she slowly scrolls through several more, all of them highlighting her naked or thong-adorned — and admittedly rather stunning — ass.

I'm possessed with enough confidence to confide that, although I'd firmly made up my mind at least an hour ago that I would never go out with this girl again, this is the only moment I waver slightly about that decision. It is *that* stunning.

But I hold firm to my former decision. I'll explain in an email a couple of days from now that I just didn't feel she was one hundred percent over her ex-husband, a charge which she will vehemently deny. But, in the meantime, I reaffirm my sacred vow to not screw things up with Sara, because tonight I've gotten a first row view of what else is out there, and, frankly, it's a gruesome spectacle. I'll make it my life's purpose over the next two days to extensively prepare for the date with Sara, and to overwhelm her with my overall worthiness when we finally meet on Friday night.

Of course, this is before I receive the phone call from José that changes everything.

21__no time is a good time for us

Friday, after I've cleaned the pool and power-washed the deck, I stop by the apartment to change into a fresh outfit. I hate walking around all day in sweaty clothes. While unlocking the door I hear, "Baby back woman, baby back woman, baby back woman, baby back woman, baby back woman," being recited from inside Thelma's apartment. God bless her. My shoulders are sore, but I'm feeling optimistic. The motel is looking the best it has in years, and with two days to spare before the Knight's Lodge people arrive. And tonight is my date with Sara.

As I walk in my phone rings. It's the motel. Weird, I was just there two minutes ago. "Hello?"

Silence on the other end, then a soft voice. "Freeg broke."

"What? Who is this?"

A sigh. "Freeg broke, ever'tin spoil."

"Wait, is this José?" I've so rarely heard his voice, and never on the phone.

"I gon' queet."

"José, what are you saying? What's wrong?"

"Ever'tin gone. I jest gon' queet. You sell de place, I lose job anyways."

Panic constricts my throat. I've already offered Cromwell's people lunch or a snack when they come to visit. Nobody's ever set foot in that kitchen besides José, and I can't cook to save my life. How am I going to find and train someone to run the kitchen in two days? "No! No, you can't quit! José, tell me what's wrong."

"I tell you. Freeg broke."

"The refrigerator broke?"

"Ever'tin spoil. All gone."

Jesus. Everything he bought for the special menu I'd asked him to prepare! Snow crab legs, shrimp, artisan cheeses—everything!

"I gon' queet."

"José, listen to me, I'm begging you. Please! You can't quit. Not with the Knight's Lodge people coming on Monday." My mouth has gone completely dry. "Listen, we'll figure this out—we'll get a new refrigerator tomorrow!"

Silence. Please god, let him be reconsidering.

"I gon' lose job anyways. You sell."

What I say next is mostly desperation, which is a euphemism for bullshit that you say and then will yourself to try and believe. "No, listen, you won't lose your job! If Cromwell wants to buy the motel, I'll just tell him the deal is off unless he promises to keep you on as chef. I swear to god."

Silence.

"Look, we'll get you a new refrigerator tomorrow, anything you want. I'll find the money somewhere, I promise."

Still no response. My stomach is churning now. I'm envisioning the Cromwell people taking me up on my offer for lunch, and me—like a jackass—explaining that we don't have any food, or a functional refrigerator, or a chef. Talk about a deal breaker.

Finally, I hear José sigh. "I help," he says.

"Yes! Wait—does that mean you're not quitting?"

He's hung up. It sounded like he's going to stay, but I'm not sure. I call the motel back to confirm, and it takes some wily cajoling to convince Quinn to work up the nerve to go back and hand José the phone. A moment later, he tells me José's not back there, and his van is gone. He must have left.

"Dammit. What does that mean?"

Although I had mostly said that to myself, Quinn replies, "Well, when he wasn't in the kitchen, and when I saw his van was gone, I just kind of assumed he had left. Unless someone stole it, I guess. Gosh, I hope not. Yeah, but anyway, no, he's not in the back."

"Yeah, I get it. Don't worry about it."

"Do you want me to check the rooms, or ...?"

"No, Quinn, you don't have to check the rooms. It's fine, just forget about it, okay?"

"Yes, okay. I mean, no, I won't check the rooms. But yes, I will forget ... I mean, I'll just stay here at the desk."

"Perfect."

◎◎◎

That night when I walk over to Mulvaney's to meet Sara, the kitchen fiasco is still occupying prime real estate in my mind. "I help" sounded positive, no two ways about it, so I'm more curious than worried about what José meant by it. But after I'd hung up with Quinn, I'd searched online to try to get ballpark estimates of what a new refrigerator will cost me. Whatever you're imagining an industrial-sized refrigerator costs, forget it. It's far more expensive than that. All the ones I saw that sort of resembled the old one fetch prices of anywhere between nineteen and twenty-eight hundred dollars. And now I think I kind of know what it feels like to be stabbed in the gut. This may not sound devastatingly expensive, but let me summarize my financial situation this way: I borrowed fifty bucks from Ethan just so I'd be sure I had enough to cover dinner tonight.

Sara is about equal to me in height. She's wearing a billowy green top that accentuates her eyes. Long, very tan, and shapely legs stretch from beneath a short black skirt. The bruises on those perfect legs remind me that she plays in a Xoso soccer league. Mental note: conversation topic. She's not carrying a purse. She smiles with half her mouth when she recognizes me and gives me a sort of prim hug, doing that fake kissing thing near both cheeks that girls tend to do to other girls, to which I respond by standing there awkwardly. I'm decked out in my favorite blue shirt that tends to bring out my eyes, black motorcycle boots, and the pair of jeans that I've been told makes my butt look good. Dressing like this usually instills confidence in me, but tonight I can tell that I'll be having trouble avoiding constant worry over the kitchen problem.

I'm more nervous than usual, and I don't think it's due solely to my anxiety about pricey refrigerators. I've built this date up in my mind into a kind of do-or-die situation, and I don't have a Plan B if I screw things up. Except maybe escaping to New York to start over. Or possibly securing some literature about becoming a monk.

We order dinner. I'm so distracted that I almost make the mistake of ordering something that comes with linguini, but I catch myself in time and order braised chicken. If there's a way to gracefully eat pasta on a first date without looking like a ham-fisted clod, I assure you I don't know about it. Sara orders swordfish, and we toast with a glass of white wine. Sara has a habit of glancing around the room regularly as we talk, and I stifle a shudder, remembering that crazy Marie shared the same inclination.

Fairly early in the conversation, Sara mentions her need for stability and desire to start a family, to which I suavely nod, in apparent assent—although I still haven't talked myself into wanting kids, truth be told. Sara's eyes are hypnotic. She currently works in marketing for one of the big investment firms downtown, but she's planning to get her Master's in business administration in order to move up the food chain. "The problem is," she explains, "that it's going to take a long time to do so, without cutting back on my hours at work."

I nod, but internally I'm wondering if any circumstance could exist on this planet that could convince me to go back to sitting in classrooms for another few years.

"I can't do that because—well, you know—I already have a certain lifestyle to maintain," she continues.

I wonder what she means by this. The jewelry she's wearing looks legit to me, and I remember her mentioning in an email that she had 49er season tickets. And she sure does take a lot of trips—she's always posting photos, from Yellowstone, Florida, even Hawaii. Damn. I wish I had a lifestyle to maintain, instead of coin-operated washing machines and a motel that could double as a lunatic asylum.

Our meals arrive. When the server asks if there's anything else we need right now, I tell him more Liam Neeson movies, just to try to get a laugh out of Sara. The server chuckles politely and agrees, and Sara gives me a tilt of her head and another one of those half-smiles, but this one seems less amused and more like she's befuddled by watching the behavior of an exotic animal at a zoo. I concentrate on not allowing my face to redden. As it turns out, I'm much funnier writing a blog post than I am in conversation.

When she asks about what I do, I use the word hotel instead of motel, and I attempt to make myself sound important. I mention needing to purchase a new refrigerator tomorrow, and I'm careful to say it casually, as if affording one isn't an issue. I even tell her I'm thinking of selling the place and buying someplace better. For the cherry on top, I lie about some publishers already showing interest in my novel. She displays all the earmarks of active listening, but once while I'm talking I notice her look past me again, and this time she smiles. When she stops to peruse the wine menu, I sneak a glance behind me. Two younger and disgustingly handsome guys are drinking Scotch at a table directly behind me. This is unsettling, but I don't have time to ponder it because Sara turns half around in her chair, scanning the back of the dining room. When she does so, the cut of her blouse reveals that she's not wearing a bra. What I spy thanks to that armhole may not officially count as sideboob, but it's close enough to temporarily expunge all data from my brain, like looking at one of those shiny light things in *Men In Black*.

As my mind reboots, I vaguely wonder if all men are as juvenile and lascivious as I am, but just hide it better. It takes me a moment to realize that she's once again addressing me. "Sorry?"

"That guy that just walked back towards the restrooms," she says. "He looked just like Bill Walsh!"

Sara is charming and fiercely intelligent, but it is now, when our conversation turns to the Niners, that I find myself truly captivated by her. She is knowledgeable and highly opinionated. I'm with her on believing our current coach to be an overrated clown, but when we challenge each other to produce a top ten list of all-time greatest 49ers, I chide her mercilessly for including John Taylor over Roger Craig. At least we agree on Rice, Montana, Young, Lott, and Willis, so I joyously point out to myself that if John Taylor is the closest this girl gets to crazy, I have indeed found myself a winner. I'm also enthralled by her descriptions of a two-month trip she took after college hiking the Appalachian Trail on the East Coast. It sounds majestic, and I vow to visit once I live on that coast. It makes me swell with pride—and relief—when I'm able to recommend the hiking trails around Lake Berryessa, a local destination which she has inexplicably never explored.

I'm a notoriously slow eater, and I know that habit annoys people, so I push myself to keep pace so that we finish our dinners simultaneously. We are having such a pleasant time that we order a couple of dessert wines, and my excitement grows over how well I'm nailing this audition. She excuses herself to the restroom before the port arrives, and as she walks away she casts a quick glance back over her shoulder, perhaps to test her theory that I'd be hopelessly mesmerized by the swaying motion of the hindquarters that give her tight black skirt its enticing shape. I don't even mind getting busted, and one peek at the guys at the table behind me confirms my suspicions that, yes, all men are precisely as juvenile and lascivious as me.

The vibration of my phone in my pocket startles me. I don't usually get calls this late. It's the motel. Since Sara is still in the bathroom, I decide to answer.

"Hi, Mr. Collins, it's Quinn Worley."

"Yeah?"

"From the Shady Spot. Quinn."

"Yes, Quinn, I got it. What are you still doing there? I thought you had the morning shift tomorrow."

"Oh. Yeah, I'm covering for Chynna," he says meekly. "She had something come up."

"Oh, really?"

"She had a RedBox video she had to watch so she could return it tomorrow." He pauses. So do I. "Late fees and whatnot," Quinn adds.

Involuntarily, I roll my eyes. The wines arrive, and I spot Sara coming back to our table. "Listen, Quinn, this isn't a good time. Can I call you back?" I give Sara the "sorry" shrug, pointing to the phone and mouth the word "work."

"Well ... it's just, I mean ...." His voice sounds worried.

"Is something wrong?"

"Well, it's José," he manages.

"Oh, god, what now?"

"I'm not sure, um, but he called to tell me to tell you that he needs you right away."

"Tonight? I'm in the middle of something here, Quinn. What does he want?"

"Yeah, I don't know. I told him you weren't here, but he just kept repeating himself. He says he needs you right away."

I try to maintain a calm veneer, but inwardly I'm calculating dozens of possibilities of what this might be about. None of them are positive. Sara's eyes are roaming around the room again as she sips her port. "Okay, don't worry about it, Quinn. I'll call you back in a little while."

"But he said—"

"I know, but I'll give you a call back as quick as I can, okay?" He doesn't respond, so I hang up. I say to Sara, "Sorry about that; it was work." I take a sip of the sweet wine. "Everything's a big goddamned hassle with them. They can't seem to get along without me sometimes." I snort, trying to downplay how rattled I am about getting an urgent and cryptic message from the employee who's been voted most likely to be an actual psychopath.

We sip our wine and make small talk, but the comfortableness has evaporated. I'm too agitated. Trying to sound nonchalant, I say, "So after these should we get the check, or did you want to get something else?"

"Oh, no, we can get the check. That's fine." She smiles.

"It's getting late," I add.

"Yeah."

I look over at our server, and he immediately approaches and produces our check from his apron. I hand him all the cash I've got on me, hoping it's enough, and he promises to return with change. I drain the last of my port. Sara's eyes are bouncing around the room again.

I roll my eyes exaggeratedly. "I should probably see what's going on over at the motel, er—hotel."

"Oh, yeah, totally. It's okay," she says. "Really."

When the change arrives, I make a show of leaving it all in the leather folder for a tip, because I'm a prosperous and immaculately polite small business owner. "Shall we?" I say, standing.

Sara stands and gives me that half-smile again. "Yeah, I think I'm going to stay for a bit," she says.

"You—oh, you wanted to stick around for another one? We can do that, sure."

"Oh, no," she says. "You don't have to."

"Wait, what?"

"No, go ahead and check on your motel," she says. "I'm just going to move over to the bar and have one more before I leave." At this point her eyes are fixed on something—or someone—behind me.

"Oh," I respond, probably sounding as perplexed as I really am. "You ... are you sure?"

"Yeah, yeah, totally," she says, smiling at me now. "I had a really great time!"

"Yeah, me, too." We are standing face to face in a still halfway full dining room. I swiftly search for the confidence to lean in for a kiss, and find it's missing. "Hey, uh, we should do it again sometime, maybe."

"For sure," Sara says, and gives me a quick hug. "Let me know!" With that, she turns, casting a subtle glance behind me again, and the black skirt positively sashays on its way to an open bar stool. I shuffle dumbly out of the restaurant with the disorienting feeling of a school boy who just found out everyone's been invited to the party except him.

Am I already being cheated on?

I go straight to the motel, where I get the story from Quinn. José has left an address where I'm supposed to go immediately to pick him up. Quinn does not possess any of the answers to my subsequent questions, such as why I need to pick him up, or whether the location is José's home address, or what in the hell this is all about anyway.

My anger swells at the lunacy of the whole situation. José didn't leave a number where I could reach him, and then I waste the better part of ten minutes locating his personnel file, which includes mostly blank spaces where things like phone number and address ought to be. With any other employee, I would curse them for an idiot and go home to bed, but such is my fear that José is going to quit—or do something much worse—that I soon find myself driving toward an address in an unfamiliar part of West Sac.

Along the way, I spend my usual amount of time obsessing over how my date with Sara actually went. On the rare occasions when I've perceived a first date to have gone well, more often than not I've been blindsided by finding out the girl's perspective was the vertical angle of mine, and she has no interest in a follow-up date. This time I think I said all the right things, and she did seem to genuinely want to see me again—as far as I could tell, anyway. But there were those curious glances around the room, and I can't shake the notion that she was making eye contact with some other dude. I have no proof of it, but why else would she want to stay after I've left?

I'm now on a gravel road, double-checking my route on my phone's GPS. There is an alarming lack of streetlights, so I switch on my high beams. Immediately upon doing so, the wraithlike figure of José is illuminated, standing on the side of the road. I stomp on my brakes and slide a couple of feet in the gravel. Now my heart is slamming kick drum beats against my rib cage. I swear if someone made it their life's mission to be as eerily frightening as possible, they would cower in deference to José. He makes his way over to the car and plops down in the passenger seat without a word.

"You all right, José?" I broach timidly. No answer. He doesn't even look at me. I look around at the vast darkness surrounding us. "Are you stuck out here? Where's your van?"

He straightens the weathered trucker cap he always wears and points ahead. "Dis way."

"Where are we going? Is something wrong?"

He just sits silently, staring ahead. I immediately regret the decision to come out here. He exhales a long, disgusted sigh until I take my foot off the brake and proceed down the winding gravel road. It now occurs to me that José is furious with me. He's convinced he'll lose his job, and he blames me for it. The sudden suspicion that I'm driving to my own execution lodges a giant lump in my throat. I try to dismiss the idea as ludicrous, but it's pointless. If I have ever met anyone in my life who's capable of murdering another human being, it's José.

My voice is unsteady when I ask José if he's angry with me. "I wasn't bluffing when I said I'd make sure you don't lose your job," I explain. "I can promise you that." When he doesn't respond, I'm struck with an immediate onset of diarrhea of the mouth. The words that start flowing uncontrollably go something like this: "I know it was wrong of me to announce the sale the way I did I should have considered your feelings all of you and thought it through better I'm sorry about that I know I'm probably not as good at running things as Remi was but you know I always liked you I mean I still do I think you do a great job and the sandwiches you make are world class quality I mean that crab salad is out of this world I'm always telling everyone how good they are ask anyone and my dad yeah my dad he really likes you too I told him what a great fantastic guy you were—"

I stop when I glance over and he appears to be smirking. Not smiling, but smirking. Until this moment, I haven't realized how truly terrified I am of death.

José nods. "Mee'ser Tom."

"Yes! Yes, Mister Tom, my dad! Yeah, he's crazy about you." He makes no response. But he kind of smiled for a second. That's got to be positive, right? I try unsuccessfully to swallow and to catch my breath. "Listen, José, can't you even tell me where we're going?"

We are back on a paved portion of road, and the glow cast by the way-too-intermittent street lights we pass reveals that his expression has gone blank again. I almost wish he had an angry or aggressive look on his face; it would somehow seem less menacing. They say psychopaths feel nothing toward their victims—no empathy, no remorse. Or is that sociopaths? Damn it, I can never keep those terms straight. I make a mental note to Google it if I'm still alive later.

I no longer have any clue where we are. We pass parking lots overgrown with weeds, boarded up buildings. I wouldn't have believed it if you'd have told me there was an area this remote so close to downtown. My mood grows more subdued. Maybe I deserve what's coming to me after all. I don't treat people as well as I should. I should have consulted with my staff before even agreeing to a meeting with

Cromwell's people. I don't appreciate my parents enough. All they've ever done is support me, and I've taken it for granted. Maybe I'm too judgmental also. Perhaps some of these Match.com women that I've written off as crazy had some very sound, rational reasons for behaving the way they did. Maybe it was just easier for me to dismiss them than to try to put actual work into developing a relation—

"Lef' after *de gasolinera*." José's voice startles me out of my self-pitying reverie. He's pointing.

I hang a left at a dilapidated building that was probably once a gas station. We're on a narrower lane now, passing barbed wire fences on our right, behind which sit a series of factory buildings, or perhaps just large garages.

"Slow down," orders José.

Looking at the darkened buildings, I consider the possibility that maybe José is just going to beat the crap out of me and sell my car to a chop shop somewhere in here. This idea does not comfort me as much as I'd hoped.

"*Aqui*," he says, gesturing toward a gate portion of the fence that's been rolled open. José directs me to park in front of what looks to be an abandoned warehouse. We get out of the car and I follow him as far as a halfway-opened garage style door.

"What are we doing here?" I ask feebly.

"Dis way."

I must be resigned to whatever's coming at this point, because I find myself ducking under the partially closed door and following him inside. In the dim light within I can make out towering rows of shelves containing machine parts, tools, old appliances, and hunks of metal things that I can't identify. We walk past several of these rows, deeper into the building. I find I can scarcely breathe as we make our way into a more open space and I step over a push broom lying across a large dustpan overflowing with unidentifiable refuse. We've reached the source of the room's feeble light—one of those light bulbs encased in a metal cage with a hook on top and a large extension cord extending from the other end. It's hanging from a metal cord, and underneath it stands a man. I stop. His stature is similar to José's, his face hidden in deep shadows beneath an oversized Giants cap. José goes and stands next to him; they nod at one another and then stare at me.

My first instinct is to run, but I'm not sure I can find my way back out of here, and besides, who knows how many more of them are lurking in the dark corners of this building?

José points at a bulky appliance that the other guy is standing beside. Sweet Jesus, is it a freezer? Are they going to chop me up and put me in a freezer!

"Four hunna fit-dee," José says. He looks at the other man. The other man nods.

I stare blankly, paralyzed with fear. José points at it again. Its stainless steel front is dinged up and scuffed pretty badly. I don't see any blood stains, though. The strange man looks at me, as if expecting me to do something. Then he looks at José.

"Four hunna fit-dee," José repeats, stepping over and reaching for the handle. I brace myself. He opens it.

It must be plugged in because it illuminates. It's a refrigerator, not a freezer, and the inside is faultless. Immaculately clean, no dents, shelves solid, nothing broken.

"Work good," José says, and looks at the other man, who nods almost imperceptibly.

It finally dawns on my idiot ass what is happening. "Wait," I stammer, "this refrigerator is for sale? This is what you want?"

"Work good. Like new."

All the tension seeps from my muscles at once, making my limbs feel rubbery as I clamber over to inspect the refrigerator. I open the other door and marvel at its sheer size. There is a large freezer section as well. I quickly put my hands behind my back so the men won't see them shaking. I cannot believe how badly I misread this situation, but luckily the room's dim light doesn't betray how flushed with embarrassment my face has become.

And now something José must have said a minute or two ago finally pierces the thick fog of my awareness. "Wait, wait—how much did you say it costs?"

"Four hunna fit-dee. Like new."

"Four hundred fifty dollars?" I practically shriek. I look at the guy in the Giants cap, and he nods in confirmation.

I grab José by the shoulder and pull him aside. "José a refrigerator like this should cost at least three times that price, if it actually works. Are you sure he's not trying to rip us off?"

"Like new. I check it out good. Use a lot of power, though."

Of the two of us involved in this conversation, the one who actually possesses the knowledge required to make an accurate assessment has given it the thumbs-up, so what am I waiting for? I look back at the other man, who I now notice looks enough like José to be a relative. I look back at José. "This seems too good to be true. Are you sure about this?"

José stares blankly at me, in the manner I've become accustomed to over the years.

"What I mean is, is this even legal?"

Blank. Stare.

"Fuck it," I blurt impulsively, "let's go get the money."

José turns back toward the man, then shakes his head at me. "We pay when Agosto deliver. Tomorrow, you like."

"He's gonna deliver it, too?" I say while looking at Agosto. He betrays no sign that he's heard or understood anything I've said.

"Work like new," José repeats. "Use a lot of power, though."

If it gets delivered tomorrow morning, that would give José enough time to go shopping and replace everything that spoiled in plenty of time for Cromwell's visit on Monday. I'm in disbelief at how well this seems to be working out, and I don't want to jinx it. I step over to Agosto and shake his hand. "You have a deal! And thank you so much! Gracias!"

When I let go of his hand, he looks at it quizzically for a moment and then shrugs. "Use lot of power," he says matter-of-factly.

"I'm not worried about the electric bills," I say excitedly. "You're really saving our butts here, Agosto, thank you again. Tomorrow morning, right?"

José answers for him. "Tomorrow morneen be fine."

"Outstanding," I say, standing there not knowing what to do next.

"We go home now," José says.

"Outstanding."

22__the day before the day

Sunday morning while I'm idly speculating about Sara, eating my daily bowl of Honey Nut Cheerios, and putting off going in to work, I receive a text from Brooklyn. It's clear that I'm firmly entrenched in the friend zone at this point, and while I'm still a little disenchanted about that I generally still enjoy hearing from her. She's making a benign comment about the new point guard the Kings traded for yesterday. She finishes by saying she hopes he's better at basketball than I am at pool, and that makes me smile.

I reply:

Well, well, the girl's got jokes. Hold on while I stitch my sides back up.

Not my best work, I'll allow, but I am subsisting on very little sleep, and, besides, what's the point of putting in effort to charm a girl who's never going to be mine? I cringe as I realize how much that sounds like something Witt would say, but I might as well be honest with myself, no matter how unappealing I may be.

My focus is on Sara. I can't stop wondering what happened when I left Mulvaney's last night. It's driving me to distraction. There's no way she would have stuck around and then hooked up with one of those young, handsome guys, right? After a first date? I mean, that would be too gauche to believe. Maybe she just has trouble looking people in the eyes for long periods of time, like a nervous thing. Maybe she wasn't looking at the guys behind me at all when her eyes wandered. My compulsive need to always know the score in any given situation takes over, and I decide to forego the customary waiting period before contacting someone after a first date. I decide to send her a very clear cut message to find out exactly where I stand.

I had a great time with you last night! Would you like to go out again later on this week?

Done. She either does, or she doesn't, and soon I'll know. It's better to know for sure, one way or the other.

When I get to the Shady Spot, Quinn is up on a step ladder with a paint brush. As usual, the look on his face suggests that I just caught him masturbating to pictures of my mother.

"What are you doing, Quinn?"

"Good," he exclaims too quickly.

"No, I mean what's going on?" I gesture to the ladder and paint.

"José's not here. Wait, what are you asking?"

"The paint, Quinn. What are you doing up there?"

"Oh!" He swallows a couple of times. "We missed some spots," he says, pointing at the ceiling.

"Wait, what do you mean José isn't here? Where is he?"

Quinn shrugs, his head trembling back and forth like it's his fault.

"We're supposed to get a new refrigerator delivered this morning," I complain.

"Oh, no. I mean, are we? I—I'm sorry!"

"It's not your fault, Quinn. I'm just saying." Good old Quinn. He worked the night shift because Chynna was lazy, and now here he is, on duty again, up on a ladder with a paintbrush trying to spruce the place up. Wait. A paintbrush? I walk over to take a closer look at his touch-up work. The brush strokes he's added contrast noticeably with the original coat that we applied with rollers. My eyes dart to another portion of the ceiling where his brush strokes have dried, and they look even worse. I immediately notice a half dozen others. "Shit."

"What?" Quinn says, visibly panicked.

I take a moment to compose myself. He's only trying to help. He can't help the fact that he's a moron. "We used rollers to paint the ceiling, Quinn, remember?"

"Right! I mean, yes."

Drawing a deep breath, I explain, "But now you're using a brush. See how the brush strokes stand out against the rest?"

He inspects the ceiling. "Yes. I mean, oh. Oh, boy. Gosh, this is bad." He looks at me timidly. "Is this bad?"

"Well ...," I can't find words that don't seem scolding. "It's just that it doesn't look all that *professional*, you know?"

"Oh. Shoot." He looks at the ceiling, then back at me. "I—I'm sorry, I didn't—"

I hold both my palms up in a calming motion. "It's okay, Quinn. Don't worry about it. Look, just go wash that brush out. We'll get the rollers and I'll help you paint over it."

He nearly tips the ladder over scrambling to get down, dropping the paint brush. Luckily he remembered to put down plastic, so no harm is done to the carpet. Good old Quinn. He may not be brilliant, but to me he's an ideal employee. No matter what menial task you ask him to do, he never cops that haughty attitude like my other workers have, like you're keeping them from doing something important to do the unimportant. Quinn has a well-developed sense of insignificance.

I hear the door open. "Uncle Mick!"

I turn to see Keegan and Maddy rushing toward me, arms outstretched. My sister steps inside the doorway with a cumbersome bag under her arm. I stoop down to receive the kids' embrace while avoiding the inevitable head butt to the testicles that usually accompanies Maddy's hugs.

"What are you rascals doing here?"

"Coming to visit you," Maddy cries.

"Awesome!" I glance over at Maggie, and the look of consternation on her face is not one I recognize. Something's wrong. "Hey guys," I say to the kids, "how about a Little Debbie?" I look at Maggie and she gives a single, stern nod of assent.

"Yeah!"

"Go ahead, you can pick out one each." They race to the coffee and snack station. I stride quickly over to the doorway. "What's up, Mags?"

Her jaw is set firmly. "I need a room."

Miss Better-Homes-and-Gardens staying here? I seem to remember "dingy" being the most positive adjective she's ever used to describe my motel. Something is up. "What's going on?"

She avoids my gaze. "Just for a couple of nights."

My sister would never leave the comfort of her luxury apartment to go slumming on 16th Street, not even for a couple of nights, not even if there was a national emergency that involved two-headed space predators. I want to point this out to her, and I want to prod her for more information, but the look in her eyes stops me. There is pain behind those eyes. This is uncharted territory. "Is everything okay?" I say instead.

She withdraws her pocketbook from the travelling bag. "Just give us the best room you can." She still won't meet my eyes. Something is very wrong.

Understand, the Collins siblings do not *do* vulnerable. Ever since childhood, we do not show weakness, we do not acknowledge emotions. We deal strictly in sarcasm and effrontery. By all accounts, a moment like this should have me needling her, pressing her for information, and lording over her the stunning turn of events that's got her asking her doofus little brother for a favor. This is something I've vaguely dreamed about ever since I became aware of the inherent power she's held over me since my arrival into this world. Instead, I'm now avoiding her gaze. I want to know what's going on, but somehow, instead of feeling superior, I'm experiencing cloudy sensations of shame and embarrassment.

I look over at the kids, arguing over the TV remote. "Just ...the three of you?" I ask sheepishly, trying to face her full on.

She's concentrating too hard on fishing some bills out of her pocketbook. "Yes," she says firmly.

"Jesus Christ, Maggie, you don't have to pay."

"I'm sure you could use the money."

This time, I make her look me in the eye, and the redness that immediately flushes her cheeks is enough of an acknowledgment of the inappropriateness of the comment. I spin around and head behind the counter. She follows. I slip her the key to a first floor room a few doors down from Mom and Da. "So," I begin, not really knowing how to approach the subject.

"Not now, Mick. Okay?" She doesn't wait for a response. "Come on kids," she calls.

"I want to stay with Uncle Mick," Keegan protests.

Maggie doesn't break her stride toward the door. "If you guys want to go swimming, we have to go change into your swim suits." That gets them scampering toward their mother. I promise to come hang out with them soon, and they happily wave goodbye on their way out of the lobby.

Quinn reemerges from the back, toting the paint pans and two rollers.

"Let's spread out some more plastic so we don't drip anything on the new carpet," I suggest.

Quinn salutes — I swear to god, he salutes — and heads out toward the supply shed. The front door jingles open again and a short, plump, middle-aged couple that look almost like brother and sister enter the lobby, beaming gregariously. Well, the man is beaming at least. His wife's expression strikes a balance between confusion and being on the verge of taking offense at something.

"Hi, there, folks. What can I do for you?"

"Whew," the man says, withdrawing a handkerchief from his pocket to dab his forehead. A twinge of sunburn colors his bald head. "Hot one out there!"

"You bet. Welcome to Sacramento in the summertime. You folks interested in a room?"

The man stuffs his hanky back in his pocket and leans on the counter with both arms. His smile so completely engulfs his entire face that it's a little disconcerting. "For two nights, please. With air conditioning, right?"

"Yes, sir. And a pool, if you should feel so inclined."

"Ya hear that, Babs? A pool," he says to his wife, who now reflects his wide grin. He calls her Babs, really?

Quinn returns and starts clumsily spreading the plastic tarp across the carpet. I ask the guests to excuse our remodeling mess and go through my usual spiel about the amenities, pet policy, pool hours, and the rest, and the man keeps grinning at me like a creepy puppet, pausing only to fill out the form.

When we're through and I hand him the room key, he leans toward me. "Say, fella, have you heard the good news?"

If there weren't so many things going on I might have recognized this worm hole. Instead, I jump right into it. "What's that?"

As inconceivable as it sounds, his grin manages to widen. It looks like it's about to swallow his entire face. There's something otherworldly about how white his teeth are. "The Lord Jesus Christ died for you, so that you might live," he says.

Shit. Not one of these guys. "Oh," I manage, "yeah. *That* good news. Yeah, I'm Catholic."

His smile narrows, just slightly, and he casts a quick glance at Babs.

"But have you been born again? Jesus gave up his own life so that you could be."

"Yeah, for sure. Yeah, that was really ... altruistic of him." I nod vigorously. "Yeah, we're big Jesus fans around here. This is a family place."

Rollie bursts in through the back sliding doors. "Goddamit," he barks, "whoever put in that pool pump had to have his head so far up his fuckin' ass—" He stops as he steps onto the plastic, nearly tripping over Quinn. "What the hell are you doin' now, Scarecrow?"

Babs' eyes are saucers. Her husband's jaw hangs like a gate that's come loose from its hinges. I sprint from behind the counter and snatch the couple's suitcases. "Let me help you with these, folks," I say, ushering them toward the front door. "Don't mind him; he's ... he's not ... he doesn't even work here." I lean close to the man and whisper, "He's a lost soul. I've been working on him, but you know how it goes."

The couple exchanges a look, and the man nods sadly.

I cringe as Rollie approaches behind them. "Mick, how long has it been since the pump tube assembly's been changed on that damn chlorinator?"

"Rollie," I say sharply, "what have we talked about with the language?" I'm furiously signaling with my eyes at the horror-struck guests.

"Huh?"

The squat bald man places a reassuring hand on Rollie's shoulder. "God loves you, son," he says.

"That a fact?" Rollie replies. "Weird that he'd create sin and pain and stuff like that then, huh?"

"Right this way, folks," I interject, herding them out onto the front sidewalk.

After I get the couple settled into their room and repeatedly reassure them that they won't run into Rollie again, I knock on my parents' door. I have to knock a second time before the door opens. My dad's holding a half empty tumbler of whiskey, his usual glazed expression smeared across his face. He's wearing a white, short-sleeved, button up shirt, polished dress shoes with black socks pulled up nearly to his knees, and blue and white striped boxer shorts.

"Ahoy there, Captain," he says merrily.

Oh, and his flaccid member is protruding indifferently from the fly of his boxers.

"Good god, man," I say, averting my eyes. I gesture toward his crotch. He continues to look straight at me, his expression unchanged.

"Don't you feel a breeze?" I say, pointing directly at his exposed penis.

"We have the air conditioner on," he says.

"Da, your penis is hanging out of your shorts."

He tilts his head to inspect. "Oh," he says. "Yeah, that'll happen." As he tucks it in with his free hand he adds, "I can't find my glasses, so that's probably why."

I lower my voice. "So what's going on with Maggie?"

He looks up and to the left. "Ah, *The Moon is Blue*."

"Not Maggie McNamara, Da. Your daughter Maggie!"

"Oh, Maggie. What about her now?"

"Is Mom in there?" I ask, losing patience.

My father grins. "She's taking a bubble bath."

"So what's going on with Maggie? Why is she here?"

"She's here?" He peers around my shoulder.

"At the motel, yes. Her and the kids just came in, asking for a room. Without Marc. Now I know you guys know what's going on with her."

Dad's smile wanes. "Your mother says whats-his-face is running around," he mutters, barely moving his lips as if he's afraid lip readers are lurking nearby.

"Marc's cheating on her?" I whisper. "No way!"

"I have half a mind to give that boy a talking to."

That would be a laugh. My dad confronting Marc. My dad confronting anyone! If there was a fly on his sandwich, my father would wait patiently for it to depart before he took a bite. Maggie, on the other hand ... it occurs to me that maybe Marc isn't here because she's already murdered and buried him. "Holy shit. So she's leaving him?"

"She is?" Pop asks.

"I don't know; I was asking you. She's here, though."

"She's where?"

"She's in 109, with the kids," I say, pointing in the direction of her room.

"The grandkids," he says softly.

A loud engine approaches. I turn to see an enormous flatbed truck pulling into the parking lot. Our new refrigerator is strapped to it with what appear to be about a thousand small ropes, tied in intricate patterns.

"Listen Pop," I tell him, "I gotta go see about this fridge. See what you can find out about Maggie, okay? But put some damn pants on before you go over there."

"Oh, I'll let your mother talk to her." He sips his whiskey.

I head over toward the truck, from which Agosto and José have just emerged and are mumbling to each other. "Hola, fellas," I call cheerily. They stop talking and squint at me. "So here she is, huh? How do we unload her?"

Stares.

"Should we drag the old one out of there first?"

Agosto looks briefly at José, who has not taken his eyes off me.

And once more I fear for my safety. Well played, José. "Or maybe you don't need my help?" I venture.

Perhaps I'm in a staring contest, and no one told me about it.

"Okay, well," I continue, "I'll go get your money together, Agosto. You guys let me know if you need help or anything."

I had forgotten to hit the ATM on my way in today. I doubt I'll be able to scrape together four-fifty in cash, but I walk to the office to see what I can find.

Quinn has moved the sofas, tables, and chairs out of the way and covered the entire lobby with plastic tarp. He is squatting, carefully pouring out paint into the pans. Rollie is standing over him, chewing on his toothpick. "You gotta stir it better'n that, Scarecrow," he advises.

"Leave him alone, Rollie," I say. "Hey, you know what? Why are you even here today? Who called you?"

"It's called helpin' out a friend, Mick. That pump tube assembly wasn't gonna replace itself. You're welcome, by the by."

I decide to back down. I hate admitting this, but it has been nice of him to come check on the maintenance things around here. Lord knows he's better at it than I am. "Yeah, all right, you've got a point. Thank you," I say, not taking my eyes off the bills I'm counting from the register. I just hope he's not going to surprise me and tell me he's been charging me by the hour for all the time he's spent here lately.

José and Agosto come in and march solemnly back towards the kitchen, avoiding eye contact with everyone.

"Oh! Right there is José!"

"Got it, Quinn. Thanks."

The front door jingles again. This time it's Abonice. I immediately lose track of how much I've counted. She approaches the counter, and I feel the same surge of excitement I do every time I realize she's about to talk to me. "Mister Collins," she says quietly, "I have a problem."

"What's wrong?"

Rollie appears at her side. "Anything I can help you with, little princess?"

She smiles shyly. She looks back at me, from the corner of her eye, and says, "DaLisa, she say we used the wrong shampoo on the carpets. It changes the color. Now she say they don't match the bedspreads."

Rollie leans in. "But does the carpet match the drapes?" he says, waggling his eyebrows up and down like an imbecile.

Abonice smiles and offers a faint laugh. Was that a coquettish laugh? Surely Rollie's lewd overtures aren't actually *working* on her. Are they? I slam the cash drawer shut. Coming out from behind the counter, I place a gentle hand on Abonice's shoulder and lead her away from Rollie, toward the front door. "Let's go figure this out," I say, casting a severe look at Rollie.

When we're outside I tell her, "Sorry about that guy."

"It is all right."

Maybe his nonsense *is* starting to work on her. Maybe that's why he's here every damn day. "No," I tell her, "it's not all right. Look, Abonice, you're young, and you are a very sweet young lady. Very pretty too. God, if I was about a hundred years younger ...," I stop. I've strayed badly from my point and made this personal. I will my face not to flush.

"How old are you, Mr. Collins?" she asks.

"Old enough to be your ... well, let's just say that I'd be quite a few branches above you in the old family tree."

She laughs with good nature. I smile without it. Getting older sucks.

"Look," I continue, "what I mean is a man like Rollie, he's not a good person for you to be around. I don't think he has your best interests at heart. Do you know what I mean?"

She looks at me from the corner of her eye. Through a prim smile she says, "Yes, Mr. Collins."

I've given up trying to get her to call me Mick. "Look, if he bothers you, you just tell me, and I'll make him stop. Okay?"

"Yes, Mr. Collins."

"Now, what's this about the carpets and the bedspreads?"

She looks up towards the second story. "DaLisa, she is taking the bedspreads off. They don't match, she say."

"What! No, no, no! I don't have time to deal with this now. Not the day before the big visit! Tell her to leave the bedspreads the way they are for now, and we'll take care of it after tomorrow's visit. Okay?"

"Yes, Mr. Collins."

"Okay, you go help her put those bedspreads back on. I have to go see about this refrigerator."

She nods and heads up the stairs. I will myself to *not* watch her perfect ass ascend to the top, and thus establish moral high ground with Rollie. Intending to chastise him, I head back into the lobby, but I see that he's helping Quinn paint, so I let it drop. With one pushing and the other pulling, José and Agosto are dragging the old refrigerator out from the back, probably scraping the hell out of the hallway carpet.

"Whoa, whoa, guys," I plead. "Don't you think you should use a hand cart for that?"

They stop. José stares daggers at me. I immediately regret having said that. He looks at Agosto, who yawns in response. Then he turns and walks out the front door. I watch him go, seized with panic that he has just quit and I'll never see him again. He disappears around the truck, but then he reemerges, rolling a hand cart. I let out the breath I hadn't realized I'd been holding and return my attention to the cash drawer.

My phone's text message alert sounds, and my heart drops past my knees when I see it's from Sara. Finally some clarification. But she's only written three words.

You are sweet.

Thus avoiding answering the question about whether she wants to see me again or not. I am sweet? What the hell does that mean?

Angelina was ... deliberately ambiguous.

23__the day

Summertime in Sacramento can be brutal. A soulless, unseemly heat descends upon the downtown grid and slows everything down. My neighbor's dog abandons his mission of berating passersby with angry yelps and lies still under the porch, defeated. Stoplights change more slowly. Breezes lose their will to blow. Unfortunate pedestrians will walk blocks out of their way just to stay in the shade. The relentless sun screams in terrifying silence from above; it stings your skin upon contact.

Instead of sleeping, I'd opted to spend last night obsessing over today's meeting with the Knight's Lodge people, so I arrive at the motel much earlier than usual. I've already produced a sheen of sweat during the short walk; it's past eighty degrees. It will climb another thirty before it peaks. Chynna isn't at the counter. I find her half asleep in the back office, and she groggily asks me if I'm here to relieve her.

"No, Quinn will be in soon. It's still early." Trying not to sound overly anxious, I inquire how the night went, if there were any emergencies.

Chynna wrinkles her forehead. "What kind of emergency could possibly happen on a Sunday night?"

Last night in bed I'd come up with sixty-two different possibilities. "Just making sure," I reply. "It's the big day today. I just don't want anything to go wrong."

She turns her attention to her phone. "Oh, yeah, good luck with that."

Her tone is mean-spirited. She's probably angry with me about wanting to sell, just like everybody else. I don't see why it should bother her, though; she's a young girl working here part time. If she harbored any notions of a career in the hotel industry I'm pretty sure she wouldn't spend all her time here messing around on her phone. She probably couldn't even tell me the color of the lobby's walls.

Since José's not here yet, I can safely set foot into the kitchen. What I notice immediately is that the new refrigerator is only slightly quieter than a coal train. When I peer inside I'm delighted to find that José has stocked it with fresh seafood, steaks, extravagant-looking desserts, salad materials—everything our visitors could want. I feel reassured that he'll come through on the special lunch I'd asked him to prepare in order to impress our guests. To hell with how much electricity the old girl is sucking out of that wall socket!

Walking through the lobby, I scrutinize the ceiling's paint job. Pretty close to flawless for amateurs, I'd say. I straighten some tables and chairs. For the fourth time in two days, I rearrange the free magazines and the pamphlets in the visitors' information rack. I make fresh coffee and restock all the creamers and sweeteners.

I proceed through the sliding doors to the pool area. The freshly-repainted supply shed looks good. The new plastic loungers situated around the pool gleam in the early morning sunlight, as does the concrete, which I recently power washed. The sun hasn't hit the pool water itself yet, but I'm confident when it does that it will sparkle. I make a mental note to point out to Cromwell's people that we're the only motel in this part of town with a pool. Every time I look at our swimming pool I'm reminded of the great pride Remi took in it, the hours he'd spend cleaning and maintaining it. I wonder if he'd be proud of my working out a deal to sell his run-down little two-star motel to one of the biggest and most reputable motel chains in the country.

I move along the downstairs passageway, rehearsing the route I'll take when I give our VIPs the grand tour of the premises. I emerge at the other end, out the glass exit door and into the front parking lot. I stop to take in a panoramic view of the front of the motel, the first thing our guests will see upon their arrival. I wish we'd had time to repaint the parking stripes in the lot, but that hadn't occurred to me until this moment. I'm sure they'll be focused on the office and the motel itself, rather than the parking lot, right?

Using my master key, I take a peek inside an unoccupied room on the first level. Everything appears polished and bright. It even smells clean! I check the bathroom, and it looks — well, it looks as good as anybody has a right to expect. Ever since Rollie and Stacy replaced those pipes, all the toilets have been working faultlessly. Retreating back out onto the front sidewalk I'm startled by the presences of DaLisa standing by the doorway, her arms folded across her chest, and her face set in a disapproving expression.

"Oh, hi, DaLisa." I nod at the room from which I'd just exited. "I was just checking out one of the empties."

"Mm-hmm."

"Great job, by the way," I say brightly. "Looks good as new."

"Except for the bedspread not matching the carpet."

"You know what, I didn't even notice. I don't think it's that bad."

"Mm-hmm."

She's making me feel like a naughty schoolboy again. She excels at that. "I mean, we can definitely still discuss it. Just not until after today's visit, okay? We'll talk about it tomorrow."

"Mick, don't be traipsing in and out of the rooms while I'm cleaning."

I know she's frustrated with me, but this sounds downright

disrespectful. "Hey," I charge back, "this is my motel. I'm allowed to go anywhere—"

"Just not while I'm here working," she cuts me off. Then she dips her head and looks at me over the top of her glasses. "For however long that ending up being."

There it is. She hasn't spoken directly to me about it, but I've known all along that it was there. "Look, DaLisa, I know I should've talked with you before even taking a meeting with the Knight's Lodge people; I realize that now." She purses her lips, making her appear even more censorious. "But, listen, if the talking should get serious today, I'll ask them point blank about staffing. I promise I won't leave you high and dry. I *promise*." And I mean it, although I realize that I might not have any real say in who Cromwell decides to keep, if anybody, no matter what demands I make. I just hope DaLisa doesn't realize that too.

"Mm-hmm."

"Okay, good," I say, pretending the issue is resolved. "So how is everything around here at the moment? Anything wrong, anything not working?"

"Everything's fine."

"Are you on your own today?"

"Young Abonice will be coming in later."

I nod. "As soon as I walk away from this door, you're going in there to make sure I didn't mess up the room, aren't you?"

She nods. With fervor. I walk back towards the office, and I hear the room door open and close behind me. I check my watch. 8:30. They should be here in an hour and a half. With each passing minute the nauseous discomfort in my stomach inches up to a higher level. Then I walk into the lobby, and it inches up at least a foot in a matter of seconds.

Rollie is leaning against the counter, blowing softly through his toothpick into a cup of coffee. "Rollie," I nearly shriek, "what are you doing here?"

"Mornin' to you, too, Mick. Say, you look tired."

"Why are you here?" I demand. "Today's the big day. You can't be here!"

"You ashamed of me or something?"

Precisely. I rifle through a list of alternative answers to that question and come up with, "Man, the Knight's Lodge people are gonna be here today, in like an hour! I can't have a plumber hanging around here. It makes it look like things need repair."

"You know your hot tub ain't runnin'?"

"Yeah, it's summertime. Nobody uses a hot tub during summertime in Sacramento."

Rollie whistles. "I don't know about that. Some of them cool nights, a hot tub make things *real* hot. And steamy, dependin' on the company, if you catch my drift." He winks.

"Rollie, you have to leave, man."

He grins. "Relax, Mick, I just came in to give everything the once-over and make sure it's all runnin' smooth for your big day. I'll be outta your hair by the time your friends show up."

This sounds like a thoughtful, kind gesture. I squint skeptically. "You promise?"

"Speakin' of your hair, that's how come you're losin' so much of it. All you do is worry, brother."

"We're not having this discussion," I say, heading to the back to make sure Quinn is here, but then I stop. "You're the one losing your hair, Rollie, for Pete's sake! What's your excuse, huh? The stress from running from the cops after you expose yourself to school children?"

Rollie throws his head back and laughs. "You see, Mick, that's called projection."

"Oh, for Christ's sake." I give up. I turn to head to the back, but then I spot my mother coming through the front door. "Morning, Mom. Everything okay?"

"Good morning Michael," she says. "Hello, Mr. Pendershoot."

I look at Rollie. "Is *that* your last name? For real?"

"Michael, I'm going to the farmer's market, and then over to check on the house. Do you need or want anything?"

"You're going right now? Is Dad going with you?"

She rolls her eyes. "He's got Keegan trying to show him how to put songs on his phone. Neither one of them has a clue what they're doing."

"I'm a vinyl man myself," says Rollie.

"Mom, you have to take him with," I blurt desperately. "And the kids. You can't leave him alone here. Today's the big day, when the prospective buyers are coming."

"Oh, Michael, I can't take him to the farmer's market. He always starts sampling the fruit and then walks away without paying for it."

"You have to." I'm pleading now. "He can't be here!"

"He won't get in the way. What are you worried about?"

"What am I worried about? What if he comes strolling in here for a cup of coffee without his pants? You know? Like he's already done twice in the past week!"

Rollie snorts. "You think that kinda stuff don't happen at Knight's Lodges?"

Mom nods. "I see your point, Michael. Okay, then, I'll bring him and the kids along. Lord help us."

"Thank you, Mom. I owe you big. And, no, I don't need or want anything."

"They have those plums that you like so much."

"Pluots," I correct her. "But no, thanks."

"I'll take some plums."

"Rollie!" I turn to my mother. "He's kidding, Mom. Go ahead, we'll be fine."

She leaves, and about twenty minutes later I see her pile Da and the kids into the car and take off. I spend the next twenty minutes after that going over the plan with Quinn and José. Which is to say, I go over the plan with Quinn while José stands there not acknowledging my presence in any tangible way. I remind myself that our gregarious chef has never let me down before and force myself to trust that lunch will be ready at the designated time.

The next half hour or so evaporates while I'm pacing around the lobby in a fugal state of half-formed thoughts and unspecific nervousness.

At ten o'clock exactly—how do people *do* that?—a long black Cadillac pulls into the parking lot. I find that I'm unable to swallow. I think my tie is choking me.

"Whew, nice ride," I hear behind me.

I spin. "Rollie! You're still here?"

"I'm going, I'm going."

I manhandle him through the hallway and out the back door. As I rush back into the lobby I see three well-dressed people—two men and a woman—looking around as they approach the front door. I clear my throat about a thousand times and open the door for them, welcoming them as they step into the lobby.

The oldest of the three, a gray-haired gentleman in an immaculate pin-striped suit, extends his hand. "Hello, I'm Richard Cromwell."

Holy crap. The man himself. "It's an honor to meet you, sir," I say, trying to keep my voice steady as I grasp his hand.

He motions to the forty-ish bespectacled guy on his left. "This is David George, our vice president of finance." We shake, and I notice Mr. George does not smile.

The woman on Cromwell's right, a heavily made-up woman in an ecru pant suit who looks to be slightly older than me, smiles thinly and reaches for my hand. "This is Hannah Greenwood," says Cromwell, "our chief development officer."

I smile back and give her one of those fingers-only half-shakes that I don't know why I always do to women instead of regular handshakes. "Michael Collins."

Her eyebrows lift. "Like the astronaut?"

I swallow. "Um, yeah?" I guess I don't know my contemporary American space program history.

I introduce them to Quinn and talk a little about my history with the motel. I'm so nervous that I will later recall very little of what I'd said during this time. I explain that I'd planned to show them the grounds and then we could talk over a light lunch. Walking them into the back, I briefly show them the office, which I'd tidied up after Chynna left this morning, and hurry them past the kitchen, where José stands silently, tensed as if ready to scrap his way out of a street fight. Almost shouting to make myself heard over the low roar of the new refrigerator, I summarize the lunch plan and ask if they'd prefer any alternatives. They have no objections to the planned menu, and I describe José as an integral part of the motel and call him the "best chef in the Sacramento hotel scene." I wink at him as I say this. I'll let you guess how he responds.

Walking back out through the lobby, Mr. George asks how many guests are currently staying with us, a number Quinn is able to quote without looking it up. Cromwell tells me they're interested in more statistics and records and suggests George stays here to get the information he desires from Quinn while the rest of us continue the tour. For a second it looks as though Quinn is ready to dive headfirst through the glass window to avoid this scenario, but I assure Mr. George that Quinn is his man and can get him whatever he needs. Which is actually true, by the way. Quinn is the computer whiz of the staff and understands the software we use better than the rest of us put together.

I lead the other two past the vending machines, where I make some stupid, incoherent comment off the cuff about how we plan to stock them with healthier snacks, and out to the pool area. No guests have come out yet, and the undisturbed pool water shines pristinely in the sunshine, looking picture-perfect.

"Is that a ... brassiere?"

Except for the comically-oversized black lacy bra floating in the shallow end.

I'm beyond mortified. What is it with random bras popping up around here? As both Cromwell and Ms. Greenwood turn to face me, I'm powerless to stop the deep shade of crimson that is now flooding my face. Cromwell's expression is quizzical, but Greenwood's could be more aptly described as revolted.

"Uh, um ...," I stammer, my desperate mind racing for an explanation in an attempt to stave off total humiliation, but I'm coming up empty. My eyes rise to an open, screenless window on the second floor above where we stand.

"Shoot, there it is," I hear a voice say.

Rollie.

My reeling mind doesn't immediately register what I'm seeing. Rollie, inexplicably dressed in jeans and a tucked-in polo shirt instead of

Franklin's jumpsuit, is on his knees beside the pool reaching in to fish out the giant black bra. How did I know he would somehow have something to do with this?

"I was just walking by with our laundry," he explains while he wrings the excess water from the bra. "Didn't realize I'd dropped it until I got back to our room."

Wait. What exactly is happening here?

"Boy, would my wife ever be embarrassed if she knew you folks had seen her undies floatin' in the dang pool," Rollie says, getting back to his feet. "Don't think I'll be mentionin' that part when she wakes up. She's feelin' much better today, though."

He seems to be directing that last sentence at me. I stare incomprehensibly.

"Say, Mr. Collins, I just wanted to thank you again for lettin' me use your laundry facilities," he says to me. "I know it ain't your normal policy, but you really helped us out of a jam. You don't run into that kinda customer service everywhere, and believe me we won't forget it."

Cromwell and Greenwood look back at me. I force a smile and shrug. "Well, yeah ... okay. Thanks."

"I'll be leavin' one of them good Yelp reviews," Rollie continues. "I'm gonna let people know what kind of a fine establishment you're runnin' here." He grins, waves, and disappears with the bra around the corner.

Cromwell is nodding at me in what appears to be some sort of affirmation. I'm so floored by Rollie's superhero-esque appearance to get me out of that jam that I can't think of what to say next. "Um," I start, clearing my throat, "you know we're the only hotel in this section of town that has a pool."

Although the look on Ms. Greenwood's face only changes from appalled to slightly perturbed, the rest of the tour is thankfully uneventful, and Cromwell himself doesn't appear too bothered. Although he did make a passing remark on the lines in the parking lot needing to be repainted, dammit.

By eleven thirty, it's already over ninety degrees outside, but we're back in the comfort of the air-conditioned lobby. We have been rejoined by Mr. George and are seated at one of the tables in the dining area as Quinn—right on time—brings us garden salads and shrimp cocktail. Despite the hiccup at the pool that may prompt Greenwood to ultimately vote against us, I'm pleased that things have gone as smoothly as they have. Mr. George says Quinn was extremely helpful, and he was able to get all the information he needed. Quinn, sweating like he's just completed a half-marathon, nods gratefully and shrugs. Although the new fridge is now humming so embarrassingly loudly that it can be heard from our table, lunch starts out well, and by the time the crab cakes arrive, my heart has resumed its normal beat and I no longer feel on the verge of throwing up. Cromwell is complimentary about the food, especially José's specialty vegetable medley, so I take the opportunity to once again talk up my chef and mention that I hope he could keep his job should they decide to buy.

Mr. Cromwell evades commenting directly about José, but he does wipe his mouth with his napkin and say, "I suppose this would be an appropriate time to start discussing particulars in what we're hoping to do."

And that's the moment the front door is ripped open and the lobby is filled with angry shouts.

We all turn to see the squat, middle-aged Christian couple accosting Quinn at the front desk. "I demand my money back," shouts the husband, whose angry face is now a much darker red than his sunburned dome.

"Oh, Stanley, my blood pressure!"

"Let me handle this, Babs!" He jabs a finger at Quinn, who recoils as if it's a bayonet. "Where is that manager of yours, young fella?"

I have a bite of squash in my mouth, and it takes considerable effort to swallow it. "Uh," is all I can manage to say when Quinn meekly looks my way.

"You," Stanley cries, and basically stampedes across the room at me.

My impulse is to stand and walk him away from the table of shocked faces, but I don't manage to budge before the irate man is standing over me, wagging a finger in my face.

"Family-friendly place, my keister," he shouts. "Just what kind of an establishment are you running here, sonny?"

Babs is beside him, clutching his sleeve. "A brothel is what it is," she spits. "You should be ashamed of yourself!"

"What's wrong?" I say, bewildered but trying to appear calm. "Tell me what happened."

"What's wrong?" Stanley sputters, inadvertently spitting across our lunches in his fury. "Just that we come back after a morning prayer convention to find Sodom and Gomorrah happening right inside our room!"

"What?"

"Having immoral relations right there on the bed in our room," Babs shrieks, fanning herself. "Your own cleaning staff!"

Holy. Shit.

Rollie.

He finally made it into Abonice's pants. At the worst possible time and place. I'm going to kill him!

"Is that what kind of place you're running here?" Stanley demands.

In my life up to this point, I do not recall ever having seen an expression on someone's face that could accurately be described as *aghast*. But that's the precise word to describe the countenances of Cromwell and his two associates at this moment.

Damn that Rollie. If I don't have the guts to kill him, I'll sue his ass for everything he's worth!

Stuttering badly, I start to say, "I assure you ... he ... he's not—"

"And the worst kind of immoral relations!" Babs interjects. "A woman and another woman! The Bible calls that an abomination you know! An abomination!"

Wait. What?

Stanley seethes. "Just what do you intend to do about it, huh?"

And that's when the electricity goes out.

24__the aftermath

By two o'clock the next afternoon, I've finished off the bottle of Powers that I didn't quite kill last night and started on the second bottle, and I find myself listening to Pink Floyd's "Wish You Were Here" on repeat. To alleviate the suspense, no, Richard Cromwell will not be purchasing The Shady Spot Motel.

I had decided to try writing a little poetry this morning, as I'd heard from others it can be quite therapeutic. The blank white screen staring back at me taunts me as a fitting visual metaphor for the progress I seem to be making in life. In my drunken despair last night I'd emailed Sara — which is always considered a winner of a move to make while in such a state — and demanded to know where I stand with her. For the third time in the past twenty minutes, I read her response.

Hey, Mick,

I hadn't realized I was being evasive, so I apologize for that. After having thought about it, I'm going to have to reluctantly say that I don't think we should see each other again. The reason is I don't think we are at the same place in our lives. For example, you had mentioned your aspirations of one day living in NYC. I think that is exciting and daring and wonderful, but it's not what I want for myself. My family is here, and I want to start my own family here. Remember how you said you wanted to wait until you were older to have kids? I've begun to suspect lately that when guys say that, it really means they're not crazy about the idea of having them at all, because they consider them a hindrance to their freedom or whatever. I'm not saying that's where you're coming from or not, but to be honest that's the impression I got. But I WANT the responsibility. More than anything in life I want to bring new people into the world, and love them, and teach them right from wrong, and to love the NINERS!! I want to start soon so that once they're old enough I'll still be young enough to play and hike with them and show them all the wonderful places I've seen. That's why I'm working toward my Masters, so that I'll be able to provide for my family no matter what. Anyway Mick, I think you're a great guy, and I'm not just saying that. I think your funny and charming and clever and kind. I just don't think we'd be great for each other. If I'm way off base about all this and you actually do want a girl who wants the things I want, then I'd be willing to talk about it some more. Let me know. Oh and in regards to your question: I wanted to stick around after you left the other night because the bartender was a friend of mine from college, and I wanted to catch up with her without feeling like I wasn't giving you my full attention.

Best, Sara

I don't want to try to list all the negative emotions my brain is teeming with after reading this, for fear of inadvertently leaving one or two out, but they're all vying for the pole position. Once anger takes the lead it gets tempered by the nagging notion that she might be right. About everything. Disappointment is a strong contender as well. I truly thought I had done and said everything right on that date. Turns out I just don't know a damn thing about women, or maybe even myself. Maybe I *am* afraid of responsibility in some way, and that's why I want to unload this wretched motel and not have to worry about making sure my staff can keep their jobs no matter how bad business is getting. Maybe having my family around here makes me feel tied to this area, and that's the main reason I want to move, because I resent my responsibility to them. Why should I have to be burdened with responsibilities towards all these people? What am I getting out of this deal, anyhow?

You're right, Sara—we're not at the same place in life, because I'm nowhere. I'm stuck in a rut off the side of the road. I don't even know where I am. I've always wanted to accomplish something important in life, something noble, but where is that, exactly? And how do you get there?

Hell, maybe I should just forget about women entirely. All they bring me is frustration. When a girl you've had dinner with one time seems to know more about what kind of woman you're looking for than you do, it's probably time to give up. Damn you for being right about everything, Sara! Plus you spelled *you're* wrong, so there!

The phone rings. Quinn says he needs me right away at the motel. Speaking of bullshit responsibilities.

I walk over, and halfway there I'm dying for a Gatorade. It's so hot outside I feel like double checking the road signs to make sure I haven't accidentally taken an escalator into hell. And it's far too early to be this drunk. As I reach the motel, I nearly walk right into the path of an SUV pulling into the parking lot. As if that would've been some great loss for the world.

There's no one at the front desk, of course. The blinds are still pulled, covering the sliding doors to the pool area. It looks like we're not even open. I storm to the back, ready to curse out Quinn, just because I feel like yelling at somebody, but he's not there, either. I walk back out into the lobby. A thin, thirtysomething man is coming in the front door, followed by his very pregnant wife, holding the hand of a young boy. Looks like I get to cover the front desk. Fantastic.

"Help you?"

"I hope so," the man says earnestly. "Have you got any vacancies?"

I check the screen. "Yep, I have a two bed."

The man and his wife exchange a relieved smile. "Thank goodness," he says. "This is the fourth place we tried."

"Really?" Although it doesn't surprise me that we weren't in their top three.

The man indicates his son. "This little guy's been begging us for a couple of years to come visit the State Fair," he says. "I guess everyone else had the same idea to come to Sacramento this week."

I check them in. After he fills out the paperwork and I give him the key, he smiles at me. "Thank you so much." It sounds like he genuinely means it.

"No worries."

"I was afraid we weren't going to be able to find a room we could afford." He casts a glance at his wife, who looks flushed, maybe overheated. "I just don't know what we would've done then."

He shakes my hand as if I've done him a big favor, then he leads his wife and son out to the parking lot to get their stuff. Nice people. I watch them go, surprised to notice my mood has lifted a bit.

"Now if that ain't noble work, I don't know what is," comes an unmistakable voice from behind me.

I sigh. "Hey, Rollie. Do I dare ask what you're doing here today?"

"I got somethin' you need to see."

"Oh, Jesus. I'm not sure I can handle it today, Rollie. Can't it wait?"

He shakes his head grimly. "Naw, you need to see it right now."

If someone walked in right now and offered me a dollar for this motel, I'd take it. I rub my head. "What is it?"

He motions with his head. "This way. Out by the pool."

I follow him, vaguely expecting the worst. I left my sunglasses on the counter, so the brightness of the sunshine is absolutely shocking. But not as shocking as the screamed word "Surprise!"

Nonplussed, I look around at the group assembled beside the pool, shielding my eyes from the sun. It takes a moment for it to register. For the first time in my life, I have entirely, genuinely forgotten my own birthday.

Everyone is here. My parents, with Maggie and the kids. Ethan and Georgelle. Stacy and Terry. Witt and some curvaceous blonde girl who looks barely out of high school. Quinn and DaLisa and Abonice and Maria. My old buddies Derek and Charlie from high school. Even Molly from the coffee shop, with one of her friends. For Christ's sake, even José is out here!

I am beyond stunned.

Rollie claps me on the back. "Happy birthday, pal," he says.

Keegan and Maddy rush me with hugs and drag me over to a table set up beside the pool, where my mother is lighting candles on a cake that's shaped like a football jersey.

"Who's Perry?" Georgelle asks.

I take a closer look at the cake. The uniform number is 34, my age today, and above the number is the word Perry scrawled in frosting. "Joe

Jeff Gephart

'The Jet' Perry," I mumble in disbelief. None of my family is as big a 49ers fan as I am, so how in the world did somebody come up with the name of a player from before my dad's time? Maybe I've had too much to drink, but the thought of someone putting in the time to research such a thing brings a lump to my throat.

"All right everyone," Mom says, "let's sing Happy Birthday and then, Michael, you blow out the candles."

"Make a wish, Champ," my father adds.

As the group sings, my eyes go from face to face, and I try to come up with a wish. It's probably because I'm still in shock, but by the time the song's over, I've come up empty. Me—who two days earlier thought he knew exactly what he wanted out of life—when I'm put on the spot I'm unable to come up with a single wish. There's something about this moment, with everyone I care about standing here, that renders me unable to muster the ability to wish to be rid of this damn motel. I know; I can't believe it, either.

I blow out the candles and everyone applauds. Mom and Maggie start slicing and serving the cake, and I'm inundated with birthday greetings. Molly has brought a small fleet of fancy iced coffee drinks topped with whipped cream and begins passing them out.

"Happy birthday, handsome," she says, serving me first.

"How in the hell did you know about my birthday?"

She rolls her eyes and smiles. "You're not the only one in your family that frequents the coffee shop, you know."

I wasn't bluffing when I said I didn't want anything to be done for my birthday, but as I stand among this assorted group of people who've all gathered at two-thirty on a weekday afternoon—many of whom don't even know each other—I'll admit that I'm touched. Suddenly the boulder that fell on me yesterday has shifted a bit, and I can see a glimmer of sunshine.

"How in the world did you get this motley crew together anyhow?" I ask my mother.

"The surprise party was Mr. Pendershoot's idea," Mom explains. "He brought it up to Maggie, and she just ran with it."

"You're kidding me." I look over at Rollie, who's using exaggerated hand gestures as he's telling some probably preposterous story to Abonice, and I smile. Good old Rollie. My friend Rollie. Jesus.

It's not long before the kids are splashing around in the pool, and in the middle of a conversation Stacy says, "Yo I gotta get in on that!" and jumps in fully clothed.

Everybody laughs, Maddy shrieks with delight, and Terry shrugs and says, "What can you do?"

"Nothing," I say. "That dude is perfect."

"Did he tell you what we got you for your birthday?" she asks.

"What? You guys didn't have to—"

"Oh, hush up," she chides. "We got tickets to opening day. Niners and Seahawks."

Those tickets are impossible to find. "You're messing with me," I say.

"Nope," Terry says. "And the best part is, I'm not bringing along any of my girlfriends for you. Stacy was adamant about that."

"Ha! He's a good man."

"However," she continues, "I did get a fourth ticket, just in case you decide you want to bring someone along." She winks and strolls over to the pool.

Derek and Charlie approach, and we catch up for a few minutes, but soon we're retelling lurid stories about our wild high school days. I laugh so hard my eyes tear up. They're both shocked and dismayed when I tell them I'm not planning to come to the reunion.

"Oh, come on," Derek pleads, "everyone would absolutely *love* to see you!"

"Hell, it won't be the same without you," Charlie adds.

I tell them I'll think about it. And maybe I actually will.

Soon Derek must go back to work, and Charlie says he thinks he'll head to the Torch Club for a beer. Quinn and Abonice have already disappeared back inside, and I see DaLisa heading that way, too. I step into her path.

"You and I need to have a serious talk soon," I say.

DaLisa sighs, and for the first time I win a staring contest with her. "I made a mistake; I know it," she says softly.

"I'll say."

She shakes her head. "I got the room numbers mixed up, I guess."

I blink a couple of times. "Uh, that's not what the mistake was."

She looks off to the side.

"That was your bra floating in the pool, wasn't it?"

She looks back at me quizzically. "In the pool? How it got all the way down there, I wonder."

I'm not really up for having this conversation right now. To tell the truth, I'm still more flabbergasted than upset by the whole thing. I see DaLisa in a whole new light now, but I'm not sure it's one I particularly like.

She crosses her arms across her chest. "You know, regardless the reason, I'm impressed by the effort you put into this place in the past few weeks. Look better than it has in years."

"Don't try to change the subject, DaLisa."

"Remi would be proud," she says nodding, her lips pressed firmly together.

I don't know what to say. The image of Remi smiling at me pops into my head, and in my precarious emotional state it almost brings me to tears. I slurp the last of my iced mocha whatever-it-was. "Well, I guess you've got things you need to do," I say, stepping out of her way.

She seems relieved to be ending our talk. I am, too.

"One thing, though," I call before she reaches the sliding door. "How ... I mean, what ... when did you ...?" I stop. I'm not sure how to say it. "But you said Abonice was too young for *me*," I say in a voice far whinier than I'd hoped.

DaLisa emits a hardy laugh and shakes her head. "The heart want what it wants," she says. "No explaining it."

Some things are just too stupefying to ponder.

I rejoin my family and receive my birthday hugs. Maggie is last, and when we release our embrace, I hold her arms and make her look me in the eye. "How are you doing?" I ask gently.

She swallows and gives my hands a quick squeeze. "I'm gonna be okay." She nods, and it seems nothing more needs to be said.

Feeling slightly awkward, I turn to my father and shake my empty plastic cup. "Seems like a birthday would warrant something a little more exciting, don't you think?"

Pop brightens. "That I can handle, big guy." He winks and heads inside.

Molly says she must get back to the coffee shop. I thank her and her friend for coming. "And thanks especially for bringing those drinks. Delicious."

"No problem," she says. "Happy birthday." Then she surprises me with an excitingly warm embrace.

"Wow, take it easy," I say. "You're gonna give an old man like me a heart attack."

She slaps my arm and grins. "Don't be such a dork!" Both girls turn back and wave before they disappear through the sliding doors.

My dad soon returns with a fresh bottle of Jameson, which catches my mother off guard, and she interrogates him. She finds most of his hiding spots, but every now and then he manages to stay one step ahead.

After a while, the party has thinned out. José had gone back inside shortly after the party began, but get this: he actually stopped and gave me a nod before he left. Quinn has returned and is chatting up Maria, the maid I don't know very well. I decide maybe I should make an effort to get to know her better. She's one of my people, after all. Stacy and Terry have just left. Mom, Maggie, and Rollie are relaxing under a shade umbrella while Pop horses around with the kids in the shallow end of the pool. I'm sitting between Ethan and Witt on the edge of the pool, dangling our feet in the deep end. We've imbibed one too many drinks to make any attempt to conceal our staring at Witt's girl, who's sunbathing on a floating lounger, wearing a bikini that could probably fit into a Ziploc sandwich bag.

"She's an intern at the station," Witt explains, his voice drowsy and thick with whiskey.

"She sure is," Ethan and I say at the same time, mesmerized by her sun-bronzed body.

"Remember when we didn't have any body fat?" Ethan muses.

"She's twenty-one," Witt says.

"Wow," Ethan and I say, and then we both giggle because it's the second thing in a row we've said simultaneously, as if we'd rehearsed it.

"It's a shame your girl had to jet," Witt says to Ethan. "I bet she fills out a bikini rather nicely."

"Hey now."

"Ha, just messin' with you."

"I bet she does, though," I add, grinning.

Ethan shoves me good-naturedly. "Knock it off."

"So, Mick," Witt says, "what's this I hear about you trying to sell this place? You trying to move out of town, or what?"

I look around before I answer. "What? And leave all this?"

Witt says, "Shit, I'd love to have a place like this."

I scrutinize his face to try to gauge whether he's serious. It has never occurred to me that any of my friends actually envied me in any fashion, especially Witt.

"Well, I was considering it," I say. "But I don't know." I look over at Ethan and drape my arm across his shoulders. "A wiser man than myself once said that change isn't always necessary."

Ethan smiles at me. "Or an improvement," he adds.

◎◎◎

"Who would you hang out with anyway?" Rollie is saying. For the thousandth time, he's explaining why moving away is a terrible idea. It's getting dark now, and all the party guests have gone. My parents, Rollie, and I are having a cup of coffee in the lobby. Chynna is slouched in a chair near the front counter, giving her thumbs a vigorous workout on her phone. Maggie has gone to put the kids to bed.

"I'd make new friends," I respond.

Rollie snorts and looks at my mother, who blows softly on her coffee, staying out of it. "Well, hell, man," he says, "you could bake a new cake, too. But why not just eat the one that's already sitting there in front of you?"

I look at what's left of the Jet Perry cake, which was admittedly delicious. "Have you ever seen the girls in New York City, Rollie?"

He snorts again. "You ever seen the girls around here?"

I shake my head. "Nah, I think I'm done with California girls."

"Oh, Michael," my mother says disappointedly.

"I just don't get them," I say, suddenly feeling like I'm under the spotlight. "Or they don't get me, maybe. Or else they just want to be friends." I say this last part in the same tone of voice a lot of people reserve for talking about Donald Trump.

"Heh, sounds like your mother," my dad says, smirking.

"Oh, Tom, stop."

"Wait, what do you mean, Da?"

"Well, you know, it's like everything else," he starts. This is a favorite phrase of his, and I've never known what it means, or if it means anything at all. He says it a lot when he's drunk. The ruddy hue on his face betrays how far gone he is at present. "When I met your ma," he says, "I tried to impress her and all, but she was convinced she didn't want a man like me. Said we'd be friends, and no more than that, so don't get my hopes up."

"I didn't phrase it like that," Mom cuts in.

"No kidding?" I say. "How come I never heard about this?"

"Heard about what?" Maggie says as she enters the lobby. "What are we talking about?"

"About your mom only wantin' to be friends with your old man when they first met," Rollie says.

"Oh, yeah," Maggie nods. She knows all the stories. Nobody tells me anything.

"Friends or nothing," my dad continues, "'take it or leave it,' she said."

"Now, Tom, I didn't say it mean like that."

"And you took it, huh?" I ask Da.

He shrugs. "I figured better to have her as a friend than not have her at all."

"And he used to embarrass you by singing that song outside your window," Maggie adds.

"Oh, heavens," Mom says, rolling her eyes.

"Got drunk and sang it once at the wrong house," Pop says.

"What song?"

"When Love is Kind," Da says wistfully.

"Red is the Rose," corrects Mom, rolling her eyes.

"And after that you changed *your* tune about him, eh, Ms. Collins?" suggests Rollie.

"Well, a girl has the right to change her mind," Mom says, blushing. "And besides, lots of relationships start out as friendships."

I glance at Maggie. Her face is set in a scowl, and she's studying the floor.

"Anyway," I say, changing the subject, "I really did want to thank you all for the party. I know I told Mags I didn't want one, but it was really nice." This gets a slight smile from Maggie.

"You only turn thirty once, old sport," Da says, and drains his coffee. Mom cradles her forehead in her hand and shakes her head.

"After yesterday," I continue, "I was just kind of down in the dumps, you know?"

"That damn refrigerator." Rollie shakes his head. "Blew out the whole damn circuit board."

"Well, it was a combination of things really," I clarify. "I was just kind of ... I was ... well, you know, that overall general state of malaise, I guess."

"Ohio," my dad says softly.

"I just felt like I'd never get in a good mood again," I continue, "but today really cheered me up. So thank you."

"We love you, Michael," Mom says.

"We sure do," Rollie says, putting his arm around my shoulders.

I lean out of it. "Okay, Franklin, we're not quite ready for all that."

A car's screeching brakes draw our attention to the parking lot.

"Oh, shit," mutters Maggie.

Marc clambers out of his car, and we watch him approach the lobby. He's almost stomping, but his stride is a little unstable. It looks like he's been drinking. He flings the door open. "I should've figured you'd be here," he almost spits.

"Marc," Maggie says, but doesn't make a move toward him.

"For two days you've been gone," he barks. "You couldn't have even told me where you were going with my children? I've been going out of my mind over here!"

Maggie scrunches up her features. "I *did* tell you. I left you a note."

"Where?"

"On the refrigerator." She's using the stern voice she usually reserves for me.

He blinks, then cocks his head to the side. "On our refrigerator?"

"Good god," Maggie mutters.

He walks up to face her. I don't want to be here for this, but there doesn't appear to be a graceful way to exit. "We need to talk about this," he says.

"We will," Maggie says, clearly struggling to maintain a civil tone, "but now is *not* the time."

"Well, when *is* the time?" he nearly shouts.

"Marc, you're drunk. You shouldn't be here right now."

"I said I'm sorry," he bellows. "I told you, it didn't mean anything!"

"It meant something to me," Maggie retorts, matching his volume.

He seethes. Then he explodes, "Jesus! Why do you have to be such a fucking cunt about this?"

The next thing that happens is over before I fully comprehend it happening. With astonishing quickness and tenacity that I didn't know he possessed, my father delivers a right cross that sends Marc toppling backwards. He bounces off a table and lands on the new carpet hard on his butt. He puts a trembling hand to his jaw and gazes up at Da in utter disbelief. Which matches the way the rest of us are gawking at him.

I hear the sound of an iPhone camera clicking behind me. Chynna is wide-eyed and grinning. "That was so dope," she says.

I look at my dad, who stands there with no discernible expression on his face. "Jesus, Pop," I half-whisper.

He looks at me. "Nobody talks that way to one of my kids, Mick."

25__and in the end

It's a slow afternoon at The Shady Spot. Life is one of those maddening ambiguities that you have to keep figuring out over and over again. It's like an impenetrable fluid that keeps changing forms on you. I've decided to put women, and dating, and future plans out of my mind for the moment and just focus on telling Angelina's story. I was growing pretty weary of dwelling on my own story anyway. I've got the laptop fired up, and I'm making good progress.

Angelina was

Yes, that third word, that elusive adjective, is hovering somewhere nearby, and today I'm going to find it. My mind feels clear, for once. I have no dating prospects on the horizon, the motel is currently without a functional refrigerator, and I've made no decisions about what comes next for me, yet I feel oddly at peace today. As if I've solved some sort of puzzle, but I don't know which.

Maggie strides into the lobby, dressed in a grey pinstriped business suit, her hair and makeup flawless.

"Whoa, what are you all dolled up for?"

"I'm going to a job interview," she says.

"Holy shit, really?" I ask. "What does this mean?"

"It just means I'm adding a little more structure to my life. It's only a part time position, at a corporate law office at 555 Capitol Mall."

"The building with—"

"Yes," she cuts me off. "The building with the giant white hands sculpture out front."

I shake my head. "Maggie Collins working in an office building. And to think you once believed corporations were the root of all evil."

She softens, and for a moment I spot my sister under all that makeup. "Bringing them down from the inside," she whispers, winking at me.

I laugh.

"Listen," she continues, "what time does your shift end today?"

"Why?"

She rolls her eyes. "I'm taking you out for a birthday dinner. Just me and you."

"None of your single friends will be unexpectedly showing up?"

"Just me and you," she repeats.

"Wow. We haven't done that in ... have we ever done that?"

"It's been a long time," she admits. "Too long."

"Deal," I say. "And, hey, good luck with the interview."

She nods, turns to go, but then stops. She doesn't turn back to fully face me, but she kind of glances at me from the side and says quietly, "Thanks for being here for me, Mick."

I'm taken aback. I don't stop to craft a clever response; I just say the first thing on my mind. "I always will be, Mags."

It feels surprisingly right to say this. She smiles and exits the building. Folks, you have just witnessed the most authentic moment between the Collins siblings in several years. For the next couple of minutes my brain tries on this brief interaction and strolls around the block with it, trying to acclimate to what could possibly be a new dimension to our relationship.

The front door jingles again, and in walks Brooklyn with a friend of hers I recognize from pub trivia. It seems incongruous to see her in this room, as I associate her strictly with other settings in my life.

"So this is your hotel, eh?" She looks around, nodding approval.

I'm baffled and pleased to see her, despite the unfortunate fact that my breath still catches in my throat at the sight of her. "Brooklyn, wow. How did you know where my motel was?"

"There's this new invention called the internet. I'll show you sometime."

"What are you doing here?"

"Well, if you're not gonna respond to my texts, what am I supposed to do?"

"Oh, yeah," I say, feeling myself blush slightly. "It's been a crazy couple of days."

"We're gonna go watch the Giants/Dodgers game at the bar where Bonnie's boyfriend works tonight," she says, gesturing to her friend. "You should come along."

She came to track me down to hang out with her? "Oh, I can't," I respond. "I'm going out to dinner with my sister tonight."

The girls exchange a look, which naturally I have no idea how to interpret. Brooklyn says, "Well, it's a three game series. What about tomorrow night?"

My initial reaction is to say no. I mean, you don't go to a bar to watch a ballgame with a girl. At least not one towards whom you continually have to smother your attraction. Then again maybe I'm overthinking it. I'm tired of overthinking things. Hell, I *like* to watch baseball at bars.

"Yeah, sure," I hear myself say.

Brooklyn breaks into that incredible smile. "Great," she says. "I'll text you tomorrow then."

"This time I'll respond," I say, smiling mischievously.

And that's that. She and Bonnie say goodbye and leave.

Angelina was a friend.

Promising. What's wrong with the book at least starting out that way? I keep thinking of what my dad said about he and Mom starting out as friends. Who knows what will happen? Wait. No. Even better:

Was Angelina a friend?

Now we're talking. This could be interesting. The protagonist doesn't know whether he trusts her or not. He doesn't know whether she's a friend, or potentially more. Or even an enemy. His confusion drives the story. It's what consumes him. And hey, they say to write about what you know, right? I could teach Confusion 101 at Sac State.

Maybe you *can* go to the bar to watch a ballgame with a girl. At the very least it'll be nice to share some time with a girl who isn't crazy. There I go again with that word. I suppose I've been using the word crazy a little too much lately, particularly in my depictions of women. I know I've used it to describe my sister. But seeing her go through this situation with Marc has reminded me that underneath this fierce façade she's created, she's still just plain old Maggie, still capable of being hurt, still struggling with confusion like the rest of us over what to do next. Sure, she's been a little overzealous in trying to set me up with a woman, but her actions haven't been without reason or logic. She just wants me to be happy.

And Sara isn't crazy, either. As disappointed as I was over her not wanting a second date with me, maybe I was just looking at the situation from a different level than she was. Maybe she's just too deep to be swayed by superficial, fleeting things like a fun time or a charming personality. She knows who she is and what she wants, which is more than I can say for myself.

Hell, maybe none of them were crazy.

Georgelle *seems* crazy for being devoted to the children of a man who's her spouse in name only, but maybe she's just a lot more caring than I am. Maybe she's not afraid of taking on the responsibility of loving those kids, even though she doesn't have to. I don't know if I'd have the guts to be like that.

Clare certainly wasn't afraid of taking on the responsibility of having kids, even if she had to do it on her own. I wonder if she ever went through with it. If so, I wonder how different she is now because of it.

Maybe having kids changes you in ways that I just don't understand yet. Perhaps that's why Alice *seemed* psychotic for calling her daughter by a fake name, but in reality she just wanted to connect with her child on her own terms instead of compromising on behalf of an ex that she didn't feel was worthy of factoring into the equation.

At least she was able to come to that decision, which is what poor Marie was unable to do. She seemed preposterously naïve for repeatedly falling for her useless ex's lies, but maybe she's just too trusting. As far as character traits go, is that such a negative one with which to be saddled? Maybe it's because of this that she feels compelled to keep all those photos of her ex on her phone; maybe she needs visual reminders to make sure she doesn't repeat those types of mistakes.

And Jen Paup. Maybe she wasn't as crazy as I thought; maybe I just didn't understand where she was coming from. Certainly our past experiences help formulate who we are, and I really knew very little about her background. Who's to say that if I worked in an extremely dangerous environment like she faces every day I wouldn't be far more suspicious of others' motives? And who's to say I wouldn't adopt certain—ahem—*extreme* measures to ensure my own safety?

And then there's Ruth.

Well, no, Ruth is just fucking crazy.

Maybe if and when I decide to date again I should be less judgmental, slower to jump to conclusions, and focus instead on trying to attain some level of understanding. Maybe I'll never decide to date again. Who knows? If that's the case, would I really be incomplete? I still don't know what I think about this whole "fractions" mindset. Maybe we are only halves, after all. But maybe our other half doesn't have to be that one special person. Maybe my other half is my small but worthwhile group of friends. Or my family. Or this stupid motel. Or maybe just humanity in general, once this book gets published. Whatever it turns out to be, I think I'm okay with it.

But then again, maybe I'll meet Princess Leia at the supermarket, and she'll turn out to be my other half. I'm certainly not closing any doors of opportunity.

the end

Special thanks
to all the lovely ladies
who provided me with the inspiration
to comprise these tales of woe.

About the Author

A California transplant from Pittsburgh, Pennsylvania, Jeff Gephart is the author of two previous novels: *The Second Life* and *Out of Dark Places*. He has worked professionally as a graphic artist, elementary school teacher, and editor. With a background in performing arts, Jeff has spent time both in front of and behind the camera in a variety of independent film projects and a weekly cable TV show. When he's not writing, Jeff can be found hiking, traveling, playing sports, annoying his friends with too many movie quotes, and being grateful he's no longer internet dating.

Learn more at jeffgephartwriting.com

ALL THINGS THAT MATTER PRESS

FOR MORE INFORMATION ON TITLES AVAILABLE FROM
ALL THINGS THAT MATTER PRESS, GO TO
http://allthingsthatmatterpress.com
or contact us at
allthingsthatmatterpress@gmail.com